LEE'S LESSON

DITCH LANE DIARIES 4

D. F. JONES

COPYRIGHT

Cover Art, by Jones Media, images provided by Shutterstock © 2017

Editing by Alicia Street

Formatting by Jones Media

Published by Jones Media

❀ Created with Vellum

DEDICATION

To my loving parents, I will miss you forever.

ALSO BY D. F. JONES

Ruby's Choice (Ditch Lane Diaries 1)

Anna's Way (Ditch Lane Diaries 2)

Sandy's Story (Ditch Lane Diaries 3)

Lee's Lesson (Ditch Lane Diaries 4)

Spinning Time (a time travel romance)

The Witches of Hant Hollow (Jonathan's Curse)

Antique Mirror (a Halloween short)

Happily Ever After, Again

'Tis The Season: Sweet Romance Novelettes

ACKNOWLEDGMENTS

Writing the Ditch Lane Diaries saved me.

I tried writing fiction many times over the decades, but the day I downsized my company to care for my mom, the floodgates opened.

My mother read the first three books in the series before her passing. My dad followed her to heaven six months later. Caregivers, especially at-home caregivers, often develop PTSD. Lee and Harry helped me work through my grief. I laughed, cried, and cheered.

Lee's Lesson is a tribute to my loving parents.

I'm not a biblical scholar, but I'm fascinated and intrigued by the stories in the Bible. The collection of ancient texts is considered inspired by the divine. Numerous biblical canons have evolved throughout the centuries. Many ancient texts are omitted, like the Book of Enoch; 1 Peter, 2 Peter, and Jude mention it.

Books, movies, and television explore the possibilities of otherworldly beings, both in theory and fiction. I recently came across one show, which suggests the Vatican possesses scrolls that would rock the world.

Faith and belief are individual experiences. It is not my place to judge, agree, or deny another's belief system.

The Ditch Lane Diaries, including Lee's Lesson, is fiction. I love Lee and Harry and trust you will too.

I want to thank my critique partners and my launch team for your suggestions and comments. I thrive working with other creative individuals. I can't thank you enough. I want to thank my developmental editor, Alicia for punching plot holes and pushing my craft to the next level. A shout out to Amanda for creating stellar covers and marketing collaterals.

I want to thank my sweet husband for putting up with my elaborate ideas and overlooking the madness that comes along with the creative process.

I would be remiss not to thank The Creator, The Prince, and Spirit of Man for listening to my prayers and lifting my soul during some of the darkest times of my life and for helping me to move on.

May love light the way!

D. F. Jones

Special note: Song titles are listed for every chapter in the Ditch Lane Diaries. Check out my Spotify playlists for each book. Spotify Search, D.F. Jones, author.

PROLOGUE

*1*986
    The Battle of Arrington

Lee's heart hammered wildly as she walked out of an abandoned hunting cabin to join the other warriors in the wooded area. A misty fog rolled in from the nearby creek. She looked up into the inky sky, watching it turn a pale blue. The sun barely peeked over the horizon.

She didn't fear for her safety, but she did for those she loved. Her adrenaline kicked in as she looked at her daughter, Ruby, and her husband, Reed, and her childhood friends, Anna and Jerry. They had enlisted with the Angel Armed Forces (AAF), and this would be their first angelic battle to save their friend Sandy who'd been kidnapped by Luc and his army of the fallen.

Lee double-checked her weapons. She had a divine sword calibrated to her energy fields along with varying sized daggers plus death stars for hand to hand combat.

She'd dreamed of this battle many times over the last three decades, and each dream ended with the same outcome. Sweat trickled down her spine as her mouth went bone dry. She'd trained with Ruby and her mortal friends. They knew the drills and the angels they would fight alongside.

"Mom. Breathe. Your face is turning red." Ruby squeezed her hand.

"Keep your eyes open. Fight to kill. Do not second-guess your instincts. Remember, demon angel wings are solid black."

"I'm ready." She pointed to Reed, Anna, and Jerry. "We're all ready."

Row after row of fierce warrior angels stood wearing golden armor, their wings shimmering bright light. Each angel carried various divine weapons of mass destruction, and they waited on instructions from their commander, the Archangel, Michael.

Most angels were tall except Michael. He wasn't short but stocky. He was also the most seasoned warrior in Heaven. Lee knew they'd be victorious in battle with him leading them, but at what cost?

The thought of losing her daughter filled Lee with such anxiety. Ruby's infant son needed her. Reed needed her too.

And the idea of never seeing her darling Harry again, took her distress to the next level. She fought the urge to scream but tamped down the feelings so she wouldn't give the demons an upper hand in the pending conflict.

Last night, Harry and Lee had said their goodbyes in their bedroom at Everglade Farms. Unable to sleep, he held her in his arms through the night and into the early morning hours with no mention of the battle or the possible outcomes. Instead, they reminisced about a lifetime of fond memories.

Harry was her rock, and he knew what she faced today.

Oh, my sweet husband, I must push you out of my thoughts so that I won't falter.

The time had come to foster bravery, to wipe out all negativity, and to focus her eyes on the prize.

Luc.

Her teeth clenched. She should've used her powers to kill Luc years ago, but the Spirit of Man forbade it. Luc feared her because, even in her aging mortal suit, some of her abilities exceeded the Morning Star's, and he knew it.

The difference—Luc was immortal, and she was not.

She'd fought with the Angel Armed Forces before and knew the protocols. Most of her encounters in the previous years were skirmishes at best. Only once had she fought in Hades, after learning who and what she was. That had been over thirty years ago. She'd been so naïve, and inexperienced, but ready and willing to give her all.

Thunder rumbled, and dark clouds rolled swiftly across the sky.

Lee watched with her unit as Michael signaled to the AAF.

Sounds from the trumpet blowers shook the ground.

Shrieking battle cries of the warrior angels filled the air.

Lightning bolts struck the ground and crackled.

She blocked out the noise and zoned in on the enemy.

The whipping wind lashed her face as she raced toward Luc's foothold with daggers in each hand. She released a deep guttural roar the moment she made lethal contact with the first demon. "Die beast."

The surprise attack gave the AAF a temporary advantage as her team ripped through the unsuspecting demon angels.

In minutes, the demons regrouped and unleashed chaos.

During battle, Lee's supernatural strength and speed kicked in. She didn't take time to swipe the dead demon's blood from her weapons before moving onto the next one.

Ducking a blow, she slid on her knees and plunged her dagger deep into the demon's sternum with a jarring pain that went up her arms. She pushed the brute off with her right foot, rolled, and reached for the sword sheathed at her side.

The demon took a chunk of her shoulder before she sliced off his head with her blade. Her adrenaline kept the pain at bay.

To the left of Lee, the AAF archery division released flaming hot arrows of blue energy in rapid succession, dropping the human guards stationed on the roofs. The guards flesh exploded and disintegrated before hitting the ground.

She fought hard against the demons with her divine sword and daggers, weaving in and out with precision, cutting the demons to ash. She clashed with body and blades against the next beast.

His mouth split open in a terrifying grin revealing jagged teeth oozing saliva. "We meet again, crossbreed."

The demon lost his footing in the mud, and she knocked the saber out of his hands.

"Yeah, I don't remember you." She plunged divine steel into his heart.

Blue energy spheres with nuclear fission properties hit the ground, spraying debris into her eyes. She blinked several times.

Lee's guardian angel, Erinelle, fought beside her. She blew into her eyes, and her vision restored.

"Thanks." Lee moved forward and didn't look back as another legion of warrior angels entered the playing field of horrors.

On the other side of the meadow, her daughter fell to her knees in combat against a female demon.

Lee screamed, "No, no, no."

She raced toward Ruby. She had to reach her in time.

Please, Lord, help me.

A crushing blow to her side stole her breath. She tumbled to the ground and rolled several times before regaining her momentum.

Erinelle attacked the shrieking demon. "Go to Ruby. I'll be right behind you." She sliced the demon's midsection severing his torso from his trunk.

Lee and Reed reached Ruby at the same time.

Frantic, she yelled, "Ruby, Ruby, are you alright—"

"I'm okay."

Relieved, Lee glanced up to find demons circling them.

By the saints, they'd used Ruby as bait. The demons attacked from the sky and the ground. Surrounded by enemy forces with no way to retreat, they must fight to the death. The demons would not take them prisoner.

Lee had dreamed about the battle. She'd witnessed the moment of truth. Regardless, and without hesitation, she forged onward to save her daughter's life.

Erinelle and other AAF warriors unleashed on the beasts. Lee looked at Reed. They were gaining ground.

Maybe her dream had it wrong. Perhaps everything would be all right.

Suddenly, Hell's fire spread through her.

A demon's blade had pierced her back.

She was burning inside and out.

She looked at Ruby. Thousands of images flooded her mind. Her parents, Harry, George and Ruby's births, their childhood, so much laughter and joy, giving way to her sinking heartache and pain.

Life was precious, and too many mortals wasted time on stupid stuff. Not Lee. Her gifts from The Creator had saved many. Her blessings overflowed. Little Joe in Harry's arms was the last image revealed.

"Mama, don't leave me," Ruby cried.

She smiled at her daughter as tears slid down her cheeks. "I love you," she mouthed.

Everything went black.

Seconds later, she woke in Erinelle's arms. They flew above Luc's compound, above the clouds. The brilliant blue sky seemed endless.

Her eyes flickered. "Is this Heaven?"

The angel smiled. "Oh, my darling girl, Heaven is so much more than blue skies and sunshine. Heaven is love."

"What's next?"

"You're going home. Stay with me," Erinelle pleaded.

They materialized inside her bedroom at Everglade Farms. Erinelle laid her gently on the bed. She cried out in pain.

"You knew what would happen today?"

Lee wept. "Did I? It freakin' burns. I'm not ready to die. My family needs me."

The angel knelt beside the bed, placing her hand on the entry wound. She grimaced. "Saints and sinners. We need a healer. I'll call for Raphael."

"He's fighting with Jerry," she sighed.

Erinelle went down on bended knees and bowed her head. Blue light emitted around her form. She closed her eyes and prayed in an indecipherable language of the angels.

Lee didn't believe in accidents or coincidences. She did believe in divine intervention. She prayed for Ruby and Reed. She prayed for Anna and Jerry, and she prayed for Sandy's safe return.

She wasn't afraid of death in this realm because death would take her to Heaven.

Destiny brought her guardian angel, Erinelle.

Divine Providence brought Lee a life full of love.

The years seemed to fade away.

She had no regrets.

CHAPTER 1

"COMING IN ON A WING AND A PRAYER"

*1*950
Everglade Farms, Tennessee

LEE QUICKLY DRESSED and jogged down the front stairs. She met her
father, Joseph, in the kitchen where he sipped black coffee and read
the morning newspaper. She leaned over and kissed his forehead.
"Good morning, Dad."

He folded the paper, then placed it on the table. "Sleep well?"

"Like a baby." She poured herself a cup of coffee.

"Are you ready to go and pick up your mother?" Dad looked as
though he hadn't slept in days.

"I'll drive." She quickly ate a banana and gulped the rest of the java.

Without much chitchat, they left the house and got into her
father's 1947 Plymouth Special Deluxe four-door sedan. She backed
out of the garage and drove down the drive and onto Campbell Ridge
Road.

Two weeks earlier, her mother, Jenny, had collapsed from a debili-
tating headache while working in her herb garden. Everglade's doctor
had moved his practice to Nashville so one of their family friends,

Blaine Glenn, suggested Sacred Heights Sanatorium specializing in various maladies.

Reluctantly, Dad took mom to the sanatorium while she finished her final semester in college. Mom seemed to respond well to the treatments, so Lee returned Easter weekend to go with her father to bring her mother home.

Dad tapped his foot impatiently. "I've never been away from your mother more than one day since the day we said our I do's. I didn't want to take her to Sacred Heights, but I didn't know what else to do. The county hospital kept pumping her full of drugs and then sent her home. It's awful watching someone I love in pain, and there's not a dad-blame thing I can do about it."

At the stop sign, she looked both ways before taking a left onto Highway 99 for the forty-five-minute journey to Sacred Heights. "You did the right thing. I got in so late last night. What did the doctor say when he called yesterday?"

"Not much. The physician used electroshock therapy on your mom. Did I mention that? It seemed to work. The staff wouldn't allow phone calls during her stay. Of course, I called anyway, but the doctor repeated the same thing, no calls or visitors while undergoing treatment. I didn't want to worry you at school, but I've been going stir crazy without your mother."

"You should've called me. I could've come home. Murfreesboro is not that far of a commute. And I'm sure Mom's fine."

She had a few lingering doubts. She'd scoured the college library regarding sanatoriums, and one of the most recent articles mentioned electroshock therapy (ECT or electroconvulsive therapy) as well as hydrotherapy treatments used for a variety of medical conditions. However, one noted medical journal stated concerns over the abuse of ECT and possibly long-term memory effects, but she kept those thoughts to herself.

Joseph linked his fingers together, rotating thumb over thumb. "If they hurt your mother in any way, I'll kill that doctor."

"I did some research at the library, and Sacred Heights is rated one of the best in the state of Tennessee. We must trust the doctors and staff did their best, and if she's coming home today, that's good news. We'll celebrate Easter together. I'll bake a ham and cook all of mom's favorites."

He gave her a weak smile. "I hope Jenny doesn't think I abandoned her. She was furious when the nurse took her away. She screamed vulgarities at me. I didn't know she even knew those words."

"She was in pain. You know, most of the time, when her headaches pass, she doesn't remember what she's done."

Lee bit her tongue.

No need to tell him how mean her mother had been in the throes of such pain. She hated to go off to college and leave her mom's care to her father, but on the other hand, she wasn't subject to her tirades. The painful memories still burned inside her.

CHRISTMAS MORNING *while her father gathered wood for the fireplace, Lee walked into the den next to the decorated evergreen. She stopped in her tracks when she looked into her mom's dazed dilated eyes.*

She wore a grim expression indicating her unstable condition and spoke in a heated voice. "That dress makes you look like a whore, and your lipstick screams Jezebel. Go upstairs and change before your father comes inside."

With caution, she said, "Mom, you bought the dress and the lipstick."

Jenny reared her open hand to smack Lee's face, and for the first time in her life, she stood up to her mother, grabbing her wrists. The look of shock or possibly fear reflected in her mom's eyes, but she had no choice but to subdue her.

"I'm sorry. I'm so sorry. I don't know what makes me lash out. Oh, please forgive me, darling. I never want to hurt you."

Lee pushed the hair away from her mom's face. "No need to apologize. I can't imagine having a headache for two straight months."

"I don't know if it's the headaches or the pills. I don't feel like myself anymore." Her mom plopped onto the sofa and stared into the crackling fire. "Don't tell your father, but when my headaches are in full swing, I try to

sleep, but I have horrifying dreams. The devil is out to get us, well, more specifically, he is out to get you, and I fight him until I wake."

"Our dreams sometimes create distractions to hide our deepest fears." She noticed the dark circles under her mother's eyes. "I hate you're going through such a hard time. I wish there were something I could do to help you. Have you taken your medication this morning?"

Jenny shook her head. "It makes me sleepy. I'm afraid to sleep."

"Does your head hurt?"

"Uh-huh. All the time. I can't remember the last time I went a whole day without pain."

Lee went to the kitchen cabinet where they stored medicine and a first aid kit. She picked up several bottles before finding the one marked, Percodan. She poured her mother a glass of water and gave her the pill. "You don't have to be afraid. I'll be right here. The meds will relax you. You don't have to sleep just rest your eyes, and I'll bring you a cold compress."

Mom's brows furrowed. "But it's Christmas. The turkey and dressing."

"You taught me well. I'll cook, so don't fret. Do you want to go to your bedroom?"

"No. I'll stretch out on the couch. You'll stay close by?" She took Lee's hand and kissed it.

"Of course, I will."

"You're a good daughter. I love you. Don't ever forget it even when I'm snappy."

Her mother dozed on and off for the rest of Christmas Day. Father was none the wiser.

LEE ROLLED down her window allowing the warm fragrant breeze to flow inside the car, releasing the stagnant air. She loved driving down Highway 99, especially in the spring. Blooming trees cascaded down the hills with shimmering colors.

She flipped on the radio and fiddled with the dial until landing on Perry Como's, "Some Enchanted Evening" then leaned back in the seat and hummed the tune.

"Harry Glenn's discharge is around your graduation day." Dad grinned.

Her stomach fluttered at the mention of his name. How did her father know she was thinking about Harry? It'd been two years since he came home on leave. She didn't like talking about her love life. "Hm, that's nice."

Joseph chuckled under his breath. "Hey, stop by the flower shop. I want to buy your mother a dozen yellow roses. She loves them."

"You're such a romantic." She parked in the space at the end of the building. Her father went inside and appeared a few minutes later with a large bouquet of yellow roses and white lilies.

"Gorgeous. Mom will love them."

A few minutes later, they drove up and around a winding road. Several road signs pointed to the visitor's station upon entering the impressive Sacred Heights Sanatorium brick entrance with giant magnolia trees full of buds. The facility reminded her of a European Castle instead of a hospital.

She parked and cut the engine, then grabbed her purse. She rummaged inside until finding the tube of soft pink lipstick, applied, then blotted her lips with a tissue. "Ready?"

"Been ready." Joseph exited the car with the flowers in his left hand.

Walking along the sidewalk and up the steps, she marveled at the Victorian-inspired architecture with four towers, turrets, and even a couple of gargoyles resting on the outer edges.

Several patients milled around outside with staff on the second-floor balcony. Joseph opened the door for Lee and entered the grand lobby with a four-level open atrium framed by intricately designed railings topped by a domed skylight. A room to the right held rows of books on cherry bookshelves.

A perky brunette receptionist worked the check-in desk. "Welcome to Sacred Heights Sanatorium. May I help you?"

"I'm here to bring my wife home. Jenny Campbell."

"Oh yes, Dr. Brickman is waiting for you in his office, Mr. Campbell, if you and your guest will sign in."

"This is our daughter."

The woman nodded. Her piercing dark eyes changed to light blue with oblong pupils like a slit in the center.

Lee did a double-take, and the receptionist's eyes returned to normal.

What the heck?

He handed the bouquet to Lee and pulled out his pen from inside his summer jacket. He leaned down and wrote their names on the page of the brown guest ledger. "Where is Jenny?"

The receptionist looked at the nine-foot-tall mahogany clock trimmed in gold against the wood-paneled wall. "It's art day. She's in the craft room on the second floor."

"Is it okay if I go and surprise her?" Lee inquired.

"Certainly. The elevators are at the end of the hall." The woman pointed in the right direction.

The receptionist picked up the phone. "Mr. Joseph Campbell is here for Dr. Brickman." She hung up. "His assistant will be here in a moment to take you to his office."

He turned to Lee. "I'll meet you upstairs after I speak with Dr. Brickman regarding your mom's release."

She handed her father the flowers, then kissed his cheek. "See you soon."

The grandeur of the facility surprised her as she walked along the corridor, then noticed there were no patients on the main floor. She pressed the button to the dome-shaped elevator doors and stepped inside the cherry-paneled walls with brass handrails and hit the second-floor button.

The elevator rose steadily, then silently slid open. A rotten scent hit Lee so hard she nearly vomited but quickly covered her nose and mouth with one hand while looking for a handkerchief in her purse with the other. She exited the elevator looking around for someone to ask for help.

A large mural of angels and demons covered the foyer wall. Suddenly, the celestial beings in the painting began to engage in a battle scene with three-dimensional effects.

Her heart raced, and her throat constricted.

She closed her eyes. Stress did strange things to the mind. She took several breaths, counted to ten, then opened her eyes again. The mural didn't move, but the angels and demons depicted in the image stared at her.

A cold shiver ran down her spine.

She walked briskly down the hall, looking for the art room. The large windows to the right revealed she was on the top floor, not the second. She stopped at the door and peeked into a small window.

To her utter amazement, a man appeared in a cage with large chains around his neck, wrists, and ankles. She pressed her hands to the door. Visions of the man in grotesque scientific experiments hit her brain with a jolt.

The patient screamed, "Evil is coming. Evil is here. RUN."

Lee sensed the presence of darkness, something she'd been able to do since her childhood but never spoke about it. Prickles of fear rippled on the back of her neck. She glanced to the left and right but didn't see anyone. She investigated the next room through another small window in the door, finding a patient wearing a straitjacket and foaming at the mouth.

Holy crow.

Cold air enveloped her.

The top floor was a far cry from the opulence of the main lobby. Wails from the patients made her tremble.

A handsome man dressed in a doctor's white coat stepped out of one of the rooms with hair as dark as onyx and eyes the color of turquoise blue. "Are you lost?"

"I'm looking for the art room, and somehow I landed on the top floor."

"You're on the acute patient floor," he said. "No visitors are allowed. The art room is on the second floor, not the fourth. May I escort you to the elevator?"

"I pushed the second-floor button. How did I end up here? Those poor patients. Why are they here?"

"The top floor of the sanatorium holds our most severe cases.

Patients with schizophrenia, paranoid delusions, and psychopaths reside on the floor. Absolutely no visitors are allowed." He had an air of superiority about him. And, something else nagged her.

She'd met him before, or possibly dreamed of him. Sometimes her dreams came true.

"But one of the patients is in a cage with chains. Why?" she asked, adamant. "No one should be treated so disrespectfully regardless of their condition."

"You must be mistaken. Which patient?"

Lee pointed to the room. "He's in there."

She looked again. The room was empty. Her heart sank.

Am I delusional?

"I swear there was a patient in that room just seconds ago."

"Do you believe in the supernatural?" the man asked with a raised brow.

"I do." She had to believe because weird and unexplainable things happened to her all the time.

He gave her a grin that would've melted most female hearts, but it held no warmth. "I've been told by the staff the fourth floor's haunted. A patient died a violent death in that room over sixty years ago."

She wanted out of here, pronto. "I am sorry to intrude. It wasn't intentional." She went inside the elevator again, and the man pushed the second-floor button as he stepped inside. "Have we met? You look familiar."

He gave her a look. His eyes held a message. She couldn't help but stare. She could've sworn he said, "Yes, I know you." But the man hadn't spoken a word.

Was he a real doctor or a patient?

Either way, she had some seriously bad feelings about the darkly handsome man. She rarely disregarded her instincts. She could spot the good from the bad nine times out of ten. She had a keen intuition. The man riding in the elevator with her was bad with a capital B.

The short ride to the second floor didn't last long. The man held the door open. "Here you go. The art room is down the corridor on the left side. You can't miss it. Do you think you can manage to find it, or would you like me to take you?"

She blushed. "Um, no, thank you. I'll find it. I did press the second-floor button. I'm not sure how I landed on the fourth floor, but I appreciate your help."

He grabbed her hand and held it firmly. "There are no accidents. I'm sure we'll meet again."

With the touch of his hand, Lee had a more sinister vision—a vision of this same man as one of the beings in the mural with the battle scene. She had an impulse to go back to the fourth floor, but something told her not to.

She exited the elevator and swiveled back to glance at him. The man had simply vanished.

Geez, Louise.

Something eerie, dark, and bizarre lived within the walls of Sacred Heights Sanatorium. The elevator doors closed behind her, and she sighed in relief. Thank God, her mother was leaving the place today. Lee would make sure she'd never return.

Luc used the fourth floor of Sacred Heights Sanatorium as one of many portal entries around the world which led him and the fallen to Hades. But it was the first time he'd sensed the presence of a celestial angel in the place.

The scent from his real home in Heaven was undeniable. He materialized only to find a mortal, but the female wasn't just a mortal. She was something else entirely.

He waited in spirit form for Daglan, one of the generals in the army of the fallen, to materialize. "Did you recognize the woman walking into the art and craft room? I know her scent but can't place it. Only angels possess that scent from Heaven, but she also smells of a mortal. I want to know everything about her."

Daglan steepled his fingers. "Rumors have surfaced from our spies within the AAF that our father, The Creator, has made a new species to help in the angelic conflict. Maybe, she's one of them."

"Hm. I hardly think the girl is a warrior angel, but she did see Malcolm's ghost. Maybe she's a medium, and her scent is not of this world. I want a full report." Luc watched as the young woman went into the room. "She has untapped powers rolling off her form that I can't quite put my finger on, and I didn't see any guardians accompanying her, which is odd. If she's a fluke of nature, then I want her on the team. If she is one of The Creator's new projects, I want her even more. Are we clear?"

Daglan bowed low to him. "We are clear, my lord. I'll find you as soon as I complete my inquiries from our spies on the other side."

He grabbed Daglan's arm. "I want to know about her family, friends, anyone we can use as leverage. Got it?"

Daglan nodded and vanished, leaving a slight trace of mist in the air.

Luc floated through the walls into the art room to find the young woman with a patient, Jenny Campbell. He'd interviewed the woman upon her arrival at Sacred Heights once he'd read her file regarding her gift of dreams.

The mortal mind had many components, and he'd learned centuries ago, he could exploit mortals with delusions and other susceptible brain disorders to his benefit in the angelic war that he'd been waging against his father for thousands of years.

Luc had monitored Jenny's dreams and learned they were of him and his fallen angels, so when he first interrogated her, he appeared as an angel of light. She eventually figured out his real identity.

Was the girl her daughter? The one she'd been protecting against demons. He inched closer to eavesdrop on their conversation.

"Mother, you look beautiful. Are you well?" asked the young woman.

Jenny stared right at him.

He placed his forefinger to his lips, transmitting a silent message. *"You mustn't tell her you see me."*

The female clenched her teeth. *"My daughter is off limits. You may do as you wish to me, but leave her alone."*

"I am interested in you. Your good health is my utmost concern. No more headaches. No more visions. But I can change it in a heartbeat. Is that your wish?"

Jenny didn't reply.

He smiled at her. *"Good girl. I'm not going to hurt your daughter. I am only interested in her gifts as I am interested in yours."*

"She has no gifts. Leave her be."

"Then you have nothing to worry your pretty little head over. You're going home today."

"Mom, what's wrong?" The girl glanced over her shoulder, then looked back at Jenny. "What do you see?"

Jenny blinked several times before standing, then hugged her daughter. "Just looking for your father."

The girl's expression softened. "He's signing your release paperwork. Are your headaches gone?"

"Yes. I haven't had one in over a week."

"So, the shock treatments worked?"

"Yes, they worked."

Luc narrowed his eyes at Jenny. *"Good. No need to share with your daughter about our arrangement. All is well. We'll talk very soon."*

The presence of an AAF warrior entered the area as Luc was about to leave the room. *"Erinelle, my old love. What may I do for you today?"*

The fierce-looking female warrior drew her blade and pointed it at his chest. *"At the bequest of The Creator, you are to desist in your arrangement with Jenny Campbell. She and her family are under the protection of the AAF. Any violation from you or your lackeys will be deemed a threat and may result in swift action."*

Luc held a firm stance, then reared back his head laughing so loudly the more demented patients under his control looked in his direction. *"You have no power here. Tell Father, if he has a problem with me to come Himself next time."*

"You have been warned, he who has no name." Three more AAF

warriors descended surrounding Jenny and her daughter just as her husband entered.

His brows popped. *"My, my, my, the girl isn't mortal, but she isn't immortal either. She has the scent of Heaven. I really should thank you for helping me do my work."* Daglan and Luc's wife, Sazae, a demon warrior, flanked him. *"Do we really want a battle here around these poor unfortunate souls?"*

"You prey on the weak-minded. Pick on someone your own size for a change." Baldric the Warrior flexed his muscled biceps.

Luc laughed again, as Daglan and Sazae drew swords. *"Now, now, children. Baldric's still a fool. No need to disrupt the serenity of my mood."* He emitted a low growl. *"But the day is coming when I alone will rule all of the Earth and its inhabitants. Remember the ancient text, my old friends."* His wings jutted toward the ceiling. *"I'll bide my time until we meet again."*

Luc, Daglan, and Sazae materialized inside his lair. "Alert the generals; a battle is brewing regarding this girl and her family."

Daglan bowed. "As you wish," then left the room.

"My lord, rest with me. Forget about the AAF and The Creator." Sazae trailed her long, slender fingers across his chest.

"Damn it. Do you think I want to live on this planet indefinitely? I can't forget them." He backhanded her across the face. Her head snapped to the left. She straightened, then she licked the blood from her lip.

"How can I rest? The AAF is taunting me. I will destroy the girl and her family." He poured a drink at the slate bar with star embellishments. "Come, Sazae, I will heal your wound."

She went to him, and he placed his hand on her mouth, then kissed her.

"All is well, my lord."

Luc's former allies would pay dearly for entering Sacred Heights.

CHAPTER 2

"SENTIMENTAL JOURNEY"

*L*ee rode her mare, Princess, to the top of Campbell Ridge with the rising sun on her face and the warm wind in her hair. The last few weeks, her mom seemed stronger, with no signs of headaches.

Life was good.

She leaned into the gallop, pushing Princess faster and faster up the ridge. She would graduate from college in a few hours. With a renewed sense of purpose, she shouted, "Freedom!"

One chapter in her book of life was closing, and a new chapter about to begin. Her parents wanted her to get her master's, but she wanted money and independence.

After dismounting, she ran her hand over the mare's mane, then slipped the bit out of her mouth. "Good girl." Lee rubbed her muzzle then reached in her pocket for a couple of sugar cubes. Princess whinnied in delight, scarfing up the sweet treats. The mare had been her thirteenth birthday present from her father.

She giggled from the memory of his harebrained idea to break the mare without help. He and Princess gave each other their money's worth. After many failed attempts and a badly beaten ego, he succeeded.

Brushing off her riding pants, Lee glanced to a strange blue light emitting from the entrance of Campbell Ridge Cave. Dad had warned her never to go into the vast cave system alone, but her curiosity got the better of her.

She skipped over the small stream, entering the mouth of the cave with enormous stalactites and beautiful rock formations. She followed the bright light and came to an abrupt halt inside a room covered with ancient drawings.

Her eyes widened at the sight of a tall woman with long, flaming auburn hair, and armed to the teeth with weapons. "Hello, Lee." The woman stood.

Her mouth gaped. "Ah, you know me?"

The woman took a step toward her, and Lee took a step back.

"Do not be afraid, for I have been with you since birth. My name is Erinelle, your guardian angel." The angel expanded her shimmering wings in a kaleidoscope of colors.

"Oh, my goodness." Lee smacked her hand over her mouth in complete shock. She'd attended church most of her life and in her heart believed in the divine, but coming face-to-face with the angel made her heart skip a beat. She swayed, and Erinelle scooped her up under her right arm with ease, removing her from the room and taking her out of the cave into the sunlight.

The angel shimmered like sparkling diamonds as she placed Lee on a raised flat rock. "I don't want to overwhelm you more, but I have important news to share with you. Are you strong enough to listen?" She leaned in and searched Lee's eyes.

"You're real? I'm not hallucinating, am I?" She straightened her spine. "And I'm stronger than I look."

The angel laughed. "Yes, you are strong. Do you need a drink of water?"

"No. May I touch your wings? They're beautiful." She lifted her hand, and the wings disappeared like magic. For some unfathomable reason, she wasn't afraid at all when she knew she should've fallen prostrate before the celestial being.

"Do you mind if I sit?"

"By all means, sit. So, you've been with me always, huh?"

"I was assigned your life before you left Heaven. The Creator bestowed many gifts on you, Lee. You're one of The Chosen of Campbell Ridge, and your divine gifts come with specific obligations."

Erinelle wore gold and bronze warrior armor reminiscent of a Greek goddess of war or maybe a Roman gladiator. She reached inside a side pocket of the body armor and withdrew a semi-precious stone with the brilliance of an autumn sunset and placed it in Lee's hand. "The carnelian stone merely triggers a release of supernatural powers given to you in the heavenly realm. Keep it with you. Close your eyes then tell me what you remember."

"In the heavenly realm? I don't understand." She followed Erinelle's instructions and closed her eyes. The stone warmed in her hand, allowing the energy to flow from the top of her head to the tips of her toes. "Um, I'm a warrior and not just any warrior, but I fight demons. The stone represents my strength, courage, and leadership qualities from The Creator, and something else—I think I'm different. I've always felt different too."

She opened her eyes and shook her head. Her calmness started to erode, and she found herself on the brink of hyperventilating. "What...what did I say?"

"Take slow breaths in and out." Erinelle placed her hand on Lee's shoulder.

A sense of peace overcame her from the angel's touch. "I feel a little dizzy."

The angel propped her boot on a nearby stump. "How much do you know of the Bible?"

"Um. I've gone to church all my life. I've read the Bible cover to cover. Why?"

"The Morning Star, the brightest of The Creator's angels, incited a rebellion within our realm. He wanted to overthrow our Father. The Archangel, Michael, cast Luc and a third of the angels out of Heaven."

She tilted her head to the side. "You mean, Lucifer, right?"

"We aren't allowed to say his name, but yes. For our purposes, we'll refer to him as Luc." Erinelle looked around the surrounding area. "We don't want him here."

She reached out to touch the beings forearm. "You are here, aren't you? Why? What's so special about me?"

The angel extended her hand in a sweeping motion. "The Creator made all species on Earth, including humankind. He created humans in His image, but there's been a constant struggle between good and evil ever since humans listened to The Serpent and gained divine knowledge, so The Creator exiled the mortals from Eden. He still loves humanity and sent guardian angels for guidance, and the still small inner voice helps humans to discern right from wrong."

Lee pulled her knees up to her chest and wrapped her arms around them. "The creation story. I've always wondered about the scripture regarding making us in His image. Does it mean The Creator is not a spirit?"

"The Creator can be both ethereal and corporeal And, it's not just a story. Ever since humankind left paradise, warrior angels have fought Luc and his army of the fallen over Earth and the mortals. The war escalated when humankind detonated the atomic bomb. Lee, you are the first of your kind. He created you with powers of the angels, along with divine knowledge to help us win the war. If you succeed in your destiny, more of your kind will enter the world, and with His blessing, we will win the war once and for all."

"My kind? I don't get it. I'm human. And why can't He get rid of Luc and his fallen? Wouldn't that answer all His problems? And ours?"

"Luc and the fallen belong to The Creator. He doesn't want to destroy him. He wants Luc to admit he was wrong and submit to His authority. But he has a taste for power, and uses his gifts of manipulation to gain ground in the fight." Erinelle looked up to the sky before locking eyes with Lee. "And you're so much more than a human. You are a lethal weapon. A hybrid messenger from the heavenly realm with mortal parents."

"You have the wrong girl. I'm average at best. I like sports. I love dancing and laughing and having fun. I don't fight. Heck, I hate confrontations."

Lee's head spun, her stomach rolled and lurched emptying the contents of her breakfast on the ground.

Erinelle handed her a linen handkerchief which materialized out of thin air.

She dabbed her mouth, then the white cloth disappeared. It took several minutes before she regained composure.

The angel cupped her hands, leaving several inches of space in between. Swirling light produced an exquisite crystal sculpture with the most amazing sapphire eyes. "Hold it."

She held the weighted crystal image in her hands. It pulsated. It couldn't be possible. Flashes of her past life in Heaven opened inside her mind—white walls and a laboratory with Him replicating her chromosomes and placing her genetic information with His into a mortal's. She traveled with the speed of light down a long tunnel and came out as a human baby, and into the arms of Joseph Campbell.

Her chest heaved. Everything in her life turned upside down. "I'm —I'm not a warrior. I'm not. I'm not worthy of the task. I'm—I'm afraid."

"All the Chosen in the world have had similar emotions, but you are His Chosen to help penetrate Luc's forces disguised in human form. You will still laugh, dance, and have fun. You will also fight."

"But how?" It seemed ridiculous to think of herself as a supernatural warrior. She'd never fought anyone. She'd never killed any living thing except maybe flies.

"I will train you." Erinelle stood and stretched out her hands. "The fallen angels are highly territorial by nature, and sometimes internal battles between groups break out. The demonic forces are grouped based on human characteristic flaws like jealousy and greed. The warrior angels like myself, and The Chosen throughout the world, use the demons' territorial nature to divide and conquer. We fight one battle at a time. And many battles are going on every second of every day."

Erinelle stared intently into her eyes. "You're receiving a lot of information at one time. The process is sometimes difficult to take in. Humans often live in ignorant bliss of the angelic conflict taking place around them daily. But I promise you, you are worthy, and you will help us to win the ongoing fight between the warrior angels and the cast outs."

"I've been taught not to question His words in the Bible, but did He see all of this happening in the grand plan?" Lee paced while wringing her hands. "Couldn't He stop the process before it started? How did it get out of control in the first place?" She stopped and looked at the angel.

"He did with The Flood, but mortals didn't change despite their second chance. The Creator has given mortals opportunities more numerous than the stars in the galaxies, but humans repeat the same mistakes over and over again."

The angel extended her hands, palms up. "Look, humans, after gaining divine knowledge in the Garden of Eden, also gained free will like the Supreme ones, and it's not in His or our power to change it. Since time began, one person's free will has affected another's positively and negatively. I don't make the rules. I follow them. We watch out for Earth and mortals, and my job assignment is you."

Erinelle sat down on the flat rock, placing her forearms on her knees. "You are smart and strong. I've been instructed to give you details on a need-to-know basis, so I don't place undue influence on your decision-making skills. It's part of our ongoing conflict, and you have a major battle heading your way based on the intel from our headquarters, but you don't have to figure it all out in a day."

Lee couldn't breathe. Her chest hurt. It was too much to take in.

"One note," Erinelle continued, "Luc's fiercely jealous of humans and uses his higher levels of consciousness to manipulate them. We work to counteract his destructive operations. We don't want to lose souls, but as the end of an age is coming more and more are falling into the darkness."

"What do you mean the end of an age? Are you referring to the end of time?" Her level of anxiety continued to escalate.

The angel's wings ruffled. "End of an age is different from the end of time. Humanity has undergone several eras known as the end of an age. Famine, disease, war, pestilence have nearly wiped out humanity many times like in the Little Ice Age, the fall of the Roman Empire, and the Black Death."

"Sounds like you're talking about the Four Horsemen of the Apocalypse."

"You do know the ancient text. That's good. It'll help you understand how close we are to ending this age."

This fierce and beautiful angel spoke about ending the world as she knew it. Lee had even wondered the same thing during the midst of World War II.

Erinelle jumped to her feet and unsheathed a blinding sword of light. "Leave her be, or show yourself."

Lee jumped off the rock and cowered behind her guardian.

Another supreme being appeared before them. "Come on, Erinelle. Where's your sense of humor? She's such a cute cupcake." He edged toward Lee. "Wanna play with me? I'm a lot more fun than her." He waggled his long fingers toward Erinelle.

"In the name..." Before Erinelle finished her sentence, the being disappeared. She turned to Lee and said, "Luc has found you."

"Was that Luc?" Lee had the urge to flee the scene, but what good would that do?

"Fear opens the door to demons. It's very destructive. Redirect your thoughts to something more pleasant." Erinelle sheathed her sword.

"It's hard to comprehend everything you're telling me. Everything I've seen today changes who I am. I can't help my emotions."

"But you can learn to control them and not the other way around. Redirection of thought to joy, happiness, or love will always send demons running away. Positive emotions shield you and mortals from the fallen. Singing is another great way to cast them away. It reminds them of the home they will never see again. It creates pain for them." She placed her hand on Lee's shoulder.

"And to answer your question, he's not Luc. Daglan is one of his generals. He's no ordinary demon warrior either. I knew him when he served The Creator before he turned traitor. And if he's watching you, we must train straightaway." The angel's hands cupped Lee's cheeks, releasing her fear.

"But-but, I can't train today. I'm graduating from college, and Carol Ann is having a party with a band, and everyone who's anyone will be there."

"I'll refrain from sharing with you the story of Jonah. Oh, you're so young." The angel sighed. "I'll be around if you need me, but remember, tomorrow morning, we start training. Meet me here at dawn for your first lesson."

Erinelle dematerialized, leaving Lee dumbfounded.

She glanced at her watch.

Dang it.

She was going to be late for graduation if she didn't get moving. She'd think about being a lethal weapon later. She looked to the heavens in wonder. "Are you sure you didn't make a mistake?"

A voice echoed from the clouds, "The Creator doesn't make mistakes."

Holy cow.

With an inhale of breath, she placed her forefinger and thumb into the corners of her mouth and whistled for Princess. The red beauty galloped toward the cave entrance but stopped short, rearing its front legs and releasing a cry.

"Whoa, Princess, calm down, the pretty angel lady is gone." She remained steady and reached inside her pocket for more sugar cubes.

A little skittish, the mare approached Lee with caution, then nibbled up the sweets. She placed the bridle bit into her mouth, grabbed the reins, and mounted. She squeezed her thighs into the beast, then shouted, "Yah."

Thundering hooves echoed in the hollow. Princess took off toward Everglade Farms. The vibrant blue sky held no clouds, and gorgeous greens spread over the hills and valleys of the two hundred-acre farm. She tried focusing on the ride, but the mental snapshots of Erinelle and Daglan prevented it.

Approaching the barn lot, she noticed her father working on the tractor next to Granddaddy Campbell's log cabin. He looked up as she and Princess entered through the iron gate.

He swiped his hands with a red bandana. "How are you; my soon-to-be college graduate?"

She pressed her lips together as she got off the mare. She held the reins in her hands. Part of her wanted to run to her daddy for one of his big bear-like hugs. She needed to hear him say everything would be okay. Another part gave her a warning not to discuss the divine encounter. "Um, I'm fine, I guess."

"Want to talk about it?" He raised a brow.

"Not, now, Daddy."

"Come on, and meet me at the barn. I'll help you put up Princess. Give me the reins, and you get the brush."

Inside the barn, he placed Princess into one of the empty stalls. He took the saddle then removed the horse blanket and hung them in the adjoining tack room.

She went into the stall and began brushing the mare. "Dad, do you believe the creation story?"

"Of course, I do. Don't you?" He leaned on the wooden gate.

"Do you believe in angels and demons?"

"Why all the questions? I'm not a biblical scholar. However, I do believe in them. I believe in the supernatural too. And I believe we're both going to get our butts chewed out if we don't get to the house and get ready for your graduation."

Lee laughed. "You're right. We can talk about it later."

"Honey, remember, each person on the planet has the choice to choose right from wrong. Each of us has the chance to make our planet and the Universe a better place. One person changed the whole world with His message of love."

"Jesus, right? Yeah, He did, didn't He? I have so many questions, and I'm not sure I'll find the answers."

"Aw, Cricket, you'll find the answers once you figure out the right questions." He leaned over and kissed her forehead.

"How do you know?"

"Humankind has strived to figure out the answers to life's questions since the beginning. But I believe in each generation; every person must figure out what is right for them. Through research, prayer, and meditation, enlightenment may happen."

Her smile went wide. "You're a philosopher."

"I read a lot. Now, child of my heart, go get dressed, or your mother will have a hissy fit."

"About, Mom."

He shooed her away.

"Dad, I'm still worried about her."

"Me, too, but if we're late for your graduation, your mother will skin both our hides."

She raced inside the house.

Mom met her at the back door with a large wrapped gift box in her hands. "No running in the house, young lady."

"What's this?" She slipped off her boots in the mudroom.

"Your graduation gift." She handed Lee the box wrapped with white paper and tied with a pink ribbon.

The woodsy scent of her mom's perfume reminded her of childhood. "I love it when you wear Chanel. May I open the gift?"

"Sure, but at least wash your hands first."

Lee placed the gift box on the sofa in the living room and rushed into the bathroom under the stairwell to wash up, returning less than a minute later.

She tore into the gift box. "Mama, you shouldn't have. The dress is beautiful, and I love the robin egg color." She touched the garment with its full, billowy skirt, yards of sheer fabric, and a tight bodice. "I can't wait for Carol Ann to see it. The dress looks just like the one in the window at Estelle's on the square."

"Well, to be honest, I bought the dress at Estelle's. They dyed your shoes to match. And you may wear my mother's pearls and use my Chanel."

She leaped from the sofa and kissed her mom's cheek. "I love you so much."

"I love you too, but you smell of Princess. Bathe, and then I'll help you with your hair."

"How's your head today?"

"I'm having a good day so far. There's a new doctor in town who's helping me."

She hugged the gift box next to her chest. "New doctor?"

"I met him at Sacred Heights. He's started a practice here. Go on and get dressed, or we'll be late."

She froze at the mention of Sacred Heights. She wondered about the new doctor because of the supernatural experience she encountered on the fourth floor. That event and today couldn't be a coincidence.

Luc has found you.

Remembering Erinelle's words made the spit in her mouth dry up. Was the new doctor good or evil?

With no time to dwell on him, she ran upstairs and bathed in record time. She slipped on the dress with feather-light material that hit at her ankle. She turned as her mom entered the room. "The dress is gorgeous. Thank you."

"You're quite welcome. Whew, I'm glad we set your hair last night, but the tangles from your ride this morning are going to require a miracle worker."

Lee plopped down on the tufted stool in front of her dresser. Her mom carefully started from the bottom of her hair, brushing out the tangles then secured jeweled combs that matched her dress. The ends of her hair turned under in a soft roll.

Her mom kissed the top of her head, stepped back, and placed her hand over her heart. "My girl, the belle of the county. It seems like yesterday you just started school, and now you're graduating college."

"You're partial." Lee winked.

"That may be true, but I'm also right. Are you still seeing the Dyer boy?"

"Lord, no. I haven't dated him for ages and ages."

Joseph knocked on the door and peeked inside. "I hate to interrupt, but we need to hurry. You don't want to miss the 'Pomp and Circumstance March.'"

"We're ready, Tootie. Get the car, and we'll be right down." Her mother waved him off.

He nodded and left the room.

"So, do I pass?" Lee twirled in a circle.

"You most definitely pass, my beautiful daughter. Give me a second to grab my purse, and we'll walk out together."

"Hey, Mom, thanks for everything you do for me, for us. You and Dad have been the keenest parents ever."

Tears glistened in Jenny's eyes. "We tried our best, and you make us very proud." She squeezed Lee's hand, then walked down the hall.

Lee glanced at her reflection in the window. The same window where she'd dreamed and planned for a different kind of life. Her life changed this morning. For better or for worse, The Creator needed her to fight. Deep within her soul flowed a burgeoning willingness to please Him, releasing a white glow around her shoulders. She blinked, and the illumination disappeared.

She'd add it to a growing list of questions to ask Erinelle.

She gazed at her dress. She'd need new clothes and tennis shoes to train—until then, she'd make do with what clothes hung in her wardrobe.

Posing in front of the mirror, she made two fists. "Good grief, I look ridiculous. Give me strength, Lord, because I'm going to need it."

Lee couldn't wrap her brain around the concept that one day soon, she would fight demons.

Real ones.

CHAPTER 3

"IT'S BEEN A LONG, LONG TIME"

*A*fter graduation, Lee met her best friend, Carol Ann Glenn, under the big maples in the university courtyard. She couldn't recollect a single word from the ceremony. The morning encounter with Erinelle kept her mind preoccupied with life-altering implications. She forced a smile. "We did it, Carol Ann. We graduated from college."

Carol Ann linked arms with her. "We did, and guess who made it home just in time for the graduation?"

Her stomach dipped. She'd fallen in love with Carol Ann's older brother, Harry, before puberty, but he didn't know she existed. Well, except maybe that one time during summer break, right before he was deployed to the Philippines. She'd spent the night with Carol Ann.

Lee woke thirsty in the middle of the night and quietly slipped down the back stairs and slammed into handsome Harry.

He caught her in his arms before she took a tumble.

Time stopped.

She inhaled his masculine scent with a trace of cinnamon and heather. Her heart raced as he bent close to her cheek.

"Be careful of things that go bump in the night, darlin'." His touch made her weak in the knees.

The thought of his hands against her skin made the air around her crack with electricity.

All thoughts of the apocalypse vanished from her mind watching Harry stride regally across the campus grounds looking dapper in his Service Dress Blues.

Everything about him was profoundly erotic, and she did love a man in uniform. The line of his face, the tilt of his head, his strong, broad shoulders, and tapered waist made her sweat with a heat that had nothing to do with the weather.

He wet his full lips, and she inwardly groaned.

"My little sister, *magna cum laude.*" He picked up Carol Ann and hugged her. His eyes locked with Lee's as his sister pushed him aside.

Shaking her head, she looked at Lee and Harry. "Are either of you ever going to make the first move? Get with it."

He tousled Carol Ann's hair. "Yeah, well, Lee, you're looking mighty pretty today. Are you riding with us to the party?"

"Ah, no, I'm riding with my parents, but I'm spending the night with Carol Ann."

"That so? Well then, the day holds some promise." Harry said with a smile.

Carol Ann gave him a mock elbow to his ribs. "Don't tease Lee. She's my best friend, and you know it."

"Don't have a cow, sister." He winked at Lee. "Save me a dance for later?"

She nodded. "I'll see you later, alligator."

"After while, crocodile." Harry grinned.

For as long as Lee could remember, the Glenns and Campbells had been friends. Harry, five years her senior, had dated the most beautiful girls in the county. Everglade's hometown hero, he'd been E.H.S football, basketball, and baseball captain back in the day and recently received the Distinguished Service Cross medal.

Tall, dark, and incredibly good-looking were adjectives she used to describe him. The scar over his right eyebrow was the only imperfection on his chiseled face. And the way he wore that uniform should be a downright sin.

She fidgeted in the back seat of the four-door sedan. "Do you have to drive so slow, Dad?"

"Honey, we don't have to rush. Harry's tour is over. He's not leaving anytime soon." He glanced in the rearview mirror at her.

How did her father know what she was thinking? "What?"

"Never mind, precious."

"You could always ask Harry over for dinner one night." Jenny winked at Joseph.

"Good grief, Mom. Would you not..." Her face flushed.

Mom turned in the seat. "If Harry's interested in you, which I believe he is, then he'll let you know soon enough."

"Ugh. Please, I don't need love lessons from my mother." She rolled her eyes.

Was her torch for Harry so visible?

"Lee Campbell, don't be impertinent. We raised you better."

Dad parked in the grass next to the other vehicles. Most of their friends and neighbors came to celebrate both Carol Ann's and Lee's graduation.

Glenn Hall sat on a large hill with a very long and steep drive surrounded by hundred-year-old oaks. The 1849 Greek Revival-style mansion had survived the Civil War. The Union commandeered the estate to run their outskirt operations, and the Glenns fully restored the house with many of the same period pieces. Carol Ann and Harry were the fourth generation to live under its roof.

She'd spent many nights in the spacious rooms reminiscent of a bygone era. Eva and Blaine Glenn were like a second set of parents to her, and Carol Ann, the sister she never had. But Harry, well, he was a different story. He held her heart forever and a day.

"Hey, I'm going to take my overnight bag upstairs. I'll meet y'all in the back yard with the other guests later. Thanks again for the dress and shoes." She turned the car doorknob, exited the vehicle then raced across the lawn and up the front steps.

Mild breezes swept through the open windows and doors of Glenn Hall. Hired servants ran to and from the kitchen with silver platters of crystal flutes filled with champagne and appetizers. Family, friends, and neighbors mingled in the lower rooms of the mansion while other guests filtered through the back yard.

Linen-covered tables dotted the gardens with pink rose center-pieces. The swing band set up next to the pool house, using it as their makeshift stage with an adjoining parquet dance floor. Lanterns strung from tree to tree, adding to the ambiance of the evening.

She took the foyer stairway. Down the hall, she entered Carol Ann's bedroom and placed the overnight bag on the floor. "What are you still doing up here?"

"Shush." Carol Ann's fingertips touched the curtain sheers, she turned and motioned to Lee. "Come over here. See that dreamboat next to the pool house? His name is Dr. Oliver Pedersen. He's the new doctor in town, plus he's single."

Lee stepped over to the window and peered out over the lawn, shifting angles for a better view. So, that was the new doctor. Thank goodness he wasn't the man she'd met at Sacred Heights in the eleva-tor. "Have you met him?"

"Not yet, but as soon as the sun sets, I'm dancing with him." Carol Ann's high standards ensured her no ordinary local yokel would ever be enough to tame her wildness.

"You don't know a thing about the man." She eased down on the edge of the bed. "He could be a cold-blooded killer for all you know."

Or a demon. Or Luc. Oh, god, help me.

It was as if two separate people lived inside of her. The mortal part wanted nothing better to do than to dance in the arms of the man she loved, and the warrior wanted to find out if the doctor had anything to do with her revelations in the cave.

"Well, I simply must dance with him, and of course, I want to know him too. Will you help me?" She grabbed Lee's hand and pulled her from the bed.

"Of course, I will." The girls left the room, and she glanced toward Harry's bedroom. "Is he upstairs?"

"No, silly. Harry's at the bar in the parlor with some of his old high school buddies, and—Catherine Blount."

Ugh. "Catherine? What's she doing here?" Catherine and Harry dated through high school.

"She rode with Pugs. Don't worry. Catherine doesn't hold a candle to you. My goodness, your new dress compliments your eyes. And your hair is swell. You know, there's something about your ensemble that's very Elizabeth Taylor."

"You think so? Mom did my hair. You like it, really?" She touched the smooth curls.

"Uh, huh. Swell."

Descending the grand staircase into the main foyer, Lee watched Harry laughing and talking with his friends from high school, including Catherine, who seemed glued to his every word with tales of his naval travels carrying across the room.

She lifted her chin and straightened her shoulders then walked by the group with Carol Ann. Several young men whistled. She rolled her eyes and kept walking.

The double French doors led to the back yard. Dr. Pedersen waited just inside and bowed to them. "Congratulations on your graduation, Miss Carol Ann." He turned to Lee, and the way he looked at her made her check to see if her boob had popped out of the bodice of her dress.

"There's something not right about the doctor," Erinelle *whispered in her ear.*

"I knew it. Is he a demon?"

"No. We'll talk later. Keep your eyes and ears open."

"And who's your lovely, friend?" Dr. Pedersen asked with a slight foreign accent, perhaps Scandinavian.

Carol Ann touched his forearm. "This is my oldest and dearest friend, Lee Campbell. She graduated today too."

The doctor took a step toward Lee and pressed a kiss to the back of her hand. "You must be Jenny Campbell's daughter. May I offer my congratulations to you too on your achievement, and please, ladies, call me Oliver."

She tried to withdraw her hand, but he held it a bit too long, brushing his thumb over the delicate skin between her thumb and forefinger.

Instinctively, she took a step back, reclaiming her hand. "So, you're the new doctor in town?"

"Guilty as charged." Oliver slid his right hand into his pant pocket. A cinched black belt accentuated his narrow waist.

She picked up on his body language. Something about him seemed a bit too confident. Nice looking, no doubt about it. He wore his hair cropped short with a wave of blond hair parted on the side. He had deep-set blue eyes, his mouth full, and his nose prominent but not terrible.

He took in every inch of Lee, making her a tad bit uncomfortable.

Harry stared at Oliver, and she inwardly laughed. If eyes could kill, the Doc would be a dead man.

Then Harry locked eyes with her. His stare was breathlessly impassioned. He didn't divert his attention away from her, and just for a split second, the world halted.

Everything and everyone disappeared out of existence except for Lee and Harry.

He strode across the room and draped an arm around her shoulders. "Walk with me." He nodded to the doctor and ushered her out the door, leaving Carol Ann grinning.

They strolled along the brick sidewalk next to the pool in silence. He snatched two glasses of champagne from a passing waiter. "Everything is better washed down with champagne. Don't you agree?" He handed her a crystal flute.

"Yes, but it tickles my nose." She sipped champagne. "Somebody's acting jealous."

"Of the doctor? Heck, no. But I didn't come across the world just to see my sister. I came to see you too, and I don't want some wannabe making dibs on my dolly." He guided her down the stone path toward the creek.

She frowned. "I'm not your dolly."

"Not yet."

Harry interlocked his fingers with hers and brought her hand to his lips, pressing a kiss. "I missed you, Lee. Don't look so surprised. You were a kid when I left, and you're not a kid anymore. I didn't want to rob the cradle. I fought my attraction to you because I didn't want to go to jail. And you're my sister's best friend."

"And?"

"I had every reason to put distance between us before I left for college. You were fifteen, and then when I was deployed, I didn't know if I'd make it back. Did you find a fellow while I was away? No, don't answer that. Just thinking about you with someone else busts my guts."

He led her toward the weeping willow beside Spence Creek. "My military service is over, and I want to spend time with you. I want to know this exceptional woman you've become, and you are exceptional, Lee Campbell. There's a magnificence about you. The way you walk and talk, and even the way you stand.

"You have this great big light bursting out of you, and I'm not the only one who notices it." He brushed a strand of hair behind her ear and leaned in closer. "I lose myself every time I look into your big expressive eyes. You and I have chemistry, baby. Give me a chance. What do you say?"

"I agree. We have chemistry, but you forget, I do know you and your philandering ways. Why should I risk my heart?"

He nudged his face into her neck. "Aw, heck, honey, because you like me."

"So, and you sort of like me?" She released a breath and tilted her head back.

"Yeah, I like you a lot." He nipped the slender column of her neck, igniting the banked fires within her.

Carol Ann raced down the path toward them, waving her hands. "Hey, hey, y'all."

They quickly separated.

She bent over to catch her breath. "Lee, hurry, your mother passed out. Dr. Pedersen is with her and your dad."

All three ran back to the house and went inside the sunroom.

Her mother lay on a gold chesterfield couch. Her forearm draped over her eyes. "My head is killing me. I don't know what happened. I've been feeling so well lately."

Her father knelt on the floor beside the doctor.

"Take me home, Joseph, please. I can't stand the pain." She wept.

Dr. Pedersen took her mother's pulse. "Miss Jenny, do you have any of the powders left that I made for you?"

She shook her head. "I'm out."

"If you'll permit me, I'll go to my office and mix a few powders, then come to your house." He turned to Lee. "If you'll ride with me? I don't know where you live."

Lee looked at Harry then at her mom. "Yes. I'll ride with you." The time with the doctor would give her insight to his personality.

Harry clutched her hand. "I'll drive you, both."

"Harry, you have guests. It's Carol Ann's party."

"So, I want to help." His eyes pleaded with her.

Stay calm.

Her desire for Harry threatened to consume her. She let out her breath slow and easy. Her mom needed her. He would have to wait.

"Lee will ride with Dr. Pedersen. Once we get Jenny settled, she can return to the party, Harry." Dad scooped Mom into his arms and carried her out the main door.

Dr. Pedersen looked at Lee. "Are you ready to go?"

"Carol Ann, I'll be back later." Lee squeezed her hand, then looked at Harry. "Well, I'll try to come back, I promise." She could sense his displeasure of her leaving with the doctor.

Carol Ann hugged her tightly. "Don't worry about me. Worry about your mother."

She gave Harry one last look, then left the front entrance with the doctor. "Where's your office?"

"In the three-story Federal-style house on Main Street. My office is downstairs, and I live upstairs." Oliver stopped next to a brand new white and teal Chevy Bel Air.

He opened the passenger door, and she slid into the seat.

"You bought the mayor's old house. I've always loved the architecture."

Dr. Pedersen started the engine and drove down the oak-lined driveway, pulling onto Versailles Road. "Has your mother experienced any headaches since coming home?"

"Did you treat Mom at Sacred Heights?"

"I did."

She placed her hands in her lap and stared out the windshield. She wanted to ask the doctor about Sacred Heights' fourth floor but didn't. "I haven't witnessed any of her headaches since she came home."

"Has your mother experienced any trauma to her head lately or in her past?" He glanced at her then turned onto Main Street.

"Years ago, she was in a car accident. Dad said she was in the hospital for weeks. She had to learn how to walk and talk again. I was too young to remember it." The car accident was also the reason her mother couldn't bear any more children.

"Ah, I see. I may need to set up X-rays at the hospital next week if she doesn't get relief. Her neck may be causing the pain." A few minutes later, he pulled into the exterior garage.

"Would you like to come in while I work in my lab?"

Oliver seemed so confident at the party, yet something about him seemed shy and not entirely sure of himself.

"Go inside with him." Erinelle said, "There's great darkness lurking in his soul, and I can't go inside to investigate without you."

"Sure, Dr. Pedersen. How may I help?"

"Please call me Oliver. Dr. Pedersen is too formal, and I want us to be friends."

Friends? He was a stranger, and she was about to enter his home alone.

"I don't have many friends here. I'm seeing new patients like your mother, but no one socially until Mr. Glenn invited me to Carol Ann's party tonight."

"Carol Ann's a brilliant scholar, plus she is the first woman to teach at the college. She's quite a catch."

"Are you a matchmaker?" Oliver turned to face her, placing his right arm on the back of the car seat. His brooding good looks bordered on the surreal. She felt a strange mix of emotions vacillating between excitement and apprehension toward the doctor.

"Hey, Everglade is a friendly place to live. I'm sure you'll have plenty of friends in no time flat." She opened the car door at the same time he did.

He waited by the black wrought iron gate for her to enter first, but she glanced at him, and froze, unable to move her feet, staring into the abyss of his mesmerizing blue eyes.

Erinelle placed her hand on Lee's shoulder. "Move. There's a demon within him reading your thoughts."

Breaking the hypnotic trance, Lee went through the gate and entered the small walkway to the front door.

Dusk settled into darkness. A soft breeze blew leaves across her feet.

Soft tinkling wind chimes combined with the heady fragrance of the established gardens on either side of the front steps suddenly came alive with chirping crickets. She sensed something else lurking within the lush foliage, making the hair on her arms rise.

CHAPTER 4

"I'LL NEVER SMILE AGAIN"

*D*riving to his house, Oliver couldn't concentrate with Lee sitting so close to him. Watching her walk down the main steps of Glenn Hall caught him off guard. She was the spitting image of Nadine Vaughn.

It'd been six months since Nadine's death, and he still grieved her.

He fiddled with his keys at the front door. A click later, and he led Lee inside his home and office. He turned on the Italian wood-and-brass lamp sitting on the richly carved oak console in the spacious foyer. The dark, walnut floors were buffed to a brilliance. He had custom-built the mahogany check-in desk and counter.

He prided himself on keeping an immaculately clean environment in the office and his upstairs living quarters to eliminate as many germs as possible.

"I developed a few headache formulas while working at Sacred Heights. Most doctors treat female patients for hysteria, but I think headaches are brought on by what we eat, drink, and other factors like stress, lack of sleep, or possible trauma. Whether her headaches are physical, mental, or emotional remains to be seen based on what I discover with your mother. The lab's in my kitchen."

Lee followed him down a narrow hallway, passing the patient waiting rooms, and entered through solid wood swinging doors.

"I worked in the biology labs at school but never within a doctor's office. I'm interested in the chemical balance of our bodies. While I graduated with a degree in the social sciences, I also have a minor in biology."

"Are you looking for a job?" He asked.

"Well, yeah, I am looking for a job. I have an interview coming up with the telephone company."

He wanted to jump for joy. He reined in his emotions because he didn't want to scare her away. "Why wait? I'm looking for an assistant. Interested?"

She seemed hesitant. "I'm not sure I qualify."

"You're exactly who I've been looking for." It wasn't a lie. She resembled his lost love, and he wondered how serious she was with Harry Glenn. "Think about it. No rush."

He turned on several different kitchen lights; then he opened one of the yellow chiffon St. Charles cabinets with French provincial trimmed-out glass doors. He pulled out a couple of labeled glass jars, cotton bandages and balls, a variety of herbs, and blue vials of morphine.

"It made more sense to turn my kitchen into a laboratory. I'm a single man, and don't need a large kitchen."

"I get it. But we need to hurry. Mom's in pain."

"Of course."

Three light oak stools were arranged around a long white kitchen table. An antique grandfather clock hung on the wall next to his doctor's certificate.

"Please sit on the stool while I work." His mind went to the first time he looked at Nadine.

She'd changed his world.

Nadine changed him.

OLIVER MOVED with his family to America in 1928. He grew up in the small town of Harnsey in upstate New York, where his father practiced medicine. After school, he accompanied his father to his patients' homes. He watched his father's unique connection with each patient, and it was during these visits he fell in love with medicine.

He didn't have the social skill set of his father, but he studied hard, and after high school, the local college accepted his admission, and from there he continued his studies and graduated from The Harnsey School of Medicine.

On December 7, 1941, Japan bombed Pearl Harbor.

Oliver promptly enlisted with most of the other young men from their community. The military assigned him to the Army Hospital Unit in Great Britain, where he met Dr. Alfred Albright, a renowned psychiatrist.

While the interests of most doctors in the psych ward lay in soldiers' combat fatigue, Dr. Albright spent countless hours researching strategies for early intervention on mental breakdowns especially for the units exposed to the most traumatic war experiences.

Oliver felt a calling to help individuals with challenging disorders. Working with the disturbed changed his life, but not until after the war when he received a job offer from Dr. Albright, the new chief of staff for Sacred Heights Sanatorium.

He caught the train from New York to Nashville late one evening. The rhythmic motion of the iron horse chugging along the tracks lulled him to sleep. It stopped periodically to pick up and drop off passengers along its route.

The next morning, he washed down a scone with a glass of milk, then made his way off the train as it hissed to a stop.

Dr. Albright waited for him on the station platform. He stored his luggage in the trunk, and they entered his car. The twenty-mile trip to the country seemed to go on forever.

"Sacred Heights Sanatorium was built in the late nineteenth century. The handsome brick buildings resemble a castle and it even has towers. The patients have airy sun-filled rooms, high ceilings with tall arched windows. Keep in mind the windows are barred, but they provide impressive views of Stones River." Dr. Albright turned left onto a gravel road outside of the city limits with rows of treelined hills littered among the landscape.

He pointed. "See Oliver, just beyond the woods, protective fencing with barbed wire surrounds the perimeter of the property. The left wing houses the female patients, and the right wing holds the male patients. Hospital staff lives in separate dormitories behind the large structure."

The winding road rounded a ravine as they proceeded up the hill toward the sanatorium entrance.

"Patients come from all over the state. Farmers, veterans, lawyers, and shopkeepers. Most of our aging patients' children either rejected them or have no way to care for them. We also have patients receiving tuberculosis treatment, while others have lost touch with reality. Some come for convalescence. The conditions vary from patient to patient."

The car came to a stop.

Oliver noticed several men working on the grounds. A couple of women washed the outside windows. "Are those patients?"

"We're doing groundbreaking work here, my boy. Patients at the end of their treatment work on the grounds, some patients work as janitors, some in the laundry, and others work in the kitchen as a positive way to reacclimatize them into society."

"I look forward to working with you at Sacred Heights. When do I start? And where?"

Dr. Albright retrieved his luggage from the trunk. "Why don't we get you settled today, and you can go on rounds with me tomorrow morning. Sound good?"

The chief of staff was the most positive person he had ever met besides his father, Jakob. He knew working with the talented psychiatrist would further his career path but also offered him a meaningful way to serve his community.

"And labs? Are they available for me to work in as well?"

"Your pain-relieving skills are much needed here, Oliver."

They walked to the dormitories in the back lot of the facility while nurses, doctors, and other staff filtered along the pathways.

He came to a complete stop, noticing a stunning female patient sitting in a white wicker chair under an enormous tree, reading a book. "Are patients allowed to roam free on the grounds?"

"Some patients are allowed. Again it depends on the degree of their illness, and we have security throughout the premises. The more severe cases are on the fourth floor near the towers. I'll try not to overwhelm you, but we're understaffed and overworked on most days. Not every doctor is willing to work with our patients. I'm glad to have you here, and I'm sure you'll get caught up to speed quickly." He left Oliver inside his new room.

He was one of the twenty physicians living at the sanatorium that served three hundred patients with varying conditions. Oliver knew his work was cut out for him.

Over the next couple of years, he worked harder than he'd ever worked in his life. He practiced medicine alongside Dr. Albright on most days. Then with no warning, the chief of staff died of a massive heart attack.

The entire sanatorium mourned his death.

Dr. Brickman replaced Dr. Albright as chief of staff. There was a darkness to the man, and he seemed to enjoy some of the procedures given to the patients.

One afternoon, he assisted Brickman with electroconvulsive therapy, known as shock treatment, with the beautiful female patient, he saw the first day he'd arrived.

Sometime after the death of Dr. Albright, the patient, Nadine Vaughn suffered a setback. She lay on the table, looking at him with the most beautiful brown eyes filled with what seemed to be fear.

He squeezed her hand. "It won't last long, and you'll sleep afterward. I'll come in and check on you. I promise."

"Dr. Pedersen, please don't coddle the patients," Brickman replied with a scowl on his face.

The assisting nurses wore white uniforms, nursing hats, hosiery, and shoes. One nurse placed the rubber bit into Nadine's mouth while the other one situated the electric panels on either side of the patient's temples before the volts of electricity fired the brain.

Dr. Brickman cranked the voltage to four hundred and sixty, and her body went rigid with a slight arch to her back. He streamed the voltage for six seconds.

"Four hundred and sixty volts? Really? Dr. Brickman, that's an extreme measure. In the past, the most I ever used was one hundred and seventy."

The voltage knocked the patient out cold. Her body convulsed on the table.

Oliver checked her vitals before nodding to the nurses. "Take Miss Vaughn to her room. Stay with her until I arrive." He waited until the nurses rolled the patient out of the treatment room, leaving Brickman and himself.

He shut the door. "Are you mad? Four hundred sixty volts for six seconds could've killed her."

The gleam in Brickman's eyes unnerved him. "She didn't die. Did she? The only way to test electroconvulsive therapy is to push the boundaries, son. Four hundred sixty volts creates an electric field inside the patient's brain. Miss Vaughn suffers from depression and hallucinations. The shock treatment should also help with her nightmares. Do not ever question me again, or I'll fire you." He spun around and left Oliver standing in the room alone.

Brickman's insane.

He must find another position, and then he'd write the state medical board about Brickman's abusive practice. He sprinted down the hall toward Miss Vaughn's room and saw one of the nurses posted outside her door.

He touched her shoulder. "Gertrude, why don't you grab a cup of coffee for both of us. I intend on staying with Miss Vaughn until she wakes."

"Dr. Pedersen, she'll probably sleep through the night."

"True, but I intend on staying just the same." He opened the door and went inside Nadine's room.

The nurses had wrapped her like a mummy in white sheets. Restraints secured her to the bed. A sedative pack lay on the table next to the door. Oliver fumed as he removed Nadine's bindings and loosened her covers. He placed a chair next to the bed and glanced at his watch. 5:00 p.m.

Gertrude brought him a cup of coffee. "May I get you anything else?"

"No. Thank you. You go ahead and take off." He took the coffee and sipped.

"I'll bring you a sandwich tray."

"No. Coffee is fine. Tell me, Gertrude, have you noticed an increase in these types of treatments with Dr. Brickman?"

She looked over her shoulder and pushed the door closed. "Yes, sir. Some of the girls think Dr. Brickman is one brick shy of a load. He scares the dickens out of me. I can't imagine being his patient, but please don't tell anyone I said so. I need this job."

"You have my word."

She lowered her lashes, then her cheeks flushed. "If you need any help with Miss Vaughn, I'll be in the cafeteria." She made a swift exit.

Oliver had more than his share of nurses wanting to go out with him. Several even invited him to their rooms after hours, but he thwarted their attempts. He worked hard for his stellar reputation, and a quick roll in the sack wasn't worth the risk.

His thoughts returned to lovely and seemingly lonely Nadine Vaughn.

Over the months, he studied her case. Nadine lost her husband shortly after the war from injuries sustained in battle, and then her only child died from influenza complications. From her file, he learned that she took her husband's razor and slit her wrists.

He picked up her thin wrist and traced her scar. She tried one other time to commit suicide during her stay at Sacred Heights, but Dr. Albright intervened, and her condition seemed to improve.

He checked her vitals. She was stable.

Oliver leaned back in the chair and watched her sleep. He wondered what happened to the brain during shock therapy. Some research suggested the treatment stimulated brain cell growth while others argued it caused memory loss and even brain damage.

He'd witnessed some improvement in several of Sacred Heights worse patients using low voltage but never the extreme amount used today and with a patient who probably didn't weigh one hundred and twenty pounds soaking wet.

The hours dragged on, and he fought the urge to sleep. He stepped into the breakroom for an apple and poured another cup of coffee.

The waning crescent moon appeared low in the sky.

Walking back to Nadine's room, he passed a dark empty cell. He heard the faint sound of a music box making the hair on his neck rise. He entered the vacant room. Bone-chilling cold descended over him. It hadn't been the first time, he'd felt an eerie presence in the sanatorium, but usually, the paranormal activity occurred on the fourth floor at night.

Returning to Nadine, he noticed her teeth chattering.

He quickly grabbed a couple of blankets from a nearby linen closet, then covered her. He rubbed her arms gently. "Miss Vaughn, it's Dr. Pedersen. Can you hear me?"

"Uh, huh," she whispered. "Thirsty."

He poured her a glass of water from the pitcher on the wooden stand beside the bed, then carefully raised her head. "Take small sips, so you don't get sick."

Her eyes were bloodshot. Her voice quivered. "What's happening to me? Please, help me. Get me out of this bughouse, please. I didn't try to kill myself. I would never do that. It was the demons, not me. Please, please believe me." She raised her hand then let it drop to the bed.

"I'll do everything in my power to secure your release." He gently stroked her hand.

With a weak smile, she said, "I don't want to see Dr. Brickman again. He hurts me. He's full of demons. I'll do anything you want."

Anger surged within him. "What do you mean he hurts you?"

"I have a secret. May I share with you?"

"Of course."

"I'm part angel sent here to help in the six-thousand-year-war. The demons killed my mortal family and cut my wrists. The drugs and shock treatment weakened my powers. The army of the fallen kidnapped my guardian angel, and I'm alone in this place. Demons run Sacred Heights, and Dr. Brickman is their messenger."

He was stunned. The woman was not only suicidal; she was delusional.

"I am not lying." She fell asleep.

He paced the floor. The meds sometimes caused hallucinations, illusions, visions. But what if Brickman abused her under his care?

The next day, he stormed into the chief of staff's office and demanded information on how he hurt Nadine.

Brickman leaned back in his chair behind his desk. "You'll find out soon enough. There's more to Miss Vaughn's condition than meets the eye. She's your patient now."

"What do you mean by that?"

"She's possessed by demons." Brickman had huge bags under his eyes. He closed the folder and handed him Nadine's file.

Not Brickman too.

What the Hell?

He had sensed a supernatural presence in the facility on more than one occasion, and it was something science couldn't explain. "Surely, you jest."

"You work with her and report to me your findings."

From then on, Oliver made it his mission to care for Nadine Vaughn. He wanted to cure her and set her free from Sacred Heights. He spent time with her every day.

One afternoon in the common room, she sat at the piano and played Mozart's Piano Sonata No. 11, so beautifully, he fought back tears. It was at that moment he knew he loved her. It broke every rule between a doctor and a patient, but he couldn't help himself. And he wouldn't give up her care in case someone else tried to hurt her.

He took her on daily walks around the grounds. During one of these excursions, she eased down into the same white wicker chair where he'd first seen her.

She shielded her eyes from the sun. "I love you, Oliver. You must know my feelings for you. It's time for me to leave Sacred Heights. I can't keep fighting them."

"Fighting who?" He wanted to tell her everything would be okay, but would it? "I placed your case before the board. If we're lucky, you could leave here by the end of the month."

"I won't last that long. Demons will kill me and drag me to Hell. I know it sounds crazy, but they are real. Sacred Heights is a portal to Hades. You've had to feel the darkness on the fourth floor. You must take me away from here before something bad happens. You're my only hope." She brushed tears from her face.

He knelt beside her and whispered, "You mustn't speak like that. You'll never get out of here speaking of demons. And if anyone suspected our relationship, I could lose my license."

"You do love me, don't you?" she whispered with a raspy voice.

He could drown in the pools of her honey-brown eyes. He wanted to taste the lushness of her pale pink lips against his and run his fingers through her silky, chestnut hair. "Yes, I love you so much it hurts my heart."

"Come to me tonight."

"I can't, Nadine. We'll be together soon. I promise."

"Please come to me." Wringing her hands, she said, "I want you to hold me like a man holds a woman. I need human touch. I'm so alone and scared at night. And what if the board declines your request to release me?"

He placed his hand over hers. "I will fight for your release, I promise. You must keep the faith; remember, I'll love you until my dying breath."

"And I you, my wonderful doctor. My friend and my...."

"My what?"

"My soon-to-be lover."

They walked in silence for a few minutes.

"Every time I look at you, my world stops spinning. You make me sane, Oliver. You turned my pain into joy." She leaned against his shoulder. "You untied the twisted knots inside my soul and allowed me to dream again, to hope again. I want to spend every night for the rest of my life in your arms and wake every morning in your embrace. I long for you."

He cupped her chin. "I'll come to you tonight."

OLIVER WENT to the dormitories and hit the showers.

In a million years, he never thought someone as lovely as Nadine would love him in return. She was worth the risk even though he could lose his license and the ability to practice medicine—the driving force in his life until her.

He changed clothes, then went to the main cafeteria for dinner. He ate by himself with a book but kept reading the same page a half a dozen times.

At dark, he left the building and strolled through the rose garden. He looked around and made sure no one was watching, then took a small pair of scissors and snipped a couple of roses scraping off the thorns before sliding them into his inside coat pocket.

He was a grown man and still a virgin.

Nadine wasn't.

His heart hammered. His pulse raced.

What the Hell am I doing? I'm risking everything for her.

He walked along the quiet corridor. Not a soul in sight. He shook unlocking her door. Beams of moonlight streamed into her room and held the fragrance of flowers.

Nadine lay in the bed with one arm stretched above her head. Her other hand slowly pulled down the sheet revealing her naked body.

His fingertips traced along her curves. "You're breathtaking. Your eyes shimmer like the stars at night, and your smile lights a room more beautiful than any sunrise. Your skin is soft as rose petals."

She arched her back as she extended her hand toward him. "Make love to me, Oliver."

His soul be damned.

He couldn't resist her.

Aflame with desire, he quickly slipped off his coat, shirt, slacks, and toed off his shoes.

To Hell with my reputation.

He slid between the sheets. Passion blazed from her eyes while he made love to her. They explored each other in the most delicious ways. An experienced lover, Nadine, guided him to pleasures beyond his wildest expectations.

Both labored for breath.

Everything seemed to click, then something unexplainable happened. She glowed with the bluest light around her physical frame. He swallowed hard in the throes of passion as an outline of wings jutted from her back.

Was she dragging him into her delusion? He had heard it could happen.

He knew he'd have to answer for his lapse in judgment tonight, but she pushed him further into the sexual storm of forbidden love, and he was lost, forever.

Much later, he kissed her gently. "I don't want to, but I must leave before sunrise or someone may find me in here."

"Let's leave this place now. Let's runaway. We can hop the next train out of here." Her seductive ways were replaced once again with shyness.

"Honey, patient rounds start in less than an hour, and I have to make arrangements for us. We'll need a place to live, and I'll need a recommendation to practice in another town."

"They're coming for me. They won't wait for your arrangements."

"Who's coming for you?" He grabbed his pants, pulling on his shirt, coat, and then slipped on his shoes.

She went on her knees. Her eyes bore into his. "The demons are real. They're here. Save me."

He helped her back to bed, opened her closet, and looked under the bed. "No one's in here but you and me, sweetheart. Be patient." He handed her the nightgown on the chair. "Here. You better get dressed. Look, I'll see you every morning and in the evenings. Keeping our same routine is important. Do you understand?"

"I do." She cast a look to the floor.

He bent over and kissed her one last time. "See you soon."

"Oliver?"

"Yes?"

"Send a message to Erinelle?"

"Who's Erinelle?"

"My leader. Tell her they're taking me to Hell." Her brows furrowed.

His heart squeezed with pain. Nadine believed every word she spoke. How could he sign her release papers?

Regardless of the consequences, he'd make the necessary arrangements to get her in front of the board this week. He'd secure her release and treat her at home. He'd investigate buying a cottage. They would move. Yeah, they'd run far away from Sacred Heights, and start over again.

He slipped out of her room and entered the cafeteria. The scent of bacon frying made him hungry. He grabbed a biscuit and poured a coffee before heading back to his room. He held the cup in his hand, watching the sun come up through the window. He was worried about Nadine.

Memories of the night flooded his mind — her soft, warm hands trailing over his body. Her lovely scent lingered. He hummed the song she played on the piano. They would marry and raise a family together.

He wanted to give her a new start in life and make all her dreams come true.

Someone pounded his door. "Dr. Pedersen. Are you awake, Doctor? It's Nadine."

He bolted from the chair next to the window and slung the door open. "What about Nadine?"

A male technician cried, "She's…she's dead, Doc."

"What?" His knees buckled.

"Someone left her door unlocked. She's, um, in the tree where she loves to read."

Oliver raced out the side door heading toward her favorite spot under the tree. The white, wicker chair was empty.

His gaze went to her lifeless form hanging from the lowest branch. He screamed, "Oh God, no." He moved the wicker chair next to the roots and leaped into the tree wrestling with the sheet. "Why, Nadine? God, why did you do this?"

A dozen or so staff members stood around watching the technician hold her body up while he loosened the noose.

He left her door unlocked.

She'd begged him for help. He hadn't taken her allegations seriously enough.

He blamed himself for her death.

"Demons are real."

Rage, anger, and hate permeated his soul, opening the door to darkness.

"WHAT'S IN THE INGREDIENTS?" Lee Campbell leaned her forearms on the kitchen table.

Her question pulled Oliver back to reality.

He locked eyes with Lee, and she materialized into Nadine. She stretched out her arms and called to him. *Come to me, Oliver. Come to my room tonight.*

Lee waved her hand in front of his face. "Earth to Oliver. Are you here, Doc?"

"Oh, I'm sorry, you just remind me of someone." The vision of Nadine evaporated. "I use several natural healing herbs crushed, the fungus ergot, and I lace the powder with morphine for patients to steep with tea. The pain reliever with the caffeine from the tea some-times halts the headache before it worsens. I adjusted the morphine level, which may give your mom added relief. I'm ready to go if you are."

"Let's burn rubber."

CHAPTER 5

"FOOLS RUSH IN (WHERE ANGELS FEAR TO TREAD)"

*a*s they topped Campbell Ridge, Lee's gaze went straight to Harry's black Monterey Sports Coupe parked in front of her house. He paced the porch, and when he spotted Oliver's car, he jogged down the steps and met them at the barn lot.

She exited the car. "What are you doing here?"

Harry glared at Oliver then looked at Lee, and his face softened. "I wanted to check on you and your mom."

Grabbing his medical bag, Oliver said, "Excuse me, but I must attend to my patient."

Lee and Harry raced to catch up with him as he walked to the main entrance of the house.

She insisted, "Go on in, up the stairs. Mom's room is the last door next to the bathroom."

Her father opened the screened door. "This way, Dr. Pedersen." He looked at Lee and Harry. "Y'all stay downstairs. Mom likes the room dark and the house quiet when her headaches are in full swing."

"We'll wait on the porch, Dad."

Red geraniums filled large clay pots scattered along the white painted porch. Mom's roses and lavender mixed with wild honeysuckle created a potent scent.

The white porch swing creaked as she and Harry sat down. She recalled fond childhood memories with him and Carol Ann, playing tag or hide-and-seek on the lawn. And, boy, did they laugh a lot. They held hushed conversations long after her parents went to bed, and sometimes, they stayed up until dawn.

"Why didn't you stay at the party?" She leaned on his shoulder, and he draped an arm about her.

"I want to spend time with you. And, honestly, I don't like the way Pedersen looks at you."

"Dr. Pedersen is establishing a practice in town, and we need a doctor. Otherwise, Mom would have to drive to Murfreesboro for medical treatment." She hesitated to tell him about her job offer.

"I'm sorry your mom is suffering. I've never experienced a migraine before except maybe once from the dynamite we used building the back pond, and it didn't last long. You're right. We need a doctor, but he's also a man interested in you."

She loved Harry's matter of fact, no bull way of expressing himself. He exuded just the right amount of confidence with boyish charm. She blushed under his intense stare.

He'd never relayed his interest in her before this afternoon. She couldn't say for sure if Oliver liked her the way Harry put it, but she needed a job.

Oliver had looked at her as though he knew her intimately, but he'd acted like a perfect gentleman. However, something about him raised red flags of doubt.

Did Harry sense the darkness around Oliver?

For the moment, the ability to sit in silence without the need of talking was a welcome respite while waiting on word about her mom's condition.

She closed her eyes and prayed for her mother.

After a time, Dr. Pedersen stepped through the front door onto the porch. He leaned against the railing while gripping his medical bag. His eyes narrowed at Lee, and a lump rose in her throat. "Your mother is resting peacefully."

He handed her his business card. "My office and home number are listed. Please call if you need me. I'll come day or night."

Harry stood.

She said, "Thank you, Oliver."

He reached for her hand and held it. "I enjoyed serving your mother, and my job offer still stands." He turned to Harry and shook his hand. "Mr. Glenn, please express to your parents my apologies for leaving the party without properly thanking them for the invitation. Tell them, I'll call soon."

Harry nodded.

"Good evening." Oliver went down the steps along the sidewalk to the parking lot next to the barn.

Dad came out of the door and let out a sigh of relief. "Mom's not in pain. Whatever Dr. Pedersen gave your mother—worked. Thank God. Why don't you and Harry go back to Carol Ann's party?"

"I'm staying. Mom may wake, and you might need me."

He leaned against the doorjamb, looking worse for wear. "Suit yourself, but what about Harry?"

"May I sit with Lee for a spell, that is if you don't mind, Mr. Campbell?"

Smiling, Joseph looked between Harry and Lee. "I don't mind. Cricket, your mom, and I are so proud of you. You're the first person in our family to earn a college degree. I'm just sorry your evening didn't go as planned." He retreated inside the house and turned on the porch light.

Erinelle whispered, "You must return to the party."

"Why? I don't want to. Harry's with me."

With a sense of urgency, the angel said, "But you're supposed to dance with Harry under the moonlight in the formal gardens of Glenn Hall. The garden is where he first kisses you. If you don't go, you'll place yourself in an alternate lifeline. It creates a wrinkle in time. I can't answer what will change, but your life's trajectory will alter."

"I don't care. I want Harry to myself, here at Everglade Farms, under the moonlight."

"It's your choice, your decision, your life. Don't be late in the morning for training exercises." Erinelle vanished.

"What's the matter?" Harry's fingers threaded through strands of her hair.

"Nothing. Um. You said something at the party about the chemistry between us?"

He chuckled and grabbed her hand, pulling her back to the porch swing. "I believe I was saying that I liked you, and you liked me, and we should see if this attraction between us is destiny or just wishful thinking."

"Are you asking me on a date?"

"Why yes, Miss Lee, I'm asking you on a date." He leaned in, nudging the side of his face next to hers. "Hey, what's this about a job?"

She reached up with both hands to caress his face. "Dr. Pedersen offered me a job tonight, and I want to go out with you, but..." She shrugged away from him.

Should she tell Harry about Erinelle?

Erinelle materialized again. "He won't believe you. Even believers have a hard time wrapping reality with the supernatural."

"Harry's different. He'll believe me."

"I'll believe what?" He raised a brow.

"Did I say that aloud?"

"Tell me what's on your mind. I see you're troubled. Is it your mother?"

"I worry about Mom, but she's not the problem. Mind you, since I was a little girl, I've had this gift of understanding people's wants, their desires, and dreams. Some good and others bad, but I mostly kept my thoughts to myself. The whisperings warned me not to share my gift or my revelations because folks get suspicious of things they can't understand."

"Lee, what's this about?"

"I found out today why I have the gift. Do you believe in the supernatural? Biblical stuff, like angels and demons?"

He scratched his chin as though to ponder her question. "I haven't gone to church regularly since leaving for college, and then I joined the Navy. I attend church when I'm home. But do I believe in unseen forces? Do I believe Moses parted the Red Sea? I'm not sure. Why?"

"What if I told you I met my guardian angel this morning before graduation near the cave entrance? Would you believe me?"

He frowned. "I want to believe you, but I witnessed some pretty horrible living conditions overseas and if there are angels, why don't they help more often? Why do some people live well and others so miserably? Where are their angels?"

She turned to the angel. "Well, why does that happen?"

Harry sprang from the porch swing like someone gave him a swift kick in the breeches. "You're speaking to an angel right now?"

Lee nodded. "Erinelle, my angel, is next to you."

He whipped left and right, then crossed his arms over his chest. "Hilarious. You had me going for a second."

"I told you he wouldn't believe it. Some humans lack faith."

Lee blurted, "Faith is the ability to believe in something you cannot see. You lack faith, Harry Glenn."

"I won't argue with you about faith. If you see angels that I can't, then I place my trust in you"—he pointed to the sky—"and the higher-ups. It's more than I can comprehend."

Erinelle clapped and whistled. "I like this boy. Ask him about losing his keys this morning. He tore through every room in Glenn Hall looking for them, and his guardian angel placed the keys on his side table next to his bed. Oh, his guardian angel is Humiel. He's standing on the other side of Harry."

"I can't see him, but thank you, Erinelle." Lee lifted her chin. "Did you tear up your house looking for your car keys this morning? And, you found them on your side table after previously looking there."

His mouth opened. "Ah. Ah. Thunderation. How?"

"I'm telling you the truth. Your guardian's name is Humiel." Her confidence level rose. "I want to be honest with you. If we have a chance of being together, it won't be a conventional relationship."

He scratched the top of his head. "Geez, now, I have a headache. I see you believe what you're telling me, but you're frightening the Hell out of me."

Erinelle gave Lee a smug grin. "I told you. Not to worry, I'll give him a memory wipe, and he'll forget about the conversation."

"Well, I guess if I'm scaring you there's no point going on a date. And, just so we're clear, my angel will wipe your memory, and you won't remember a thing." She crossed her arms over her chest, defiant.

"Come on, darlin'. Don't get testy with me." He leaned his forehead next to hers. His arms wrapped around her waist. "I want to believe you. Will you give me time to think about it? And on the safe side, please no memory wipes because it sounds mighty painful."

Erinelle chuckled. "Your call."

Lee stepped away from Harry. With a frown, she narrowed her eyes at the angel. "Are memory wipes painful? Do they cause headaches? And if so, is that why my mother suffers?"

"Daylight. Campbell Ridge. Don't be late." Erinelle vanished.

Lee stomped her foot. "That makes me madder than a rattlesnake."

He touched her shoulder. "At me?"

"No. Erinelle. My mother must've seen something, and the angels wiped her memory — *good grief*. No amount of pain medicine is going to stop a supernatural headache. Hey, I have a lot on my mind. I like you, but if you can't even conceive the story is real, then why date? No hard feelings. I don't want to fall completely in love and wind up with a broken heart." Which was already too late, she had fallen for Harry years ago.

"Hold on a cotton-picking minute. Don't put words in my mouth. I'm asking you to place your faith in me. Give me some time to take in what you said tonight, and I'll stop by tomorrow so we may talk a little more on the subject. Deal?" He bent down and lifted her chin with his forefinger. "Please. Give me until tomorrow."

"We'll sleep on it. I have my first lesson with Erinelle in the morning. I'll try to make it to morning church service. Save me a seat?"

"You got it, sugar plum." Harry jogged down the steps, paused, then turned to her. "You're not conventional, Lee Campbell, but that's what I love about you."

He loves me.

She watched him leave, then sat on the porch swing, pushing off with her right foot.

So much had happened today. She met an angel, graduated college, got a job offer and Harry asked her on a date. All in all, the day had been full of surprises and the most eventful of her young life.

Lee stayed up with her thoughts long after her parents turned in.

What would Erinelle teach her tomorrow?

Then she'd meet Harry at church. There was no better place to believe in the supernatural than inside the beautiful church of St. Timothy's.

HARRY STARTED his car and backed out of Lee's drive. She waved at him, and he threw up his hand.

Was Lee for real? Or was she nuts?

She confused him with all the hocus-pocus nonsense.

Driving to Glenn Hall, he ran through every detail she told him about angels. He'd known Lee since they were children and not once in all that time had she seemed insane.

He glanced at his watch under the moonlit sky. "Hey, Humiel, ole buddy ole pal, Carol Ann's party is probably over. You wanna grab a cocktail and sit next to the pool?"

Silence.

"I need your guidance if you're real."

He must make a crucial decision. He'd dreamed about Lee so often in the Navy.

Should he pursue the lovely lady and all her quirkiness, or let her go?

"How does the angel thing work? I mean, surely if you can help me find my car keys you can give me some insights on what Lee needs in a mortal man. She's training with an angel in the morning. Should I spy on her?" He wondered what kind of training an angel could teach a mortal.

Back in his college days, he took an elective class on Myths and

Legends. So many different religions. So many different gods. He believed all gods were the same deity; only different cultures placed their own religious spin. He never understood why so many people fought and died over spiritual teachings.

He grew up in the church. He'd been saved and baptized at the age of eleven. He also knew how gossip thrived in small churches, and most members couldn't agree on song selection much less the more significant questions of life. Anytime he'd ever inquired about scripture with even the slightest sense of doubt, the elders responded by telling him it wasn't proper to question the Bible.

Why not? How does one learn without asking questions, Humiel?

Harry parked his car in the garage and pulled down the door.

All seemed quiet on the home front.

He mumbled to himself as he followed the stone path to the pool house. "My mind is crackling with so much energy that I'll never sleep tonight."

Inside, he grabbed a whiskey decanter and poured a stout drink and threw open the double doors to allow the breeze to cool the room. "Humiel, want one? Ah, no answer, I'll drink yours too."

The inexplicable scent of warm butterscotch caramels permeated through the pool house, making the hair on his neck rise. He glanced left then right, but no one else was in the place but him.

Trembling, he raised the cocktail glass to his lips. "Are you real, Humiel?"

He greedily drank the Tennessee whiskey and placed the empty glass on the table. He took his shoes off and stretched out on the sofa, slinging his forearm over his eyes.

During high school, Harry knew Lee liked him. He fought the building attraction as she grew from a girl into a young woman. And, wowzer, what a woman.

At college, he compared every date he went on to Lee. No one could take her place in his eyes or heart. She was a knockout, but they were also friends. Seeing her today had only intensified his feelings for her.

But he had overheard his mother talking to his dad about Jenny's hallucinations.

Could Lee suffer from the same delusions?

Was he prepared to take on that kind of responsibility?

Nights on the ship, he thought of her as the waves rocked him to sleep.

He concentrated on his breathing to relax his mind until drifting off to dreamland.

Slumbering waves crashed on pristine white sand beaches. Harry inhaled the briny air. The hot sun warmed his face and cast glistening diamonds on the calm sea. The tropical forest came alive with the screeches of exotic birds and animals. He lay in a hammock swaying under the shade of the palm trees.

Lee walked along the shoreline in a sarong. A purple orchid adorned her silky chestnut hair. She ran and jumped into the hammock with him. She traced her fingertips along his jawline. "Kiss me."

Her soft, sweet lips brushed against his.

He gave her what she wanted. It wasn't a gentle kiss. It was a bruising kiss full of passion, open-mouthed, and delicious. Her fingers feverishly worked through his hair.

Shaking with desire, he lost himself in the steamy kiss.

She trailed kisses along his neck and up to his mouth. He tickled the seams of her lips with his tongue as his hand smoothly slid down her spine.

He knew he should stop kissing her, afraid he would push her too far, but he'd waited for her for so long, and what if he never got another chance?

Warmth spread throughout his body, creating an ache of awareness of how badly he wanted her, and how much he needed her.

He rolled her onto her side and placed the palm of his hand in the curve of her cheek.

She strained toward him, pleading, "Did I do something wrong?"

"You're doing everything right."

He'd dated other women over the years, but nothing quite prepared him for the onslaught of emotions, or the sheer sexual energy he created with Lee.

The silence lengthened.

She wept, and he took her back into his arms. "Please don't cry. I can't bear to see your tears. I love you, and I'll never hurt you."

"You don't have faith. You don't believe me, Harry. You don't believe in angels."

She faded away.

A fearsome female warrior angel with blazing red hair surrounded him with a pulsating blue light. "I am Erinelle. Do not be afraid to love Lee Campbell. Be worthy of her love. Believe what she is telling you. Your children's lives may depend on your faith. Do you believe in angels, Harry Glenn?"

"I believe in angels, I believe in angels, I do, I do, I do." Quivering under the glare of the angel's light, he became disoriented. The edges around his peripheral vision blurred.

Behind the female warrior, dark shadows lurked. "Humiel, to your right," Erinelle shouted.

Another supreme being burst through the air with a golden bow and arrows shooting blue fireballs turning the lurking shadows into gray ash.

A giant angel clad in bronze from head to toe went on bended knee. "Harry Glenn, I am Humiel, your guardian angel."

Harry couldn't breathe.

The images before him drifted off in a cloud replaced with soft humming. He turned, and Lee skipped along the shoreline. He ran after her, and the faster he ran, the farther she became out of reach.

"I believe you, Lee. Don't leave me."

In an instant, he stood alone on the beach. The slow waves lapped at his feet.

His dream shattered into a million fragments.

He woke, drenched in sweat, lying on the sofa inside the pool house. Relief the dream had ended eased his racing pulse. His doubts faded. The angels could've been real. He was raised on the belief of angels. It was possible.

"I believe in you, Humiel. I must tell my honey-eyed girl that I believe her too. And I'll work on the faith part." His declaration to the unseen angel spun a new world of possibilities. He'd never quite look at life the same again.

CHAPTER 6

"DEVIL MAY CARE"

Oliver drove down the main street too hyped-up to go home. He parked and walked unusually slow toward the only bar in town. Technically, he lived in a dry county, so the establishment claimed itself as a club but resembled dive bars popping up all over the country.

Antique wall sconces and floor lamps provided the only illumination in the dingy smoke-filled room. Hunting and fishing photographs lined Pugs Pub's log walls along with a couple of rustic art pieces of Tennessee landscapes. Hank Williams blared from the jukebox while two young men wearing overalls played pool.

He took a seat next to a handful of other men at the bar with a blond bombshell. He'd noticed her at Carol Ann's party.

The big burly bartender came over to him. "Hey, Doc. I'm Paul Pagett, but everyone around here calls me Pugs. What can I do you for?"

"Do you have Scotch?"

"Nah, man, we got beers and whiskey. Tennessee whiskey, the good stuff, not the rotgut. I have a bit of shine in the back, but I'm not sure you got the stomach for it."

Laughter came from the patrons, and the tall blond sauntered over and pulled out a stool next to him. "Pugs, don't scare off Dr. Pedersen. Moonshine comes in from the mountain. Stick with beer or whiskey. You'll thank me tomorrow. Hi, I'm Catherine Blount." She stuck out her hand, and he shook it.

"Hello." He leaned his forearms on the bar counter and turned to Pugs. "I'll take a whiskey. Make it a double."

Pugs whistled. "My kind of man."

"Hands off, I saw him first." She brushed her hair off her left shoulder and leaned over just enough for him to catch a glimpse of her ample bosom. "Tell me, Doctor. How is Miss Jenny? She's such a dear sweet lady to have such a snot-nosed daughter."

"I'm sorry, but doctor-patient confidentiality prevents me from saying. I also found her daughter quite amiable."

She let out an exasperated breath.

Pugs wiped down the bar counter. "Catherine's jealous of her because of Harry Glenn. But then again, most guys around here have a crush on Lee. She's feisty with a boatload of attitude. She doesn't go sniffing after every Tom, Dick, and Harry." He winked as Catherine fumed.

"You're an asshole, Pugs." She threw a beer bottle, and he caught it one-handed.

"Yup, that's what I've been told." He laughed so hard his shoulders shook.

Listening to Pugs and Catherine made him chuckle for the first time in a long while. "I'm sorry. I'll never get used to Southerner's interesting ways of expression."

She placed her hand on his forearm. "We also have colorful ways of expressing love too."

Pugs leaned in and pointed at Catherine. "Good lord, Doc, you better git while the gittin's good or that girl right there will have you marching down the aisle."

"Don't listen to him." She placed a finger to her bottom lip. "Is it okay to call you Oliver?"

Catherine was a looker with legs up to her ass, but he was starting over in Everglade, and she didn't look like a one-night stand kind of girl. He turned up the whiskey, then placed the empty cocktail glass on the counter. "You may call me, Oliver if you wish. I'm going to call it a night. I enjoyed meeting you both."

Pugs grabbed the glass and plunged it into the sink behind the counter. "Come back anytime, Doc, and I'll give you a free sample of shine on the house."

He nodded.

Catherine seemed crestfallen, so he placed his hand on her shoulder. "Miss Blount, you're a beautiful woman, and I'm sure any man would be lucky with you at his side, but I'm taken."

"You think I'm beautiful?"

Pugs bent over, hee-hawing, and slapping his knee. "Good grief, Catherine, is that your take-away from what the Doc said? Hey, girlie, get back here and help me clean up, and I might give you some shine."

She giggled. "You better. See you later, Doc." She wiggled out of the barstool and went around the bar to help Pugs behind the counter.

He reached into his pant pocket and withdrew a couple of dollars from his billfold. "Will this cover the drink?"

Pugs gave him back a buck, placing the other one in the antique cash register. He slammed the drawer shut. "We have cheaper drinks in the county. Thanks for stopping in."

Oliver strolled down the tree-lined sidewalk passing the Snowbell Diner, Buckman's Jewelry, AJ's Hardware Store, Leatherman's Dry Goods, and the town paper. The quaint small town had many advantages, but the last thing he needed was gossip.

Everglade's previous physician operated a small office in the building next to Buckman's. The space wasn't large enough for patients, his lab and living quarters, so he bought the mayor's house. Mayor Burns had purchased a farm farther out of town but continued to run Everglade General Store with a working post office located at the end of the street close to Miss Pearl's Bakery.

Nearing his home, he saw an older man with a head chock-full of greasy white hair sitting on the sidewalk with his forearms on his knees, his head bowed. Oliver approached him slowly. He crouched next to the man. "May I assist you in some way?"

Bright blue eyes locked with his. "You want to help a crazy old man?"

"Sure. Do you have any family I may call?"

With a gruffness to his voice, the man said, "Hmph. What family?"

Some family members had abandoned patients at Sacred Heights, so he didn't expound. "Come to my house. I'll make you a sandwich and a cup of tea."

The older man gave him a nod. "You are too kind, sir."

He helped the man to his feet and placed his arm around his waist to give him added support. "You're welcome to stay the night. I can make you up a bed in one of the exam rooms. What's your name?"

The man didn't answer.

"You seem to be the same size as me. I'm sure I have some clean clothes if you want to bathe while I make you something to eat."

Entering the house, the man stood upright. His laughter had a level of madness to it, and Oliver quickly thought about the gun in the foyer drawer.

Do I have time to grab it?

Then something happened before his eyes with no scientific explanation. The older man's body twisted and distorted rapidly like a cartoon character.

Terrified. Stunned. Shocked.

He couldn't move as if paralysis had set in.

Am I hallucinating?

The last six months must've pushed him over the edge. His heart pounded so hard and fast he thought he might die from cardiac arrest.

The older man peeled away layers of skin until an incredible being with waist-length, glossy, black hair appeared with striking features and sparkling eyes the color of turquoise.

Translucent wings spanned from his back shimmering and reflecting light with a rainbow of colors. The creature held an evil smile. His eyes seemed to glow. The room seemed to expand and contract. "Do not be afraid, Oliver. I have come to help you."

"Who...who are you?" He slowly backed to the front door for a way to escape.

"Come, my son, I'll tell you in your laboratory, and I'll take that cup of tea you offered. Anything sweet in the house? I love sugar."

The being's innate sense of power and air of superiority kept his mouth shut. If he'd lost his mind, then maybe he'd join his beloved Nadine.

With an abrupt turn, the creature said, "I will raise Nadine from the dead if you believe in me. If you serve me as your master, I offer you wealth, power, and skills beyond mortal capabilities. I am Luc, and Earth is my domain."

Luc waved his hand, and a hologram of Nadine running in abject darkness appeared. Her big beautiful eyes went wide with fear. She kept looking over her shoulder, but he couldn't see who or what she tried to escape.

Anger filled him. "You're— you're Satan!"

"Such an ugly name for an archangel, the Prince of Earth, and cast out from Heaven. My followers call me, Luc. Do not ever refer to me as Satan again. I fight those arrogant angels who stripped my rank. The Creator turned away from me, so I must prove to Him that I'm right about everything. Humans like you, Oliver, will help me to return home. You will help me." His statements were more of a command than a request.

Oliver mentally recited The Lord's Prayer, and Luc backhanded him so hard he flew across the room. He crashed into the wall, bringing down a large gilded mirror on top of him spraying shards of glass across the hardwood floor. He reached up and touched his brow. He felt blood trickle down his face.

Luc extended his hand and levitated him. "I'm willing to return Nadine Vaughn to the land of the living if you cooperate with me fully. Otherwise, she'll suffer day and night for all eternity."

"How—how can you bring Nadine back to life? And what are your demands?"

The devil lowered him to the floor. "Are we negotiating?"

～

LUC LEFT the physician's house giddy with confidence. He'd plant a subtle suggestion in Lee's subconscious to take the job Oliver offered and he'd use the mortal doctor to gain knowledge about the young woman. He knew the AAF had spies in his army. He'd keep his plans for her secret. He didn't want to alert the AAF of his intentions until he decided what to do with her.

The town's clock tower struck midnight.

Behind the painted fences and preened lawns of Everglade Farms, Luc spread darkness among the close-knit community. On any given day, children learned the duck and cover drills. Moms wore tea-length swing dresses with pressed aprons while cooking for their families.

The town slept except for Snowbell's. Saturday night, the diner stayed open late. Teens and college-age mortals chatted hanging on the doors of cars next to the carhop and the outside picnic tables. Waitresses delivered burgers and fries wearing roller skates.

He noticed several high school boys torturing a studious-looking bookworm sucking on a milkshake.

Rubbing his hands together, he itched for a little fun. He ducked in behind a dump truck next to the hardware store and materialized into a teenage girl wearing a pink poodle skirt paired with a tight sleeveless shirt, and a pink scarf tied at his neck. Luc sashayed out from the truck and strolled on the sidewalk toward Snowbell's.

The bullies turned from the bookworm when they spotted him. Mortal men, even the younger ones, thought with their pricks most of the time. He would enjoy torturing them.

"Hey, doll, where you been all my life?" one asked, followed by catcalls and whistles from the other teens.

Luc turned to face the three young men. He fiddled with the top button of the shirt revealing cleavage. "Boys, do you want me? I mean really want me?"

The boys circled the female manifestation. The tallest one pushed forward and draped his arm around Luc's shoulders. "Hell, yeah, baby, show us what you got."

With a high-pitched voice of a female, Luc said, "I have the keys to Leatherman's. Follow me."

He walked to the back of the warehouse, placed his hand on the doorknob, and pushed the door open. He went inside and sealed the area once the boys entered, preventing any unwanted interference from anyone passing by.

He placed his back against the wall next to a filthy twelve-foot window as the boys inched closer. "What would you give to have me?"

The tallest one replied, "Anything you want, baby."

"What about your friends? Don't they want some too?"

The shortest of the three boys backed to the exit door. "You can't have my soul, Succubus. Asher, Dick, this woman is evil. I can feel it in my bones."

Luc roared with laughter. At least one of the boys had some sense. "Carlos, you're a little dramatic." He turned to the boy with a sizable erection. He withdrew a pen and handed it to him. "Sign my breast, and you may have me in the flesh."

The young mortal took the pen, then threw it to the floor. "No. Carlos is right. Something is seriously wrong with you, doll. Come on, boys, let's get the heck out of Dodge."

"Too late. Your asses are mine." He waved his hand, freezing the three boys from movement. With a whirlwind of energy, Luc returned to his glorious self. All three boys pissed their pants. "I'm not a succubus, but I know several." He snapped his fingers, and two female demons appeared.

Carlos paled. His eyes widened then he screamed, "Jesus, Mary, and Joseph."

Luc threw his head back and laughed again. "Not quite."

Hell unleashed on the teenage boys.

The screaming didn't reach the exterior of the building. The demons dragged Asher and Dick to Hades. He turned to Carlos. "You're next, my little friend."

Carlos tripped over his feet, busting his lip and cracking his two front teeth. He fiddled with the door and ran out of the building. He screamed like a banshee.

"Run, boy, run. It's the little things that make life on this miserable planet worth it."

After a fun-filled evening, Luc time-walked to his home in Arrington.

Saggal bowed to Luc at the entry door. "Lord, we've had word there's been a breach at Sacred Heights Sanatorium."

His pleasant mood went sour fast. He had many portals across the globe, but the Sacred Heights gateway led to his castle. He kept calm. "Great work. Where's Daglan?"

"Honky Tonkin."

The walls and windows shook as he shouted, "Daglan."

Daglan instantly appeared with red lipstick smeared across his face. "Yes, sir."

"Do you ever tire of mortal females?"

"Never, my lord. I attract their attention so easily. I can't help myself. What's up?"

Luc scratched his chin, contemplating the best tactic. "Call a meeting of the generals. We need to increase our legion's presence at Sacred Heights, and in the nine circles. I want additional soldiers both on the ground and on each floor of the sanatorium. I'll send the giants should the need arise to protect the castle."

Luc and the original fallen angels craved the light from Heaven. He actively engaged in capturing The Chosen of the World along with souls of the innocent. Their light illuminated Hell.

Nadine Vaughn had been the icing on the cake. She held more than light. The explosive power within her had enough plutonium to blow up one of the major eastern seaboard cities. He retrieved her power slowly so as not to kill her and placed it into the many mirror prisms inside the castle walls.

Daglan bowed. "I'm on it." He turned to Saggal. "Did you mention if you captured the culprit?"

"I'm working on it."

"Return to me when the army is in place. I want regular updates in the meantime." He cocked his head to the side. "My wife is calling me. Sazae, dear, I'm in the living area."

She strode into the room wearing a blue and black kimono complementing her beautiful dark bronze skin which shimmered from the wall of windows. "I've missed you, Luc. I need you too."

"You always need me, wench." He traced his fingers along the majestic frame of her face, and down her long neck. Her deep azure eyes searched his. He didn't love her, but he did lust after her. Her tongue rivaled that of a water kelpie, and she knew what to do with it.

He draped an arm about her waist and looked over his shoulder to Daglan and Saggal. "Move it."

The demons vanished.

Sazae jumped in the air, wrapping her legs around his waist. "Hurry, before I start without you."

"You are a seductress." He gripped her buttocks.

"I serve only you, master."

"Good answer." They materialized into his room. He threw her on his bed, spread her legs, and plunged his rod deep inside of her. He didn't worry about the marks he'd leave. She loved the rough stuff and healed quickly.

CHAPTER 7

"DON'T FENCE ME IN"

*E*rinelle ran through drills waiting on Lee to arrive. Hefting her sword from its sheath, she made slow circle eights with her wrist. In a fighting pose, she weighted her right foot.

Lee reached the open meadow next to the cave's entrance. "Hey, Erinelle." She pointed toward her jeans and saddle oxfords. "I didn't know what to wear?"

The angel motioned to the large flat rock near the cave's entrance. "I supplied you with several bodysuits plus training boots."

"Am I supposed to change clothes in the cave?"

Erinelle shook her head. "For Pete's sake, no need for modesty."

"Do you watch everything I do?" Lee scrunched her nose.

Leaning against a boulder, Erinelle crossed one foot over the other one. "I never invade your private space unless there's an imminent threat to you. Go on, change clothes, and pick up your sword." She pointed to the sleek blade with a golden hilt.

"Turn around."

"Seriously?" Erinelle raised a brow.

"You bet your boots." With her forefinger, Lee made a circular motion.

She grimaced but complied. "You're wasting time, little girl."

A few minutes later, Lee wore a silver bodysuit with laced up black boots like her gold ones. "I love the material. What is it? It fits perfectly. May I keep the boots too?"

"You may keep the suits and boots. After today, to retrieve your sword, all you must do is think about it and open your hand. Your sword's calibration is for your energy fields. The divine blade yields capabilities of mass destruction if misused. Handwash the bodysuit with mild soap or detergent. No lye soaps. The material acts as armor and will help thwart minor injuries."

Pointing to the sword, Erinelle said, "Go on, pick it up. Get a feel of your blade by rotating your wrist." She pushed her blade between Lee's feet. "Always keep your side to your opponent."

Lee picked up the light sword making circles with her wrist, mimicking her seamless moves. "I love it. Oh, wow, I remember how to fight. How in the world? Is it the sword? Or you? How do I remember?"

"Really? You're flexing memory muscle. How exciting." Could Lee remember their friendship? Could she remember belonging to their elite organization of warriors fighting The Dragon for thousands of centuries?

Lee demonstrated. "If memory serves, there's three basic fencing moves. The lunge is a basic attack move. Parrying blocks against an opponent's lunge, and the riposte is used to counterattack."

"Excellent, Lee. There's a rhythm similar to dancing."

Lee whipped around, clashing her steel against hers. "You always reminded me to keep my sword level at the nose of my opponent while I regrouped from a lunge or a riposte."

"You do remember. Give me all you got." The angel chuckled. Anything and everything was possible with The Creator.

Lee charged her, clashing blades, echoing steel throughout the hollow. She pushed forward then retreated while parrying blow after blow.

Lee's blade quivered under the sheer force of Erinelle's strength. The bout seemed to last for an hour but only minutes by Earth's time until she lunged with a sharp sideways motion knocking Lee off balance. She fell to her knees.

After placing her blade point at Lee's sternum, Erinelle sheathed her sword. She offered Lee a hand up, but the hybrid delivered a swift side kick, knocking her to the ground, pouncing on her chest and holding her wrists to the ground.

"I remember that move too." Lee panted.

Erinelle scissored her legs around Lee's waist, flipping her on her back. "Full-bloods are always stronger. When you fight demons, always go for the kill. They will not play fair and seek to destroy your soul. Sometimes, they kill The Chosen. Other times, The Chosen are pawns, and some are held as prisoners. I will die for you, Lee Campbell."

"Angels don't die."

"Some angels are spies in Luc's army. When he captures one of our warrior angels, he places them within Hades separated from the light given by The Creator. It's a slow death with no access to the light of His love."

"Oh, I didn't realize angels suffer too. And don't ask me how, but I remember you, Erinelle. I cherished our friendship in Heaven. Is it a curse or a gift to recall such a perfect place?" She sighed. "Hey, you need to answer a few questions. Did memory wipes cause Mom's condition? What did she see that was so bad to require them?"

"Too many questions and some answers will be revealed in time. Demons have come for you many times. I protected you, and it's why I visited you yesterday. Your mother is especially sensitive to you and your unique capabilities. The Creator gave her the ability to protect you at birth until you received your powers. Jenny caught a demon trying to smother you in your bed. She jumped on its back, gouging its eyes with her fingers. Her guardian is a plain angel, not a warrior, and by the time, I entered the room, your mother neared death."

Erinelle sat on the boulder next to Lee. "I killed the demon and initiated the memory wipe. The memory wipes protect your mother and father. But the recurring and often disturbing visions Jenny sees and cannot fully understand may cause her headaches. The one flaw in our system. The healers are working on ironing it out."

"So, now that I'm in the loop will her pain ease?" Lee asked.

"We hope so."

"Have you identified Dr. Pedersen's demon?"

Erinelle shook her head. "Not yet. The AAF is working on your case, including the new doctor. I'm not sure if the demon is directly seeking to destroy Pedersen's soul or merely using the vessel to get to you. The Creator bestowed many gifts to you, and I am not privy to all your data, but Luc wants your gifts. The Chosen's gifts increase his power exponentially. He won't stop without a fight."

Lee squinted from the sun and blinked to the ground. "You said The Chosen could fall to Luc?"

"It is one of the sacrifices some of the Chosen have endured. You may choose to deny the position. The more your powers increase, the more demons will come for you."

"I would never deny The Creator." Lee placed her hand over her mouth. Her eyes widened. "My gosh. I placed Harry in harm's way. Oh, no, no, no, no. I must speak with him. Do I have time to make morning worship?"

"May I suggest testing your superhuman speed."

Lee rubbed her hands together. "With or without the suit?"

St. Timothy's Church

Lee's car came to a stop next to the rose-covered fencerow of St. Timothy's. She loved the old gray stone church and its high steeple. The melodic chimes of the bells meant service would start soon. She hurried along the brick-paved sidewalk to the front door.

She turned the knob, pushed the door open, and a rush of wind followed her inside, lifting pamphlets off the back podium, making them float throughout the sanctuary. Everyone in the pews turned to look at her.

It took a second to adjust her eyes when she spotted Harry sitting on what most church members considered the Glenns' pew. His eyes lit with amusement as he motioned for her, and she slid in next to him. She usually sat with her parents, but her mother was still in bed resting, and Dad stayed home with her.

What would she say to Harry after the service?

How could he possibly understand her dilemma?

She looked at the stained-glass windows, which told the story of Jesus with Mary and Joseph and included a few scenes with the twelve disciples. Since Christmas, the church had installed new red velvet carpet. Deep red homemade cushions covered the pews.

Across the aisle, Dr. Pedersen nodded to Lee.

She returned the greeting.

Sunlight filtered into the pulpit and illuminated the intricately carved cross with Jesus mounted on the wall behind the pastor. "Today's lesson comes from the King James version of Philippians Chapter 4, verses six and seven. '*Do not be anxious about anything, but pray with thanksgiving and let your requests be made known to God. And the peace of God surpasses all understanding, will guard your hearts and your minds in Christ Jesus'...*"

She wondered if the pastor experienced the supernatural or if he merely quoted scripture. Regardless, she couldn't stop worrying after the last twenty-four-hours' revelations.

She looked at her neighbors.

Who had demons? Who didn't?

Saints and sinners all under one roof.

She wondered why the place didn't explode from the tension.

Could anyone else sense the presence of the angels and demons like she did?

The walls quivered.

Was she the only one seeing it?

Harry pressed his thigh against her, temporarily redirecting her thoughts to him. She loved him so much, but she'd let him go if it meant saving him and his family.

She glanced at Oliver. The good doctor seemed agitated. Did his demons hate the scriptures? He twisted and turned in his seat. His eyes glowed an unnatural color.

Maybe the demon hated her? She personified humanity with a twist, not to mention being enlisted into The Creator's war to reconcile humanity's future.

She silently cheered for the angels on her team.

Erinelle placed herself between Dr. Pedersen and Lee. "The demon hates you more than the scriptures. Most of the fallen angels worshipped The Creator before following Luc in their descent to this planet. About half of those worship angels rebelled against Luc and currently work with our efforts on the ground. We call them, Earth angels."

It was weird how Erinelle read her thoughts.

She stretched her telepathy skills. *"Does Dr. Pedersen have a guardian angel?"*

"His guardian angel is Adimus. All humans have guardians, but only The Chosen have warrior angels. Sometimes, regular or plain guardians are captured and tortured to get to us. The AAF is taking measures to retrieve Adimus. Obsidian shields cloak Oliver, so we don't know how far up in the upper echelon of Luc's army that his demon ranks."

She looked at Erinelle. *"Baby steps, please, or you may overwhelm me."*

"You got it."

After the morning service, Harry leaned over and whispered, "May I speak with you in private?"

"What's wrong?"

He seemed nervous and upset.

Was he going to give up on pursuing her after she revealed her true calling?

"Nothing. Did you drive?"

"Yeah." She wouldn't let him see her cry if he chose not to love her in return.

Eva pushed by him and squeezed Lee's hand. "Dumplin', the Women's Sunday School class made lunch for your family, and I volunteered to bring it over. That's alright, isn't it, sweetie?"

"What a wonderful gesture. But Mom's not up for visitors. I'll take the food you ladies prepared." She placed her hand over Eva's with a pat. "We'll get together another time."

"Oh, darlin', I understand. The box is in the church kitchen with your mama's name on it. I'm so sorry she's feeling poorly. You give Jenny a big kiss and hug from me."

"I'm going with Lee," Harry added.

"I think that's a marvelous idea." She winked at Lee. "Oh, Carol Ann is putting your overnight bag in your car. She hightailed it outta here after the benediction to catch the new doctor."

"That's fine. Thanks again for the food."

Carol Ann was relentless at times. She almost felt sorry for Oliver.

Eva made her way down the aisle and out the door.

She turned to Harry. "Will you help me with the food?"

"Only if I can hang out at your place this afternoon. I must talk to you." He followed her to the back of the church.

They strolled down the long hall and took a right inside the kitchen. A big cardboard box held a platter of fried chicken, a bowl of mashed potatoes, green beans, and a dozen or so homemade biscuits, plus peach cobbler. The delicious scent alone had her stomach growling.

By the time they exited the back door of the church, the parking lot was empty.

"I guess the Methodists wanted to beat the Baptists to Snowbell's." Harry chuckled, and she joined in.

She opened the trunk of the Plymouth, and he secured the box of food.

With a slight hitch in her voice, she said, "Are you going to break my heart?"

"Not today." He slid into the passenger seat as she got in behind the steering wheel.

Her stomach fluttered. "Short cut or the long way, Harry?"

"The long way."

She backed out of the parking spot and waited until the traffic cleared to pull out of St. Timothy's. "What's up? The suspense is killing me."

"Honey, nothing is wrong. I had a dream last night or more of a revelation, I think." He relayed his dream from the night before while she drove the back streets of Everglade. As he continued with the tales of his dream, the tension across her shoulders eased. He wasn't dumping her after all.

"You're my destiny, Lee Campbell. I've always believed it in my heart. Erinelle said our children's lives might depend on us."

He was too adorable, but she didn't want to seem overly excited. "Most children depend on their parents. And aren't you placing the cart before the horse? We haven't even kissed yet, and you have us married with children already." She pulled into the tractor lane on top of Campbell Ridge and turned off the engine. "I'm not making fun of you, so don't look disappointed. One question."

"Shoot." He leaned against the passenger door.

"Does this mean you accept the knowledge angels exist? That there's a supernatural war going on every day ordinary people do not see? Do you believe in me?"

He inched closer and caressed the hollow of her cheeks with his thumbs.

Her heart hammered.

He glanced at her chest, heaving up and down and smiled. "I believe in you, Lee. I adore you. I want to kiss you."

"It's broad daylight."

His hot stare set her aflame with desire. "Your point is?"

She'd waited her whole life for a moment like this with Harry and wanted to savor every second of it. She parted her lips, tilted her head, and closed her eyes in anticipation.

Brushing his lips lightly across hers, he whispered, "You're mine. Do you hear me? All mine. Forever."

She opened her eyes. "No other women? Just me?"

His left arm encircled her waist, drawing her to him. "Only you."

His mouth closed over hers in a mind-bending kiss, sealing the bond between them.

She could've sworn she heard bells ringing as she melted into his arms. His kiss held a promise for the future. His kiss told her he loved her the way she loved him. His kiss validated all the years she pined for him when he was away.

But she wrestled with her conscience. Should she stop the affair? She had no clue what fighting demons entailed, but she could safely assume falling in love with Harry might place his soul in jeopardy. He mentioned saving their children, but if she ended the relationship now, no children would need to be spared.

Abstinence would protect Harry.

Promiscuity would endanger him.

She braced herself and pushed away. "I don't want to hurt you. Harry, I'm confused."

He linked his fingers with hers. "We have time to figure things out. Take all the time you need."

"We should go. My parents will wonder what's taking me so long."

"Your parents can probably guess."

She playfully punched him in the arm.

"Ouch." He rubbed his bicep, glancing at her for more sympathy.

"That didn't hurt, silly bear."

"Am I your bear?" he asked.

"Yes, my big bear." She started the engine and turned around in the field, then drove the short distance to home, parking next to the barn. She spotted Oliver's Bel Air in the front driveway, but she didn't comment. "If you'll grab the box of food, I'll unlock the kitchen door."

They walked the low-sloped hill in the back yard to the kitchen. Lee jiggled the key into the lock, and they went inside.

Her father sat at the kitchen table, drinking coffee, and reading the paper. "Did you hear anything at church about the disappearance of Asher Winthrop and Dick Shen?"

Harry placed the box on the counter.

She pulled out each dish and placed it on the kitchen table. "Not a word. What happened?"

He set the newspaper aside. "It seems they were at Snowbell's around midnight with Carlos Smith. They left with a girl, and no one saw them again."

"Who was the girl? And what about Carlos?" Harry asked.

"One of my friends from The Lodge called me. None of the folks at Snowbell knew her. And Carlos is in the hospital. He is probably getting transferred to Sacred Heights. He says one word, over and over. Succubus. Strange things have been happening around here."

That was an understatement.

Lee's back stiffened. It couldn't be a coincidence the teenage boys disappeared, and their best friend's only word was Succubus. Luc and his demons seemed bent on spreading their darkness to Everglade. She got so mad she could've spit nails.

She changed subjects. "The church ladies sure know how to cook. And look, Dad, I think this is Miss Pearl's peach cobbler too. How's Mom?"

"Dr. Pedersen just stopped by to check on your mother. She's with him in the living area."

Lee wiped her hands on the red and white checkered dish towel and made her way to her mother. "How's she doing, Doc?"

Oliver's eyes no longer glowed but shimmered blue again. "Why don't you tell her?"

Mom wore a house robe and pink fuzzy slippers. "I slept like a baby last night. And so far today, no headache."

He laid out three small sleeves of paper. "Each powder makes a cup of tea. Jenny, you need to space them out about every six to eight hours at the first sign of a headache."

He tugged the collar of his shirt when he faced Lee. "Are you going to take me up on my job offer?"

A voice inside her head said, *Take the job.*

Is that you, Erinelle?

"What offer?" Mom straightened herself on the sofa.

"I offered Lee a job last night as my assistant." He reached around his neck, retrieving his stethoscope and placing it into his open medical bag.

Harry and Joseph stepped into the room as Lee said, "I'll take you up on your offer."

"You're going to enjoy working for me. Science is evolving daily. No two patients are ever the same." He closed his bag and stood.

Harry's gaze bored a hole through her.

"What time should I arrive?" The blood rushed to her cheeks. She cleared her throat, shoving her hands into her boxy sweater pockets to stop fidgeting.

"My office opens at eight o'clock, so you should arrive at seven-fifteen, and I'll walk you through your job requirements. I see patients in the morning then I do rounds at the hospital and Sacred Heights on alternating afternoons."

"I'll arrive at the office at seven-fifteen. Thanks for the opportunity." She shifted her feet.

Why did Harry seem so angry? Why should he care where she worked? She needed a job.

Oliver reached down and took Mom's hand. "You call me if you need me, and I'll check on you in a couple of days." Jenny nodded then he left out of the front door.

Harry frowned. His eyes darkened. With a hint of sarcasm, he said, "I thought you wanted to work for the telephone company. And you took a job with him?" He pointed toward the front window as Oliver walked down the sidewalk.

She ignored his smart remark and turned to her mother. "I'm going to make you a plate for lunch."

"For Heaven's sake, I can walk into the kitchen. Dr. Pedersen's headache powders work miracles." Her mother got up and made her way to the table.

Harry hip-bumped Lee. "Stop acting like I'm not here. You took a job without telling me?"

"I don't need your permission to take a job."

He braced his arm against the doorjamb so she couldn't get to the kitchen. "No, you don't, but I thought you might tell me something that may or may not affect our future."

"You just returned home. I haven't seen you in years. Don't smother me."

"Me? Smothering you?" He shrugged, shaking his head at the same time.

She pushed by him, entered the kitchen, and began to uncover the dishes. She set out the plates and utensils, then grabbed the glass pitcher of sweet tea flavored with lemon wedges from the counter. She poured the tea into the glasses on the table. Thirsty, she gulped most of her glass in a couple of chugs and filled it again.

Her thoughts went to the local boys. She'd ask Erinelle about them.

During lunch, Harry and Joseph talked about the farm, the new crops, and his livestock. But the underlying tension between Harry and her persisted.

"Blaine told me you're training for an engineering position at the electric company." Her father slathered butter on his biscuit.

"Humph, guess you forgot to mention your job too." Lee started coughing.

Her mom thumped her back. "Don't put so much food in your mouth. You'll choke to death. Are you okay?"

She waved her mom off, then took a sip of tea. "I'm fine. That last bite just went down the wrong pipe."

Harry pushed food around his plate with his fork. "I'm heading to Bethesda tomorrow for a workshop. I passed the academic portion of the job, and still have to pass the on-site training. If everything goes well, I should start full-time later this summer."

"The electric company offers lifelong job benefits." Joseph scooped a large portion of peach cobbler on a dessert plate. "I mean if you want to raise a family, job security is important."

"Dad, I'm sure Harry has better things to talk about than raising a family."

Harry locked eyes with her. "No. Nothing is more important than family."

"I didn't mean to imply family wasn't important." Gosh, how he could get under her skin so fast. "I don't wish to discuss the topic at the kitchen table."

"Family is something that interests me," Harry said. "It should interest you too, but I suppose you're too busy worrying about your new job."

Jenny looked between Lee and Harry. "Now children, let's not get into an argument at the table, or I may have to insist you kiss and make up."

Dad spat out his tea. "That's one way to nip it in the bud."

Her mother pushed her plate to the side. "Well, they're both so young and starting in on life. Why should they argue about gainful employment? You two have time to entertain all the possibilities."

Leaning back in the chair, her mom placed her hand on her belly. "Whew, I overate. I'm full as a tick. So, I think I'll lie down." She winked at Dad, then looked at Lee. "I'll do the dishes later."

"No worries, Mom. Harry will help me with the dishes. Won't you?" She narrowed her eyes at him.

"Miss Jenny, I'm happy to help with the dishes." He took another bite of chicken, chewing with his mouth closed, and stared at Lee.

Dad yawned, stretched his arms, and pushed from the table. "A nap is a great idea." He extended his hand to Mom then he turned to Lee and Harry. "Try not to kill each other. Enjoy this gorgeous day. You both should go for a stroll?"

Lee rolled her eyes.

Her parents took regular Sunday afternoon naps, and she was nearly a teenager before she figured it out. Sex was not something a child wanted to envision parents doing. "Sure thing, Pops."

Lee and Harry cleaned up the kitchen, barely speaking a word to each other.

"Why are you so mad at me?"

He dried the dishes while she washed. "Our families plan a trip to the beach every summer at Gammie Glenn's on the Gulf. If you start a new job, will your boss give you the time off?"

"You're acting like a child, and I'm not buying it. The beach isn't why you're mad. You're mad I took a job with Oliver. And I'm not going to the beach until my mom gets better. Some of her headaches take weeks to recover." She washed the last dish, then rinsed out the sink.

"And what about you? You're going out of town for job training. Look, Harry, we need jobs. If this thing between us ever gets off the ground floor, we'll need money." She reached up on tiptoes and kissed his cheek. "Don't be mad. Let's hike the ridge. Okay?" She took off her mom's apron and hung it on the baker's rack. "Give me a minute to change clothes."

"I'll wait here." His facial features softened.

She raced up the stairs and changed into jeans, a red sleeveless top that tied at the waist, and slipped on a pair of tennis shoes. She went into the linen closet and grabbed a picnic blanket from the shelf. She jogged down the stairs, and back to Harry in the kitchen; then they went out the door holding hands.

"Let me put my tie and coat in your car." He loosened his necktie, took off his Seersucker jacket, and placed them in the back seat.

"Let's go to the cave. I love the old tree next to it. It's my favorite place to be alone."

He took the blanket and tucked it under his arm. He proceeded to follow her up the tractor lane and onward to Campbell Ridge. "I guess I needed to stretch my legs a bit after eating so doggone much, and the fresh air will help clean out the cobwebs in my mind. The last couple of days have been stressful."

She stopped in front of him and searched his eyes. "Don't be mad at me for accepting a job with Oliver. I want to work for the telephone company, but they don't have an opening."

He brushed a strand of hair behind her ear. "Dr. Pedersen likes you, Lee. He's using the position to get close to you."

The touch of his hand made her heart beat unsteadily against her rib. "He needs an assistant, and I need a job. Besides, your sister is sweet on Oliver, and jealousy doesn't suit you."

"Psst, I suppose I am a little jealous."

"Race me." She took off at a slow jog, then glanced at Harry before she blazed a trail to the top of the ridge using her superhuman speed.

A canopy of trees in various shades of green dotted along the landscape, some covered in moss, others with lichen. The branches swayed and danced in the late spring breeze.

She spotted several deer scurrying into the thicket of the woods. Frogs sang near the pond as sunlight dappled streaks of liquid gold through the trees. Large boulders shouldered against the ridge.

The valley below resembled a patchwork quilt with different shades of green. Since childhood, she'd retreated to her favorite place. The place had a spiritual quality. It was no wonder that she met an angel at the cave.

Reaching the top, Lee waited until Harry caught up with her then took the blanket from him, spreading it out on the soft spring grass close to the old willow tree.

Out of breath, he said, "I see the angel taught you a new skill. Geesh, you're like Flash Gordon."

"I tried the speed thing this morning, but I wanted to see if I could do it again." She hadn't broken a sweat.

"So, when are you trying out for the Olympics?" he chuckled.

"Ha, ha, very funny. You're a regular Bob Hope." She stretched out on the blanket, and he joined her. "Gosh, I love it up here. I can think about things up here without interruption."

The nearby stream flowed lazily over small and medium-sized rocks, gurgling, swishing, and swirling eddies out of the cave downstream.

He rolled onto his side, propped by his elbow. "I love it up here too. It's funny how fast childhood passes us. Some of my fondest memories are terrorizing you and Carol Ann on the ridge." Laughter rumbled out of his chest, lifting her spirits.

"Why do boys enjoy scaring girls?"

"I suppose even back then I had a crush on you with your silky hair, and you have the cutest freckles across your perfect nose. And scaring hypes up the adrenaline. Hey, are you scared? I mean of the demons. Do you think they had anything to do with the disappearance of those boys?"

"I don't know. Maybe. I'll ask Erinelle."

She twisted a lock of his hair. "It sounds strange, but I'm not scared. I was terrified when I met Erinelle, but she released my fears. I don't worry for myself, just for my loved ones, and that includes you, but if I can help save one soul, it'll be worth my sacrifice. I knew my destiny the moment I met the angel. Maybe, I've always known."

"You mentioned last night about your gift since childhood. What did you mean?"

"It's like homemade movies in my head. Sometimes I get glimpses of the past and other times the future. It's not a gift I can control. I may touch a person's hand, or article of clothing, and a vision will appear. Once I found a billfold on the sidewalk in town, and as soon as I picked it up, I knew who it belonged to before opening it." She crossed her feet at the ankles.

"Do you have visions about me?" His face almost touched hers — a hair's breadth from her mouth.

"Nope, but I do have dreams." She stared at his enticing lips.

He tipped his head slightly to the right. "Do tell."

"Maybe someday, I'll tell you my dreams as long as you don't think I'm loco." She kissed the palm of his hand.

"I never meant to imply you're crazy. The whole supernatural thing is a bit daunting for this ole country boy." He imitated Oliver's accent. "Do you think Dr. Vunderful has a clue about the supernatural warfare taking place over his soul?"

"I'm not sure about Oliver. Please, no more talk about angels and demons. I want to enjoy my time alone with you. And my dad always says destiny has a way of working itself out." She pushed him onto his back and placed her head on his chest. His heartbeat was a comfort to her ears.

IN THE SHADOW of the cave, Luc watched Lee Campbell with a mortal man. He had successfully planted the job offer suggestion, and she took the bait. The intel coming in suggested the young woman may very well possess all the powers of the angels, including the ability to appear and disappear at will. What the angels called time-walkers.

The thought of a mortal on the same playing field as an immortal made him furious.

But was she more than just a mortal?

It was one thing to battle seasoned warriors, another thing entirely to fight the AAF's mortal recruits. His solution was to drain The Chosen of their divine gifts, making him stronger each time.

Luc extended his hand toward the couple lying on the blanket, immobilizing them to take a better look. He froze the animal and plant life around the area— even the creek stilled.

Scanning the woods for Erinelle, he didn't sense her presence, but that didn't mean she wasn't around. He usually sent Daglan to investigate the mortals, but the thought of a human hybrid yielding such power from the Heavens intrigued him.

He crouched in front of the mere slip of a girl.

Humans seldom earned a personal visit from the Prince of the World. However, two years earlier, in 1948, the announcement of Israel's new nation forced him to up his game. The prophesied re-gathering of the faithful remnant signaled the apocalyptic battles had begun between the species to end an age. The war intensified between angelic beings.

He blamed The Creator. He had given Luc the planet then He started experimenting on other life forms including humanity. Luc and his followers carved out an existence and even marveled at the creation process until The Creator made humans in His image.

A slap to the faces of the fallen.

The fallen angels shouldn't be Earthbound in the first place and having to cohabitate with the Homo sapiens, which in his opinion were no better than the Neanderthals. The insult still made him livid to this day.

He made it his mission to destroy humans, and just maybe, The Creator would see the error of His ways and welcome him and his fallen family back to the fold. If not, he had no intention of relinquishing his reign of power on Earth. Mortals could be controlled and manipulated easily.

The blue sky opened, and a team of warrior angels from the AAF descended on the wings of the wind, shaking the ground beneath Luc's feet.

Erinelle, Baldric, Luwenia, and Raphael surrounded the humans on the blanket.

He stood at attention and gave them a mock salute. "Welcome again, my brothers and sisters. How may I assist you today?"

Erinelle stepped up to him, sticking the spear of destiny at his heart, the one divine item that could kill any angel on the spot. "You may assist us by leaving these two humans alone."

"Whoa, girlfriend, that spear is nasty. And what's so special about these mortals? Don't you ever wonder, Erinelle, what would've happened had you not left me? The world may have been a different place. Do you miss me?"

She spat on the ground. "I loathe you."

Luc spun around appearing in a pair of blue overalls and a straw farmer's hat, then took a toothpick out of his mouth. With an elongated Southern drawl, he said, "Y'all want to kill me, but you can't, and that just sticks in your craw."

Baldric the Warrior charged him, but Luc was too quick, and the giant angel slammed into the tree. "You never learn, son."

"I am not your son," Baldric shouted.

Luwenia's voice roared with the sound of a thousand trumpets. The vibration shook Luc to his core, threatening to rip him apart. "It is not your time, Dragon. Leave or face the wrath of the Lord."

"The end of an age draws near, and I relish the moment I send you all to the Eternal Darkness." He vanished.

LEE AWOKE to the presence of four giant angels hovering over her head.

Erinelle went down on one knee. "Raphael, help them."

"Hold your hands together." The warrior angels did as he instructed. He placed his hands on her and Harry. "No injuries."

"Guys, I'm awake. Erinelle? Why are you here? What happened?"

Harry stirred but did not wake.

"Luc was here." Deep lines of grief etched into Erinelle's face. A sight that made her stomach dip with fear and trepidation.

"Luc? As in Lucifer?" Lee's hands made fists.

"Do not mention his name." The warrior with Erinelle looked like a golden version of Zeus.

Erinelle said, "Meet my team, Luwenia, Baldric and Raphael."

"Are all angels so gorgeous? You're the most beautiful creatures." She came to an upright position. She was too weak to stand. "Why was Luc here?"

"We aren't creatures. We are warrior angels," Luwenia said matter-of-factly. "We have reason to believe Luc knows you're a hybrid. He wants you."

"Did he take the local boys?" Her brain was fuzzy, and she couldn't stop staring at the warrior angels. She could see why the prophets of old mistook them for Gods.

"What boys?" Erinelle asked.

"My father said two local boys disappeared last night. Another boy escaped. The only word he mutters is succubus. Can we help them?"

"Demons took the boys to Hades." Luwenia said, "Their physical bodies wouldn't survive crossing realms. The best we can do is free their souls and send them to Heaven. The other boy, Carlos, is hiding under layers of demonic cloaking. We have the healers working to remove the shields, and with His grace, Carlos will recover, eventually. Luc doesn't play fair, and he doesn't see age as a problem. Any innocent soul gives off eternal light."

"Damnation. Luc is in my town. He's been on my ridge. I'm ready to fight the bastard."

Baldric chuckled. "Enough with the profanity. You'll hurt my ears. Erinelle will help guide you as you gain new powers. You and only you will know how to use them."

In a flash of white light, the angels disappeared except for Erinelle.

"What did Baldric mean? Will I learn through osmosis? And, so that you know, I'm about at my breaking point."

Erinelle placed her hands on the top of Lee's head, filling her with calmness and peace. "You're in shock. You've received more information than most of The Chosen in a two-day window. But you're safe for now. Meet me here at dawn, and I'll work with you daily until you master your awakening powers. An end of an age is coming." She dematerialized.

"Wait!" It was too late. Erinelle was gone.

Harry stretched and yawned. "Did I fall asleep? Man, my neck hurts."

"I fell asleep too." A thousand thoughts swirled in her mind simultaneously.

The devil, that vile creature, had been on her ridge.

The idea of Luc manipulating them made her furious. A fire grew in her belly to learn all she could to save her loved ones, Everglade, and herself.

CHAPTER 8

"I'LL NEVER BE FREE"

Over the next several weeks, Lee worked a grueling schedule. She set her alarm each night and woke before the sunrise. Every morning, she worked out with Erinelle for an hour and a half, then she bathed and dressed in time to arrive at Oliver's office at seven-fifteen sharp and worked there until dusk.

He gave her a detailed notebook with a list of daily work chores. She greeted patients, set up, and organized files. And during the slow periods, she helped him in the laboratory. He made no advances, and she never felt the presence of the unknown demon.

Her mom arrived one afternoon before closing. "I have a four-thirty appointment. How do you like your new job?"

She pulled out her mother's patient file, then left her work area to hug her mom. "It's interesting. I've learned a lot. How are you feeling?"

"I'm fine, but your father insisted on me keeping my appointment." Jenny placed her purse on the counter and reached inside for a tissue.

"Dr. Pedersen is with a patient. You're the last one for the day. Do you mind waiting?"

"Of course, I don't mind. It's not like I have a boat to catch." Mom glanced at the empty waiting room with a variety of magazines stacked neatly on the end tables. "Everything is so clean. I'm impressed."

"He does most of the cleaning. He has a phobia about germs, I think."

Lee scanned the contents of her mom's file. Oliver made several notations regarding headaches and possible associations with depression, trauma, or mental illness.

Mental illness?

Her mom didn't have a mental illness, for crying out loud; she witnessed demons. It was against office protocol to discuss patients' files unless Oliver specifically requested information for her to research.

Dr. Pedersen walked out of the exam room with his patient, Mr. Desmille. "Keep the stitches clean and dry. Stop by the desk and schedule a time next week, and I'll remove the sutures. If you see any redness, swelling, or start running a fever, call me." He looked up and smiled at her mom as Mr. Desmille waited to schedule his next appointment.

"Mom's down for a checkup. After her appointment, you have the rest of the afternoon blocked."

"I always have time for you, Miss Jenny. How are you?" He ushered her mother down the hall into one of the exam rooms.

Lee flipped the page in the appointment book. "Mr. Desmille, would next Wednesday at four o'clock work?"

He shoved his hands in his overall pockets. "S'hore will. How much do I owe you?"

"Nothing today. Dr. Pedersen said he'd work out something with you in trade. Perhaps, cheese and butter? Or eggs?"

His grin went wide, revealing a missing lower central incisor. "I got plenty of eggs and dairy. I'll have the missus make Dr. Pedersen a basket."

She chatted with him about his recent tractor accident. "Dad or I could come over and help with your farm."

"No need, Miss Lee. My son is home visiting for a couple of weeks while I recover. Doc said the baler could've killed me, so I'm blessed to be alive. But do tell your dad that I said hello."

"I sure will. Take care." She filed Mr. Desmille's paperwork as he left out the front door.

She glanced at the clock. The hair on her arms rose. A dark presence entered the room, and seconds later, she heard her mother scream. She bolted to the exam room.

Jenny crouched in the corner, shivering. Her blue eyes turned a stormy gray. It was her mother, but also something else. "Mom, can you hear me?"

Mom tilted her head to the side.

Holy crow.

Mom's eyes color changed to blood red rubies. *A demon not her mother, said,* "Lee Campbell, the demon fighter? What a joke."

In one giant leap, the demon that took possession over her mother's body stood in front of her.

She'd worked with Erinelle enough to know the demon used her mom as bait.

With measured calmness, she asked, "What is your name?"

A rancid odor of sulfur filled the exam room.

"Don't you remember me, cupcake?" Jenny inched closer, searching Lee's eyes.

"Daglan? If that's you, leave my mother. Let me see your real face." She extended her right hand, mentally calling on her sword, which instantly appeared. The room seemed to narrow, but the demon must've used an illusion trick or sorcery.

Air rushed from her lungs. She went into a battle stance, her sword level at Jenny's nose.

Black sinewy substance poured out of her mom's mouth before Daglan appeared in his full form.

Her mother fell to the floor, unconscious, but she was alive and breathing. Lee had to kill the demon before checking her mom for injuries.

Daglan's cold stare fell on Lee with such intensity it nearly made her falter. His crazy as a loon grin transformed. He pulled back his lips, revealing sharp jagged teeth dripping with green saliva.

Grotesque.

His menacing quality radiated around him. Prickles of fear created a momentary doubt in her abilities. Her heart rate jacked up and electricity coursed through her veins. She flicked her fingers and arcs sparked from the tips.

"So, looks like you've learned new tricks?" He hissed. "But can you do this?" He disappeared and reappeared with high speed, knocking Lee's sword out of her hand.

He dashed about the room, knocking over the patient table, shoving the glass jars of cotton balls and bandages off the counter, sending them crashing to the floor. Shards of glass flew everywhere as Lee covered her face with her hands.

"I've learned something new about you, cupcake."

Oliver's eyes went wide with fear. He stood frozen against the wall, either unable, or unwilling to help her.

With a quiver in her voice, she shouted, "Daglan, in the name of The True Prince, leave these premises, or I will send you to the Eternal Darkness." She pointed her fingertips at his head, and sparks shot across the room, hitting the demon in the face.

"You'll pay Hell for scarring me, crossbreed." Daglan dematerialized.

Had she frightened him?

Adrenaline trumped her fear. She quickly turned left and right, looking for him. She felt Daglan's presence, but he wasn't visible. He feared her. The thought filled her with confidence, making her feel so alive. She heard the rustling of wings.

His voice deepened. "Luc is coming for you, Miss Campbell. And what he wants, he gets."

The demon was gone.

Oliver collapsed, and slid to the floor. "What-what happened?"

She let out a huge exhale of breath. "You tell me." She rushed to her mom's side, helping Jenny to her feet. "Are you okay? Are you hurt?"

Mom's hands trembled. "Dr. Pedersen was checking my pulse, and then I passed out. I-I didn't come to until I heard your voice. I'm fine, just a little shaken."

Suddenly, Lee knew how to reach Erinelle by sending a message across the telepathic lines to the In-Between command center where Michael carried out his Earthly operations.

Seconds later, Erinelle appeared to Lee. *"Daglan was here?"*

"Sparks flew from my fingertips. He said I scarred his face. Did I?"

"I bet you made his butt pucker." Erinelle laughed.

Lee wasn't amused. *"I'm pretty sure I frightened him, but how?"*

Oliver looked sick. His head swayed. She grabbed the wastebasket just in time for him to puke.

She opened one of the cabinets and handed him a small hand towel. "How do you feel?"

"Ugh. Nauseous. Exhausted. Spent. I don't understand what just happened." His head lolled against the wall. His eyes closed.

"Mom, I'll call Dad to come and get you so I can care for Dr. Pedersen."

"Don't worry your father. I'm fine. I promise. It's not my first rodeo." Jenny reached for her purse, pulled out a tissue, and dabbed the sweat beads on her upper lip. "I'll see you at home. Dr. Pedersen, we'll reschedule."

He nodded, and her mother left the office.

Erinelle materialized before Oliver. He clutched his chest. "Oh, God. Not another one."

"I'm an angel fighting for the good in this world. I'm here to help Lee, and through her, we will help you. Tell us about Nadine. Demons are using her to get to you."

Oliver slowly came to his feet. "So, I'm not the only one? Thank heavens, I'm not alone." He threaded his fingers through his sweat-saturated hair. "You're not a demon? And your name is Erinelle?" He seemed puzzled.

"No, I'm not a demon, and yes, my name is Erinelle." She sent Lee another telepathic message, *"Our goal is to save Oliver's soul. A beast larger than Daglan is pulling his strings."*

"Luc?"

"Yes, I think so."

He straightened the overturned table. "I thought I was losing my godforsaken mind. Lee, your poor mother. Do you think she's okay?"

"Mom is tough. I'll check on her later."

Erinelle tapped his shoulder. "Oliver, tell us about Nadine."

He pulled up a stool and sat down. "I wanted to start over in Everglade, but I see I have unfinished business at Sacred Heights." His shoulders slumped. "Nadine Vaughn was my patient."

Lee listened to Oliver's bittersweet tale of love and death, and she sensed his profound sadness. She had experienced despair over her mom in Sacred Heights while she attended classes. She wanted to comfort him but held herself in check.

"Nadine's last words were, tell Erinelle they're taking me to Hades. I should've listened to her. I should've believed her."

Erinelle paced about the room. "We must devise a battle plan to take over Sacred Heights. Based on Oliver's story, Nadine may not have committed suicide. Her soul may be trapped within Sacred Heights on the fourth floor, which sounds eerily like a demon portal. Nadine and any other innocent souls need our help."

"I'm in. I have the keys to all the floors and rooms," he said.

"The demons of Sacred Heights seem to be seasoned warriors. Lee, your lessons are bumped to twice a day, early morning on the ridge when the weather is agreeable, and we'll train in the barn in the evening. Oliver, you're welcome to join our planning sessions. However, you have no superhuman abilities except your intellect."

She looked at Erinelle, trying to remember the details of the demon encounter. "I developed a new skill. Baldric was right. I knew how to use it. But Daglan used time-walking, which placed me at a disadvantage."

"We'll work on time-walking, but I want to see the new skill you've developed in the morning."

"Um, we should attack Sacred Heights on a weekend when the staff is minimal." Oliver flexed then curled his hands into fists. "I want to fight the monsters that took Nadine from me. If she's trapped, we must set her free."

"What about Harry?" Lee asked. "Do I tell him the plan?"

"Harry is too involved with you to reason. He'll try to intervene and may cause problems and possible injuries. We need seasoned warriors. My team, you and Oliver, should be enough to free the trapped souls."

"I'll be ready. What do you need me to do?"

"Will discuss it during your lessons."

Lee turned to Oliver. "I'll help you clean up this mess."

He motioned with his hand. "No. I'll do it. Go home, Lee. I need to do something to keep my mind and body occupied."

"If you're sure then I'm leaving for the day." She had more questions to ask Erinelle, but the use of her powers had drained her energy.

"I'm sorry for bringing you and your mother into my nightmare."

"Somehow, I think it's the same nightmare. You and I connect in a cosmic way. I don't know how, but I believe things happen for a reason. I'll see you later, Oliver." She left the destroyed patient room, grabbed her purse, and went out the door.

"Do you think Oliver is working with Luc?"

"I'm counting on it. I read some of his thoughts, but he has a cloaking shield around him. It may take time, but we'll win Oliver over. He will help us. I am sure of it. Our job is to save souls, and he still has one."

OLIVER WATCHED THE ANGEL VANISH, and then Lee left. He locked the door and went back to the patient room to clean up the mess.

Luc materialized carrying a broom. "You should go to Hollywood, Oliver. I believe even Erinelle bought your sad sap love tragedy."

"You and I have a deal. I'll deliver Lee to you on the fourth floor of Sacred Heights, and you deliver to me, a living and breathing Nadine. No demons are to touch her. Do we agree?"

Luc spread out his arms with a sweeping bow. "As you wish, Oliver."

He didn't want to hurt Lee, but if delivering her to Luc would set Nadine free then so be it.

~

HARRY AND LEE sat on the porch, alone.

He tried to remain calm after she explained to him what happened in Dr. Pedersen's office. Her expression was unreadable. He reached for her hand. "Walk with me to the barn."

"What for?"

He glanced to the front door and whispered, "Not here."

Lee jogged down the front steps.

He caught her before she entered the big red barn spinning her around to face him. He drew in a sharp intake of breath and released it. "I did warn you about Pedersen. I knew it the moment I met the man he was bad news."

"You have no clue what's going on, Harry. A battle is brewing. The demon that possessed my mom is really after me. The only way to protect those I love and the souls of Sacred Heights is to fight."

"For crying out loud, are you listening to the words coming out of your mouth? I swear, sometimes you don't have the sense God gave a goose." He glanced toward the sky before looking back at her. The waning sunlight played against her taut facial features.

She shoved him hard. "You're such a liar. You told me you believed in angels. You said you believed what I told you. I went against Erinelle's instructions and told you about Sacred Heights. I don't want secrets between us." Lee opened her right hand, and a sword appeared miraculously. "Just because you can't understand what's going on doesn't mean I'm crazy. And well, well, truth be told, I've had enough of it."

Lee went into *en guarde* position, whipping the blade back and forth, and took off running with blinding speed, jumped the barn gate, springing onto the tractor, then catapulted into the hayloft with the ease of an acrobat. "Does this look like I'm playing or crazy, for that matter?"

"Dad-gum it, Lee. You're faster than Everglade gossip."

"I'm not in the mood for your wisecracks." She jumped to the ground, landing in front of him and released the blade, which disappeared. "Go home."

He stood speechless. He couldn't explain what Lee did. She defied the laws of nature.

His heart raced as he pulled her into his arms. "You're right. I don't understand what's going on here. I came home from service, and the world still spun on its axis, and now everything is topsy-turvy. I only know one sure thing, and that is I love you. I am in love with you. A man's job is to protect the woman he loves, and I don't know how to protect you. I don't know how." He fought the urge to cry.

"Don't you dare start weeping on me, Harry Glenn. If you love me, then believe in me. I told you a relationship with me wouldn't be conventional. Do you think my life plan was to fight demons? I wanted to work and travel, then settle down and raise a family."

She searched his eyes. "I stand before you, on this Earth, as a hybrid messenger sent from above to help fight and win an angelic war that's been going on for thousands of years. I'm not the first of The Chosen, nor will I be the last. I'm a different species. And those fly skills you just witnessed, I learned them in Heaven long before I was born a mortal. I am a warrior, and I can't explain it. I can't understand it. With or without you."

She leaned against the tractor. Her strength seemed to wane. "Go home and think about what you want in life. If what I am is too much for you to handle, I'll understand. Erinelle will wipe your memory, and we'll remain friends just like before."

He stepped over and cupped her face with his hands. "Is that what you want? Do you want me to leave and forget everything that's happened? Do you want me to forget our kisses? Don't you love me?"

"Demons go after loved ones of The Chosen. I don't want them coming for you. See what's happening to my mother? They could come for your parents and Carol Ann too."

"Life is messy and complicated, and I get that for us to move on requires a giant leap of faith, one that I can't deny. I am all in, Lee. I am willing to leap."

She wrapped her arms around herself. "I'm going to fight whatever battles The Creator deems me to fight, but that doesn't mean you have to. I don't know how it will end. But in this war, people are captured and tortured for eternity. The angelic war is a full-on fight for souls. It is a fight for everlasting life. I can't expect you really want to live not knowing one day to the next what demon could come calling. This is my cup to drink, and it doesn't have to be yours."

She took his hands into hers. "I'm giving you a way out."

"I don't want out. I admit, before I came home, I didn't think about spiritual things, angels or demons, Heaven or Hell. I did think about you and me more often than the stars in the sky. If you're going to fight, then so am I. I'm a warrior too. I'm a full-fledged mortal, but I know war. I won't allow you to go to Sacred Heights without me. I mean it, Lee. Wherever you go, I will follow." He wrapped his arms around her waist. "We don't have to decide today. A lot has happened. And, for the record, I'm not a fan of Oliver Pedersen."

"I gathered that much." She leaned her head against the crook of his neck. "Hey, you just told me you loved me."

"Yeah, I do. Can you teach me the fly thing?"

She laughed. "I have no idea. And, I can't allow you to fight with me. I need all my concentration and newfound skills to stay alive, and I can't if you're on the playing field. I won't be able to fight if I'm protecting you. If you insist on following me, Erinelle may wipe your memory of me altogether. Maybe, I'm not the woman for you."

"No memory wipes. Are we clear? I get to choose who I'm with and what I do with my life."

"No, we don't choose everything. Everything and everyone has a purpose, a reason under the sun. Humans have free will. Souls are on the line, daily." She pressed her lips into a firm line. "I got it. Try and slam me to the ground."

With exasperation, he replied, "I will not. I have never lifted one finger against a woman in my life."

"Don't be a girl. I want to show you how strong I am." She went into a fighting pose. "Come and get me."

He halfheartedly rushed her. She slammed him to the ground with such force his teeth clattered. He pulled himself up and looked at her. "Lucky try."

She motioned for him. "Come on, baby, give me what you got."

Harry brushed the dust off his pants. "I don't want to hurt you."

"You're not going to. When I'm in the fighting mode, my powers kick in gear, and I grow strong, like Samson." She winked and motioned for him to come again.

He tucked his head and ran for her. He intended to scoop her up and throw her over his shoulders like a sack of potatoes. Instead, she scooped him up with one arm and flipped him in the air, slamming his back against the hard terrain, knocking the breath out of him.

She placed her hands on his chest. "I'm so sorry. I didn't mean to hurt you. I wanted you to see I can fight. I don't need your protection."

He shoved her away and came to his feet. "You meant to humiliate me."

She leaned back on her heels; her hands slid on her thighs. "I wanted you to see I can take care of myself. Angels are much stronger than mortals. If you're determined to participate in our attack on Sacred Heights, the best I can offer you is the driver position. You may drive me to Sacred Heights, but you must stay in the car, and Erinelle must be on board with you becoming a part of the team."

He knew Lee was trying to look out for his best interests. He never thought his woman would be stronger than him. It was mind-boggling. She tried to explain to him the dangers of messing with supernatural beings.

"Angels and Demons are different than us. For crying out loud, they time-walk. I mean they use teleportation just like in science fiction, but it's real. Most celestial beings don't die from battle. Harry, you could die, and the thought of losing you frightens me."

"Well, I'm in no hurry to die, and don't forget, you're not immortal either. You may have abilities of celestial beings, but you still bleed red." He looked at the ground. "Damn. I feel so unnecessary. Useless."

She placed her head on his shoulder. "You are necessary to me. You give me emotional strength. Love moves mountains. Remember the scripture, *'if you have faith as small as a mustard seed, you can shout to any mountain, 'Move from here to there,' and it will move. Nothing will be impossible for you.'* You are strong where it counts."

"Humiel needs to get off the pot and find me some powers. I will drive you, but if what you say is true, then I can move mountains too."

"I don't think Humiel is in charge of divine powers, but I will speak to Erinelle." She wrapped her arms around his neck. He loved the way her body melted against him. They fit together perfectly. He pressed his hand on her low spine.

He kissed her slow and easy, pausing between each exhale of breath to savor the feel of her soft, full lips. His breathing labored as their kiss lengthened then his tongue took advantage of her mouth. Tingles rippled over his skin.

His hands roamed over her curves as he nibbled and licked the column of her throat. "I love you so much. Just thinking about the possibility of losing you rips me apart. Dread snakes through the pit of my stomach. I dreamed you ran with the angels with your sword, slicing and dicing the demons to gray ash. I couldn't breathe when I woke."

She curled his hair with her fingers. "I've had a similar dream except I have streaks of white hair and crow's feet around my eyes. I might've died. I'm running to save my daughter, and the demons ambush me, and everything fades to black."

"Our daughter?" He asked. "I don't want to lose you or a daughter, now or in the future."

Lee pressed feather-light kisses along his neck. "Humans die. What's important is how we live. What's important is how we love. Love me, Harry, all of me. Accept me as I am, not what you want me to be."

He would do anything to keep her. He craved her more than the air he breathed. His instinct alerted him to the dangers he faced but losing her meant losing himself. He wasn't about to let either happen. Not on his watch.

CHAPTER 9

"ANGEL IN DISGUISE"

Over the next couple of weeks, Lee worked out with Erinelle in the mornings and the evenings. Oliver made some of the morning planning sessions while Harry attended the evening bouts.

The angel reluctantly agreed to allow Harry on the team, temporarily. She argued with Erinelle for days before she finally caved in to her terms. She pleaded that Harry was her soul mate, and with him on their team was the best way to accomplish the task.

After much discussion, she requested enough supernatural powers for Harry to keep him from harm's way. He would drive her to Sacred Heights, but she didn't trust him to stay put. He needed to train, so Erinelle sent for Simon because his guardian, Humiel, wasn't a member of the AAF.

Simon looked like a child. "I'm not a kid, I assure you. I'm over three thousand years old and have seen more battles than most of the warrior angels I train. Harry will come with me. Lee, you stay here and train with Erinelle."

Anxiety filled her chest. "Don't hurt Harry."

Simon slapped Harry on the back. "Not a chance. We're going to be lifelong friends. Friends don't hurt each other. Friends make us better."

Harry's chest swelled. "Uh huh, see, Lee, now, you have a little taste of my concern for you. I requested help, and The Creator sent Simon. As you said, He doesn't make mistakes." He blew her a kiss and left the barn with the angel boy.

She sensed his pride. He wanted to help her, and for that alone she'd love him forever. Putting her life on the line was one thing, risking Harry's life made her sick to her stomach.

Erinelle set up a hologram of the Sacred Heights Sanatorium building plan against the barn wall. She circled the entry point to the towers. "The fourth-floor tower is U-shaped. The patient and visitor elevators flank the entry point, and down the hall leads to the service elevator on the opposite side of the building."

"I received intel from our command center that the fresco in the foyer of the tower is a possible portal to Hades." She marked an X in the center of the towers. "The key to our attack is to find and open the door."

"We intend to take over the sanatorium and rid it of demons. My commander is sending one of the AAF on a covert mission to find the opening to the portal." The angel paced the length of the barn. "We believe Luc is holding Nadine and possibly the innocent souls of Everglade's missing teenage boys captive within its walls. The AAF has changed our tactics to a full-scale search and rescue operation."

"Where will I be stationed?"

"Tentatively, our AAF team will enter the portal somewhere around here." Erinelle pointed to the map, then continued, "We believe the gateway enters into the nine levels of Hades. We're still working on the logistics. I'll give you orders when we solidify the plan. You will fight. You're ready. And you will triumph."

With some hesitation, Lee said, "I've never killed a living thing before."

"I've never trained someone like you. You're different than the other Chosen. You're my equal in combat. The demons haven't seen the likes of your powers, and you'll use it to their disadvantage and our advantage. I won't lie. It pains me to kill the fallen angels, but they chose Luc, and their evil knows no bounds. In battle, you must not hesitate. You must kill or be killed. Do you understand?"

"I won't hesitate. I promise."

Oliver entered the side door of the barn. His face was ashen. "I need your help."

Erinelle reached for her blade, walked up to him, and pointed the tip at his sternum. "Cough up the truth, mortal."

Lee rushed over. "What do you mean, Erinelle?"

"I'll allow him to explain, but first, I must check for demons. Be completely still, human. My blade will run you through if this is a trick." She traced the blade over his heart. "No demons are present. Speak."

"Luc is using me to get to Lee." He shivered.

Erinelle sheathed her sword, then placed her hand on his shoulder. "Luc is the dark demon within you. I knew it, but I couldn't prove it. I must request a legion to storm Sacred Heights. Oliver, if Luc senses your betrayal, he'll not only torture you but Nadine too."

"I don't think he resides in me, yet he has been persecuting me since I moved to Everglade. He's holding Nadine captive." He said, "I realized her best chance of survival is telling you the truth."

"Repent, Oliver. The Creator will deliver you from The Dragon beast."

He fell on his knees. "Oh, Lord, I repent." He steepled his fingers in prayer. "Please forgive my transgressions."

He looked at Erinelle and Lee. "I should've told you sooner. I can't imagine the suffering of souls at Luc's hands."

"Get off your knees, mortal man. The Creator has forgiven you. Chin up. We're going to set Nadine's soul free. We're going to save any other innocents too and close the portal at Sacred Heights, forever."

"Luc told me if I followed him that he'd deliver a living, breathing Nadine. Was he lying?"

"I'm sorry, but Nadine's Earth suit has expired. We're fighting to free her soul and the souls of any innocents, not their physical bodies. Only The Prince of Heaven can raise a whole person from the dead."

"I'm willing to sacrifice myself to save Nadine. She came to me for help. I used her for my desires, and she lost her soul."

"Luc and his demons used Nadine long before you came on the scene. The demons also killed Dr. Albright and they're using Dr. Brickman, not just you." Erinelle motioned for him to sit on the yellow straw-back chair. "The only way to protect you against Luc is to give you a memory wipe. You won't remember our conversation. However, Lee will need the keys to Sacred Heights service entrance."

He handed Lee the keys. "I made you a copy. The shift change is at eleven. Saturday evenings after the shift change is your best shot. There's about an hour with little or no security. Several demons must possess the fourth floor. A cold stench hits you in the face as soon as you step off the elevator."

"I can attest to that horrid smell." Lee scrunched her nose. "I went to find my mom in the art room, and I found myself on the fourth floor."

Erinelle grabbed her shoulders. "What? You've been on the fourth floor? Lee, that wasn't an accident."

"I see that now." She stepped away from the angel and squeezed Oliver's hand. "You have tremendous courage standing against Luc."

"Not courage. I'm scared to death, but eternal damnation scares me more."

"You won't feel a thing, I promise." Erinelle placed her hands over Oliver's eyes. Soft yellow light released from her palms with what looked like pixie dust, while delivering the memory wipe.

Oliver sat in silence for a few minutes. He glanced around the barn with a quizzical brow, then looked at them. "Did I miss something?"

"Not a thing. Good workout. I'll meet with the other team members and secure a date for the operation. Harry will drive Lee to Sacred Heights. Oliver, can you meet them at the gate?"

"What's the plan again?" He looked puzzled.

Not wanting to put the poor man through more trauma, Lee playfully shoved Oliver. "Aren't you a jokester. We just went over the plan."

He scratched his chin. "I guess I'm more tired than I realize. Just keep me posted. I'm available anytime."

"I'll be in the office in the morning if you have any questions, but I'm exhausted and need sleep."

"Sure. Um, I'll see you then." Oliver nodded, then left the way he came in.

～

LUC SAT on Oliver's sofa with one leg crossed over the other one, staring at the walls while waiting for the mortal to return. He'd learned the human might be working with the AAF with a possible *coup d'état*.

If his intel was correct, the AAF planned an attack on the Sacred Heights portal, which would allow him the opportunity to take out some of his formidable foes while absorbing Lee Campbell's powers. It was a win-win for him. The worst thing that could happen—he might lose a few souls, the best-case scenario placing Erinelle and her team into the Eternal Darkness.

The stairs creaked.

Luc heard sniffles. The sniveling, whiney bastard, he'd get what he deserved in time. He went to the top of the stairway railing. "I hate humans straddling the fence between good and evil. Be one or the other, man."

He flinched as if Luc struck him. "I didn't ask you. You took someone I loved and placed her in limbo. For what?"

"Oliver, Oliver. Nadine isn't in limbo. She's in Hades. She never loved you. She never loved her husband, and she killed her only child. You're pathetic."

Oliver straightened. "No, I'm not pathetic. I love Nadine. I love my parents. I love my career as a doctor. I love people. What do you love? Yourself? You gave up Heaven for your selfish gain. You destroyed paradise. You are nothing like The Creator."

Luc punched him so hard blood spurted from his mouth. "I love myself. I love The Creator. I love Heaven. I love Earth. I love my angels. I don't love humans. Out of all the intelligent species, human beings are the most destructive force on the planet and possibly the universe. I plan on destroying humanity."

Oliver pushed by him and fell on his bed face first. He rolled to his back, reaching for a tissue on the nightstand to stop the bleeding. "I agree humans are destructive. Humans are greedy and self-centered. But humans in our worst moments show compassion for one another, love each other, and many strive to save the planet. Do you think maybe if you worked with The Creator instead of against him, the whole war could've been avoided?"

Luc flew into a wild rage. He stretched his arms and extended his fingers. Glass, mirrors, anything breakable in the room exploded.

Oliver ducked and covered himself with a quilt from the bed.

Luc roared. The walls threatened to cave in.

He flew into the air and swooped in front of the mortal levitating before him. He ripped the quilt off to see the human's face. "I made a deal with you. You deliver Lee. I'll deliver Nadine. But you, Oliver, your sorry ass is mine."

He dematerialized.

THE GLASS SHARDS had torn into Oliver's flesh from Luc's tirade, leaving him in excruciating pain. Blood ran down his face, arms, and legs.

He rolled off the bed and went to his knees. "Oh Lord, hear my plea. I placed many people in harm's way of losing their souls forever. I've compromised my soul. I pray you'll forgive me. I offer my life for the captive souls. Save the innocent, and you may do with my soul as you see fit."

An angel appeared. A brilliant warm golden light filled the room. "Oliver, I'm here for you." The bronze being's black curls cascaded over his shoulders, his eyes the color of summer grass.

He squinted. "Who-who are you?"

"I'm your guardian angel, Adimus. The Creator is aware of your sacrifice. He's heard your prayers. Luc will not take your soul."

The angel's shimmering wings spread the width of the room. He bowed his head and extended his hands toward Oliver. "Take my hands and close your eyes. I will remove the glass from your injuries and stopped the pain but the scars will remain. We don't want to alert Luc that you're working as a double spy."

He did as he instructed. The angel spread warm waves of healing energy over him. His ripped and torn injuries healed and sealed the flesh.

Adimus let go of his hands. "You may open your eyes."

All evidence of Luc evaporated. "You work miracles. You saved me."

Adimus placed his arms around Oliver. "Souls who offer themselves to The Creator are never lost, my son."

The angel pushed his shoulders back, his chin lifted. "Daglan and several of Luc's soldiers captured and tortured me. The AAF found me on a rescue mission like the one they are planning for Sacred Heights. They will save Nadine."

"I'm sorry for your pain. Luc captures angels too?"

"Yes, he does. We once lived as a family in Heaven. Now, my fallen brothers and sisters capture and torture us. Many suffer at Luc's hand. But I say this with all confidence, when Heaven's Prince was murdered in Golgotha, Luc became condemned. Rest, Oliver. You'll need your strength for what lies ahead."

CHAPTER 10

"MONA LISA"

*H*arry looked forward to finally spending some time alone with Lee this evening. Her parents traveled to Nashville to celebrate their twenty-fourth anniversary, so she invited him over for the night.

He arrived at seven and knocked on her front door. His smile went wide when she pushed opened the screen door. He kissed her cheek, then handed her a bouquet full of cheerful daisies and roses mixed with white Baby's Breath. "Hey, beautiful."

A thread of amusement flittered across her eyes as she caressed the petals. "I love flowers." Her bright amber eyes mixed with specks of gold were framed by thick black lashes and hooked him every single time. Her pale pink floor-length dress swished against the hardwood while she ushered him into the living area.

Harry envied the dress, kissing her skin.

She no longer held the look of the lethal warrior facing an immortal foe but gave him a seductive look backing up the air in his lungs. He loved and adored everything about her. Her grace and elegance persevered even in the face of imminent danger, making him love her even more.

The record player blared Nat King Cole's, "Mona Lisa."

"I made pizza and picked up some sodas." Lee placed the flowers in a crystal vase with water and brought them back into the living area, placing them on the curved glass coffee table. "I thought we could eat in the den since my parents are away. It's a little less formal. Don't you love Nat King Cole's new single?"

"I am a fan." He held out his right hand, which she took and placed the other one on her low back. They swayed back and forth slowly dancing to the tune. "You smell wonderful. I've counted the minutes waiting to have you alone." He stopped and stared into her eyes. "Lee, I'm in love with you."

She pressed her face next to his. "And I'm in love you."

He held her close and shut his eyes, savoring the words he longed to hear. "I can't eat or sleep. I think about you all the time. Do you remember the night you lost your footing on the back stairs of my house? You were so young. I think I fell for you then."

"Of course. I couldn't sleep when I went downstairs for something to drink, and I slipped. You caught me. I couldn't breathe. I didn't want you to let me go. I wanted you to kiss me so badly."

"You wore that skimpy little nightgown, and I forced myself to leave you alone. I knew you had to grow up. And I did wait for you."

"Ah, but you weren't celibate," she chastised.

"It's not ladylike for you to mention, nor is it gentlemanly of me to reply."

She took his face into her hands. Before she could kiss him, he took a step back and paced the floor.

"What's the matter with you?"

He grabbed her hands, bringing them to his chest. "Marry me, Lee."

"What?"

"Marry me. We love each other. I've loved you for many years. I don't want to wait. I want you to be my wife."

"Can you live with my lifelong commitment to the war? And what about children? There's a chance what's happening to me will pass down to our children."

He crushed her with a kiss. "You are fighting for The Creator of our world to make it a better place. How could I be anything but proud of you? I will risk everything for you. I'll do whatever I need to take care of you and my family, including laying my life down."

"I believe you." She lowered her lashes and extended her hand to him. "Come with me, to my room."

"You're the most exciting woman I know, and you're not just beautiful on the outside but the inside too. You're smart, strong, and extremely sexy but as bad as I want you, I won't take your virginity."

"You're not taking my virginity. I'm giving it to you freely."

"Not without a commitment first."

She placed her hand on her hip. "You sound so old fashioned. It's 1950. Modern times and modern women."

"Yup, I'm old fashioned. You can still get married and be modern too. I promise to respect and cherish you and your decisions. I want you forever. I know you're worried about our future. I am too, but we can face anything together." The back of his hand stroked her cheek.

"I will marry you, on one condition."

"What's the condition?"

"We'll wait until I see how the Sacred Heights battle turns out. I need-to-know I can fight and win. I want to protect both of us, Harry. Then, I'll marry you."

"I agree to your terms."

"Good. Take my hand and follow me."

STREAMS OF SUNLIGHT stretched across the cherry four-poster bed. Several of Lee's favorite books rested on her nightstand. Harry followed her into her bedroom. Her breathing became labored as she closed the door, pressing her back against it.

He unbuttoned his white collared shirt.

Transfixed by his muscular chest, her gaze roamed to his navel and the single line of black hair hitting at his belt buckle.

She wet her lips. "You could've picked any woman in the county. Why me?"

"I've always loved you. Always." His lips barely touched hers. His fresh minty breath made her want to taste more. Taking her into his arms, he traced his tongue over her lips and kissed her so gently, as if he might break her.

Harry overshadowed any man she'd ever met or dated. He took her breath. She'd waited years for his attention, and now he offered her marriage. All that time, he knew she existed after all and loved her too.

He broke from the kiss, giving Lee a slow smile fanning the embers of her desire. He lowered his head slightly. The intensity of his stare and the awareness of him so close to her made her stomach somersault.

She surrendered the supernatural shields for the night and released her insecurities regarding Harry. She'd dreamed of making love to him more than once, and now he was in her room.

She considered herself as a strong woman, but Harry stripped her emotions to the bare bones. Her fingertips released little bursts of white energy. She flexed her fingers back and forth. Her heart hammered. Her blood thrummed through her veins.

She wanted him and needed him. The heat in her body pulsed. If he touched her in just the right place, she might explode.

His hands slid over her dress, caressing her breast with one and her buttock with the other.

She gripped his hand at her breast and clenched her thighs together, trying hard to control her lustful thoughts, but her body had different plans. Her lips parted. Her eyelids were heavy. Her body pulsed on the verge of climax.

His voice deepened as he whispered next to her ear, "You want me. I see it in your eyes."

"I want you, Harry, so much."

The downstairs phone rang.

With a throaty whisper, he said, "Don't answer it."

"I have to. It's probably my parents checking on me but hold that thought." She raced out the door, down the stairs, across the hall to the wall phone near the kitchen. "Hello."

Harry followed her.

She listened and paled. "No. It can't be true."

He reached for her hand. "What is it?"

She placed her hand over the receiver. "It's Linda from the sheriff's department. Glenn Hall's on fire."

He shouted, "Noooo."

"Linda, thanks for calling. Harry and I will be right over." She hung up.

"Get your shirt. I'll change into my jeans. The fire trucks and the authorities are on the scene. Where are your parents? Carol Ann?"

He turned paperwhite. "I left the house this morning, so I'm not sure. I'll be right back."

She ran into the laundry area, took off her dress, and pulled on a pair of jeans and a shirt folded on the stand.

Seconds later, Harry came running down the stairs pulling on his shirt. "We'll take my car. Wonder, what happened? God, I love Glenn Hall."

"I love it too."

They jumped in his sports coupe.

Driving like a bat out of Hell, he passed slower moving vehicles and raced ahead, fishtailing on the graveled roads.

Smoke billowed from the estate. Part of the mansion's white painted brick was covered in soot. The fire department trampled the once peaceful gardens next to the house.

Lee gripped Harry's arm after getting out of the car, and both watched in a state of shock.

The sheriff's department wouldn't allow Harry to enter, as an ambulance rushed from the scene.

He tried shrugging out of her grasp, but she held him back. "Let me go."

She pulled him away from the scene. "Honey, wait, please."

"I must find out who's in the ambulance." His jaw clenched.

Sheriff Dobbs stepped over to Harry. "Son, the person found in your house isn't anyone from your family. The victim is a young male that's badly burned. He's almost unrecognizable. We found kerosene cans, but until the investigation is complete, I won't speculate."

Harry released a sigh. "No one in the family got hurt, thank God. But who's the man?"

"Not sure," Sheriff Dobbs replied. "The suspect was unconscious when we arrived. We're gathering evidence. And I'll interview the man if he regains consciousness. I'll let you and your family know whatever we find." The sheriff turned and headed inside the house.

Lee tugged on Harry's sleeve and pointed. Eva, Blaine, and Carol Ann parked on the road and raced toward them.

Blaine's face paled. "What happened to our house?"

Harry didn't wait. He wrapped his big arms around his family. "I thought I lost you. The sheriff thinks its arson."

"Why would someone try to burn down our home?" Eva's voice quivered.

"They transported a man to the hospital. He's the main suspect. I'm just thankful you're all fine," Harry said.

Carol Ann circled her arm around Lee's waist. "Ain't that the gospel truth."

A few minutes later, Sheriff Dobbs strode back over to them. "Blaine, if you and Harry want to come with me, I'll take you inside. Most of the damage was contained in the kitchen and the back exterior of the home. The rest of the house was spared."

They followed the sheriff to the back of the house.

In her gut, Lee suspected one of Luc's flunkies set fire to the home as a warning. She must distance herself from the Glenn family before someone got hurt. She'd break ties with her best friend, and the love of her life, but not tonight.

They needed her.

"You're all welcome to stay at Everglade Farms."

Eva said, "Honey, thank you. We're planning a trip to Gammie's beach house, but we may head there sooner than we expected. Carol Ann's job doesn't start until the fall semester."

Twenty minutes later, Blaine and Harry walked past the debris on the front lawn. Blaine placed his arm around Eva. "Mama, look at this fire in a positive light. You get to decorate again. You wanted to paint and replace some of the furnishings, well, now's your chance."

Eva shrugged out of Blaine's arms. "Not funny. I love my home. And I guess I have been wanting to make changes, but not this way. We need to find out why someone deliberately set fire to the house."

Harry interjected, "I'll give Buck Hasten's a call. He's the best contractor in Murfreesboro, and we served together overseas. The fire chief said I could retrieve some clothes for everyone."

"We'll go to the beach once I meet with my interior designer." Eva sniffled.

Blaine raised a brow. "You have an interior designer?"

Eva glanced to the ground, then looked at Blaine with lowered lashes. "Well, I did meet with her once or twice with some of my ideas. We've been talking about modernizing the house."

"Anything you want, sweetheart," Blaine said. "We'll drive down to Gammies after we get the ball rolling on the renovations."

"I'll drive Mom to the beach house." Carol Ann looked at Lee. "Why don't you come with us?"

She squeezed her friend's hand. "Um, I'm working for Dr. Pedersen. But we're still planning to drive down to the beach for a visit later this summer." She had the battle to fight at Sacred Heights first.

"Dr. Pedersen? Oh, yeah. I remember hearing about your new job. I've been staying at Suggy's in Murfreesboro until I could find my own place. Harry, are you coming to Lee's too?"

"I'll stay in the pool house. We don't want vandals."

"Why don't all of you come to Everglade Farms? My parents are spending the night in Nashville. I'm sure they'd want you to stay."

Eva's hand went to her chest. "You're so thoughtful, dear. I think we will stay with you tonight."

"You may stay at Everglade Farms as long as you like."

Harry kissed the top of her head. "Thanks, honey, but I'm staying here just in case someone else shows up to finish the job."

"Sheriff Dobbs is leaving one of his deputies overnight," Blaine said. "You don't have to stay."

She looked at Harry. "May I speak with you in private?"

They stepped away from his family.

She pointed toward the corner of the house. "Someone's in the shadows." She started toward the area when she heard the *whoosh, whoosh, whoosh* of angel wings ascending into the sky, and the shadow disappeared.

Erinelle materialized next to Lee. "The mortal who torched the house is full of demons. He heard the voices telling him to burn down Glenn Hall. Luc is sending you a message,"

"*He just messed with the wrong person.*"

"Luc's responsible." She held his hands. "He wanted to hurt your family to get to me. I tried to tell you. The fallen go after The Chosen's loved ones."

His voice shook with rage. "I won't allow anyone or anything to come between you, me, and my family. Lee, I'm serious. I will not relent."

She loved his courage. "If you and I stop seeing each other, Luc will leave you alone. He'll leave Carol Ann and your parents alone. I'll never forgive myself if any of you get hurt."

"I won't allow beings that I can't see to control my life or yours. What happened here is not your fault. Do you hear me? And I get it. You have supernatural powers, but you're also a woman. My woman. I won't give you up, ever."

"I'm glad because I really don't want to lose you, and I don't want to lose your family either." She leaned her head against his chest. "I'm glad your family is going to Gammie's."

"Would you mind driving Mom and Carol Ann to your house? I'm going inside to retrieve some of our belongings, then Dad and I'll meet y'all directly."

She agreed.

The clouds rolled in, and thunder rumbled. One dark cloud seemed to funnel, but no tornado materialized. Inside Harry's car, she started the engine as heavy rain fell in sheets. An uneasy feeling uncurled like a ribbon within her soul, and she was afraid Luc pulled the strings.

CHAPTER 11

"FAR AWAY PLACES"

*E*verglade Farms

After getting the Glenns settled into the house, Lee stepped into the barn to feed and water Princess.

Erinelle appeared. "Take a load off. We need to talk."

She sat down on the tack room bench. She couldn't stop shaking. "The Glenns could've been hurt because of me."

"They weren't hurt, though. Do you want to stop before you start? This is war. You're fighting for the greater good. You must remember, all human bodies expire, but the spirit lives on. I came to tell you Michael, our commander, sent special units to guard the Glenns and your family. It doesn't mean Luc won't send some deranged individual to do his bidding. It was one of our warrior angels who stopped the man from burning Glenn Hall to the ground."

"I'm not afraid to fight. I'm not afraid to die. I'm afraid of losing those I love." Lee placed her face into her hands.

The angel gave her some time before she touched her shoulder. "None of us want to lose those we love."

"Have you lost loved ones?"

With a deep sigh, Erinelle joined her on the bench. "I never talk about my loss. Partly because I'm embarrassed, and the other part of

122

me is still angry and hurt. I fell for the Morning Star eons ago before the world existed. He's such a charmer. And boy, did he charm me. I was a young angel and looked up to him. He was second in command. He made me laugh. Back then, he was full of light and love. And plenty of angels loved him, but I found favor in his eyes and fell hard."

"After some time passed, I noticed the little inadequacies in him but ignored them at first. He'd go off on tangents about the Trinity and how unfair the system worked. He'd say things like true greatness requires extraordinary sacrifice, and he was willing to risk everything to achieve it. I listened to Luc's every word. I believed in him."

Lee listened to this beautiful, mighty angel reveal her innermost secrets and sensed her anguish and hurt.

"Time is different in our realm. Eventually, Luc tired of me when I aged." Her bright eyes watered.

She couldn't fathom Erinelle aging. The angel was so vital and strong.

The angel linked her fingers together. She stared at the dirt floor, and then she looked at Lee. "I was the one who reported him to Michael. I attended the rebellion meetings. I'm responsible for his descent. I'm responsible for the war."

She jumped to her feet. "You're not responsible for his actions. He chose to rebel."

"Some of my best friends followed Luc. But I destroyed them. I couldn't bear the thought of them turning against The Creator and turning toward evil, corrupted by Luc's leadership. I volunteered to fight him and his fallen angels." Erinelle's head lowered.

Her voice softened. "Are you still in love with him?"

The color of Erinelle's eyes turned to a burnished amber. She stood, and her wings jutted toward the rafters. "I do not love him anymore. He's no longer the angel I knew from Heaven. I'll destroy him too if The Creator permits me."

On an impulse, she enveloped Erinelle's waist. The angel was much too tall for her to hug her neck. "I'm sorry for what he did to you. Why doesn't The Creator destroy him?"

"Remember, The Creator wants him to repent and submit to His authority."

"Oh yeah, so let me get this straight. The war will continue until Luc submits, or until the end of an age which we're nearing."

"Until Luc submits or destroys humanity. The Creator said he'd never destroyed the Earth by flood again. He never said humanity would survive. Free will determines mortals actions and it's growing out of control. Humans don't like being under any kind of authority."

The radiant light spread throughout the barn filling Lee with the warmth from her love. "I'm not supposed to get so attached to my wards but you, Lee Campbell, are different." The angel vanished in a flash of light, leaving Lee bewildered.

She started for the door when the Morning Star materialized before her like a lightning bolt. She took several steps back and extended her hand, calling forth her blade of light.

He glared down at her with crazed eyes. He looked way bigger and more dangerous than she could handle. She concentrated on her breathing and kept her eyes level at him.

"You cannot defeat me, little human. I am responsible for the fire. I am responsible for your mother's illness. I am responsible for many things, but that warrior angel, Erinelle, is responsible for my descent and she's responsible for The Creator casting out a third of Heaven's angels. Haven't you ever wondered about my side of the rebellion? Is America a democracy? That's all I wanted. A level playing field where each angel in Heaven had a say in ruling."

"It always gets my blood surging, sensing the fear I cause in others, and you are no different. And Erinelle may have exaggerated a little on how much she loved me. If she loved me, she would've stood by my side. She would've fought with me, and maybe I'd still be living in the perfect realm instead of The Creator's sloppy seconds." Luc's murderous look along with his menacing demeanor had her quaking in her shoes.

With a wave of his hand, the tartan blanket from the tack room covered her. "You don't need to fear me, *yet*. Had I wanted you or your friend's death, you'd be history. I want you on my team, Leeel. Are you ready to listen to my side of the story?"

Leeel?

She replied through gritted teeth, "Do I have a choice?"

He laughed. "No, you don't." He paced about the breezeway. "I had a damn good plan. If Erinelle hadn't turned me in, my warriors and I would've stormed the Palace of Gold, and we would have held The Creator captive until He listened to our complaints, and He would've listened to me. But instead, we were condemned as traitors without a trial."

Lee pressed her lips together and remained silent.

"No comment? It doesn't matter. Do you even know who and what you are?"

"I am a warrior. One of The Chosen to fight you." She spat on the dirt floor.

"Well, well, aren't you full of piss and vinegar? That's what the AAF told you. But dear Leeel, I know who and what you are. I have spies everywhere." He stalked around her and sniffed. "You're not scared, but you should be."

He sighed. "You are fun, but enough with the chitchat. I must wrap this encounter up. I am the Prince of the World, after all." He shook his head with a little swagger. "No one ever gets my humor. You aren't a human at all. You are an entirely different species made by The Creator. You're a future warrior prototype, and should you succeed, there will be others. I can't allow that to happen, now can I?" He allowed his words to seep in. "I have a spy in the New Soul Departure Division that confirmed my suspicions."

"Don't believe me? How in the world do you think you possess the powers of angels without being one? Tsk, tsk, tsk. The Creator loves control. I'll give him that."

"And?" She knew she was different. Erinelle had told her, but she wasn't admitting anything to The Dragon.

He reared back and smacked her in the mouth so hard her teeth rattled. "Don't be brash, Leeel. You're a warrior hybrid, and I want you in my army. I met you at Sacred Heights. Remember? Your angel scent triggered my inquiries. You join my forces, and your family and friends will remain unharmed. If not, I will destroy you all."

She rolled her eyes without thinking, and he reared back to hit her again. She flinched, so he lightly caressed her face.

"Now, little warrior, I will have you willingly, or by force. It is your choice. The Creator is using His divine powers to demolish my strongholds. I need to examine you thoroughly. If it weren't for the AAF legion stationed around you, I'd take you now."

Luc punched a hole in the barn wall shaking loose dust particles in the air. "One day, I'll bring the nations of the world to my feet as numerous as the sand along the shores. They'll serve me and fight for my reign, faithfully."

"Um," She interrupted him. "Aren't you forgetting the part about The Creator destroying you and your army?"

The dirt floor beneath her feet became unstable. She may have overstepped just a smidge.

"Insolent fool." His hand extended, levitating Lee in the air. He began to choke the life from her. "I am not beyond killing you."

Lee couldn't scream but writhed in pain.

"With one thought, I can hurl you from my planet to the Eternal Darkness. The place is death to any angel, demon, or mutant like you. It's where you belong."

Suddenly an angel entered the area, taking Lee into her arms. She turned to him. "Luc, Luc, why must you harm others? Leave her alone."

He stomped and yelled, "Why? Why should I leave her alone? I have just as much right to her as you do. Why can Father forgive the mortals and not me?"

The angel shook her head. "You use people, places, and things for your gain, twisting reality to make weaker souls believe your actions are divine. You never accepted the responsibility for any of your faults. You always place the blame on others, including your father."

"It's not my fault. I should've never been cast out in the first place, and you know it." The walls trembled. "Erinelle betrayed me. And tell Father, I will continue to use the mortals insidiously to win battles.

More and more of them are coming to my way of thinking anyway. His faithful will fall to my temptations. Have you noticed? Many of the mortals don't believe in the supernatural at all."

Lee cast him one more look. He was a master deceiver. She sharpened her gaze as he flicked his fingers in and out before making fists. The fake smile glued to his face tried to mask his real thoughts. He didn't fool her. He might look like a stallion, but he was a Grade A jackass.

He arched his back and extended his arms toward her. "Be afraid, Lee Campbell. Be very afraid. Choose your alliances wisely because I will win."

Luc formed a fireball in his hands and threw it. Flames ignited in the bales of hay before he vanished.

The angel blew a stream of ice from her mouth, quenching the flames before it spread.

Lee stammered, "Who...who are you?"

"I'm the Spirit of Man, the seeker of truth. You need to understand Luc is very dangerous. You must prepare yourself to fight him. He will come to you again."

"Why can't you destroy him? Why doesn't he threaten you?"

"I took part in the Morning Star's creation. He sees me as a mother figure. That's why he doesn't threaten me. He still longs for a relationship with his father and me but doesn't care much for The Prince. As Erinelle told you, The Creator wishes Luc to submit to the Trinity. He still has time as well as the mortals of Earth, but that window of opportunity will close."

The Spirit of Man covered Lee in light, restoring her health. "Many suffer, and many perish due to Luc and his army. We must save as many souls as possible, or they too will be doomed."

"I will try. Is it true? Am I a different species from humans?"

"You must do more than try. The end of an age depends on whether you succeed, or Luc does," the Spirit of Man replied. "And yes, your DNA comprises elements of The Creator, angels, and your mortal parents. He created you as a separate species with many gifts and powers. You have enough energy inside of you to blow up the state of Tennessee."

She scratched the back of her head. "So, what am I? A prototype of warriors to come, as Luc said?"

"You are a lethal weapon. A hybrid messenger and you will gain more insight, abilities, and supernatural powers. Time-Walkers travel on the cords of light." The Spirit of Man placed her hands on either side of Lee's face. "Remember."

Lee closed her eyes and mentally traveled on multicolored strands of light. She opened her eyes and found her spirit in a garden teeming with animals, trees, and fragrant plant life. A slow rolling river sliced through the paradise. The stream of life, she thought. Peace and tranquility filled every fiber of her being.

Her second thought, the Spirit of Man sent her.

She reappeared back inside the barn. "Did you send me to the Garden of Eden?"

Soft laughter filled the barn. "No. You did that all by yourself."

"I thought the Garden was forbidden."

"The Garden is forbidden to mortals. The Archangel Metatron guards it."

"I didn't see any angels, although I saw a lion with spots of a leopard and an animal with the face of a monkey and the body of a dog."

The Spirit of Man smiled. "It is an enchanting place. Time-walking will come in handy should Luc choose to revisit you." Then, she faded away.

So much information crowded Lee's mind. She took slow breaths in and out to regain composure. She'd always known she was different. But the thought of having the power to blow up Tennessee gave her pause. She hoped she didn't accidentally blow up anything.

She needed to get back to the Glenns. She wondered why Harry hadn't come looking for her, then glanced to her watch. Only thirty minutes had passed instead of the hours it felt like since she went into the barn.

How was that possible?

Time was different for angels. Time must be different for her too. Could she manipulate time?

Could she create a fireball and put it out with ice?

She stepped outside to test her burgeoning powers. She cupped her hands and first created the fireball working out the details in her mind. It materialized in her hands and didn't burn. She leaned in and blew air from her mouth, freezing the fireball until it cracked into ice particles.

She straightened her spine then walked toward the house. She must speak with Erinelle about the events of the day, but she'd wait until tomorrow. She had enough drama for one day.

Harry pulled up and parked next to the barn gate. He and Blaine got out of the car.

He yelled, "Hey, Lee, need any help?"

She ran to him, throwing her arms around his neck. "Kiss me, Harry."

"Gladly." He wrapped his big strong arms around her waist, and she melted into his passionate kiss.

"I'll see you two inside," Blaine said.

"What have you learned about the suspect?" She broke from his embrace.

"I don't get it. The man they took to the hospital has done odd jobs for our family. Sheriff Dobbs questioned him, and he doesn't remember how or why he did it. The attending physician doesn't think the man will make it through the night."

"I think Luc or one of the fallen whispered in his ear and planted the suggestion." Lee's chin dipped to her neck. "Hm. I suppose all angels, fallen or otherwise, may plant suggestions."

"Talking to yourself, sweetie?" He draped an arm around her waist.

"It's been a weird afternoon. I'm starving."

He chuckled. "Me too. Let's see if any pizza's left."

"No worries if they ate the pizza. I love peanut butter and jelly."

"Peter Pan or Skippy, darlin'?"

"Is that a question? Peter Pan, of course." She twirled a loose curl. "Harry?"

"Yeah?" He leaned his head next to hers.

"Oh, never mind. I'm tired, and we have training in the morning." They held hands walking to the kitchen.

After dinner, Lee assigned bedrooms to the Glenns. Carol Ann slept in her room, Eva and Blaine in the downstairs guest bedroom, and Harry took the couch.

Around midnight, she slipped out of bed, and quietly descended the steps, placing her feet carefully on the planks so they wouldn't squeak.

Harry slept with his arm over his forehead.

She raised his blanket and slipped in next to him.

He woke and yawned. "This is a surprise."

"Hold me. I couldn't sleep with all the things swirling in my mind."

He placed his arm about her. "You sleep with me. I'll wake you before morning, and we'll go train with the AAF team together."

She snuggled into the curve of his neck. "I feel safe when I'm with you. You don't have to volunteer."

Harry interrupted, putting his fingers over her mouth. "Don't. I want to fight for The Creator and with the AAF team. Plus, I sort of bonded with Simon. And, for the record, I'm safe with you and all your mad skills. Don't ask me how I know, but I do know everything is going to be all right. Close your eyes and try to rest." He rubbed her back, and she drifted toward sleep.

ERINELLE MET SENECA, Raphael, Luwenia, and Baldric in the conference room inside the Hall of Moses with walls made of crystal trimmed with gold, plush crimson red carpets, and a rectangular table and chairs created from the Universe's oldest trees.

She pressed her fingers down on the table. "Luc's amping up his game. We need to strike fast."

"Sit down, Erinelle." Seneca wore his signature white tunic.

She straightened. Her sensors went on high alert. "What's happened?"

Seneca looked at Baldric. "Go to her."

Baldric wore a golden coat of impenetrable armor, and his enormous sword sheathed into his power belt. He placed his hands on Erinelle's shoulders. "Luc met with Lee."

She fought him hard.

He kept calm. "She's fine, sister. The Spirit of Man is with her. Please be still. You're hurting me."

Erinelle shoved him away. "Like I could ever hurt you. What happened?"

Luwenia's shiny raven hair was pulled back into a long braid. Her red lips accentuated her pale complexion. Bright aquamarine eyes with thick black lashes held Erinelle's gaze. "He was in the barn waiting on you to leave."

"Saints and sinners," Erinelle cried, "I've failed my ward."

Raphael stepped between her and Luwenia. "No, you did not fail her, my friend. It was meant to happen. We need Lee to understand who and what she is before the battle. Her powers strengthen daily. Tomorrow, you must accelerate the learning curve."

"What about Harry?"

Simon pushed through the double glass doors. "I'll take care of Harry. We have numerous souls on the line, and Heaven knows how many demons are in the Sacred Heights Sanatorium. Lee must be able to time-walk with ease. We'll have minutes to retrieve the captured souls and escape, or we risk becoming captured too."

The angels stepped over to the time crystal bowls spinning with perpetual motion revealing glimpses into the future.

Her jaw clenched.

To date, the AAF angels had only entered Hades a handful of times and at a high cost to the legion. Luc's generals changed strategies and safeguards to trap the AAF. "We must be victorious. Lee and Harry must marry, and their offspring must carry on Lee's line with The Chosen."

Seneca leaned back in the chair with his arms crossed over his chest. "Lee and The Chosen of Campbell Ridge will turn the tide of the war. Erinelle, only relay to her information on a need-to-know basis. We need her strong."

"But will Lee survive?" she asked.

"We've yet to determine all of the elements of His design," replied Seneca.

Baldric said, "We need a Sacred Heights dress rehearsal of the battle plan with the boyfriend and Pedersen. Campbell Ridge or Everglade Farms barn? I must inform headquarters to seal the area."

"The barn. Oliver is the conduit to initiate the plan with Luc." She looked at Seneca. "Seal all the perimeters of Everglade Farms, including the house. The Glenns are staying with the Campbells for the next few days. We wouldn't want one of the blue spheres of energy straying into the path of the mortals."

Baldric said, "The AAF using kinetic energy to create the blue spheres of energy was pure genius, and I can't wait to see the look on Luc's face when we light up his demons with them."

Seneca pushed away from the table. "We meet at Everglade Farms, first light."

One by one, the angels dematerialized from the room except for the two female warriors.

Luwenia held Erinelle's hands. "Don't dwell on the past. Luc will use it against you."

"I am trying."

"Don't try. Face your fears and put Luc behind you. Lee needs your undivided attention."

"Do the others know about Luc and me?"

"I'm not sure. You prevented his attempt to overthrow the Trinity. You did the right thing, Erinelle."

"Great. That makes me feel so much better."

Luwenia faded from the room.

Erinelle time-walked to the In-Between to catalog the weapons they'd use in battle, and she requested additional AAF soldiers for the fight.

The AAF headquarters stationed a legion of the Powers at every exterior wall of the massive white structure and inside the compound, each sentry armed with weapons of mass destruction.

She passed through the doors and walked down the hall to the weapons room. Divine bows and arrows, daggers, and swords traveled through space and time with any AAF warrior. The weapons she selected would annihilate any demon, including Luc, sending them to the Eternal Blackness. It was a place for unruly beings.

She met Michael leaving his office.

"Erinelle, how're the plans going for the Sacred Heights invasion?"

Their footsteps echoed across the white marble floor as they reached the exit.

"Sir, it would go better if I planted Luwenia as a spy on the fourth floor. The mortal, Oliver, is helpful, but he's also under the influence of dark forces."

He nodded. "Seneca is the acting informant at Sacred Heights. He's working with Luwenia and should have more details in your morning meeting with the updated floor plans. He's searching for the entry point of the portal to retrieve the captive souls. How's Lee's progress?"

"Excellent, sir. She's a fighter. Her instincts are great, but her mortal DNA creates doubts. Did you hear about Luc appearing in the barn?"

"I did. I sent the message to the Spirit of Man to intervene. Luc still listens to Her. I have complete faith in your team's success. May love light the way." He dematerialized.

She gave the In-Between one last look.

Luc's army possessed similar weapons as the AAF, and with each battle, her team faced the same possible fate as the lost souls of Sacred Heights.

CHAPTER 12

"BE CAREFUL IT'S MY HEART"

*O*liver parked outside of Everglade Farms red barn. The sun peeked over the ridge. The night skies turned a dove gray giving way to a prism of pastel colors. Golden beams of sunlight melted into pale pinks bleeding over into the deep lavender skies spreading across the horizon. A rooster crowed in the distance. He gazed upon the dew's fine mist covering the grass.

The farm was as beautiful as a Van Gogh painting.

He looked up as Lee and Harry walked down the low sloped hill of the backyard toward the barn.

Oliver knew they didn't trust him.

He didn't care.

He participated in the coup to save Nadine's soul even if he lost his own in the process. He raised his hand in greeting. "Good morning. Harry, I heard about Glenn Hall. I'm sorry. Did they arrest anyone?"

He raised a brow. "Good morning, Oliver. The suspect is in the hospital and unable to talk from what the sheriff told my dad last night."

"Changing subjects, fellas. This is our last training session before the battle. Are you ready, Oliver? Do you have any reservations?" Lee asked.

"I've been waiting on pins and needles. I'm as ready as I'll ever be. My biggest concern is for Nadine. I haven't slept much since learning what happened to her." He wouldn't think about the cost to the AAF, Lee, or Harry for that matter. His main goal was to save his lost love's soul and set her free.

The barn's main entrance had double doors. There were two entries in the back and one side door. The horses and livestock grazed in the distance.

They walked inside.

The interior changed as the angels worked in groups, fighting hand-to-hand combat. The ceiling of the barn opened to a swirl of angels developing an aerial attack.

He gasped. "How in the world? It looks like the fourth floor of the towers."

Erinelle stepped over to them. "We have milliseconds to retrieve the captives. The Powers have allowed the replication of the Sacred Heights site."

Lee tilted her head to the side. "What's the Powers?"

"There are three main sectors of angels, The Dominions, The Powers, and The Principalities. The AAF warriors work with the second sector of angels. The Powers is just another name for the Angel Armed Forces. I apologize for confusing you."

Three other angels joined Erinelle. "Meet some of our team, this is Luwenia, to her right, is Simon and bringing up the rear is Seneca."

The angel pointed to the different training stations. "We have a workout station for the blue spheres of energy, and a station for archery. Lee, you'll work with me at the swords and daggers station. Oliver, you'll go with Seneca to find the best entrance to the towers. Harry, you'll work with Simon. His assignment is to protect us from the demon ground forces."

Oliver stood with Harry and Lee among The Creator's warriors. It humbled him.

One wall of the barn replicated the angel war scene on the top floor of Sacred Heights. "Why is the mural here?" he asked.

"We believe the innocents are captive within the walls of the mural," Luwenia replied. "It's a portal to Hell."

"Is that where Luc's holding Nadine?" He examined the replication. "It's uncanny how accurate you have depicted the details."

The pale female angel resembled a porcelain doll. "You'll go with Seneca. I've given him several possibilities, but the two of you must figure out which scene holds the entry door. When did you enter the towers last?"

Oliver shoved his shaky hands inside his pant pockets. "I visit once a week. I still have patients on the floor."

"We have reason to believe all of the acute psych patients who reside on the fourth floors have been compromised and taken over by demons," Seneca said.

His eyes widened. Surely not all the patients. "Mrs. Elmer couldn't be a demon. She's got to be at least eighty-eight and in the late stages of Alzheimer's. She gets violent occasionally during the afternoons, but most of the days she's happy as a lark."

"Some demons and plain angels, or well, regular guardians interact well with the mortals and look human, but they're not," Erinelle said. "We're burning daylight. Let's break out into our teams and meet back here in a couple of hours."

Seneca reached for Oliver's hand, and he took it.

In an instant, he stood with the warrior angel in front of the exquisite mural at the fourth-floor towers.

Angelic beings depicted in the wall painting moved.

"Do not be afraid." Seneca placed his hand on Oliver's shoulder. "I placed cloaking shields around us to hide from the immortals living here. Let's search for the portal."

He reached out to touch the mural, and Seneca grabbed his hand. "Look. Don't touch. The demons would sense your presence. They can't sense mine."

Clouds within the mural swirled with lightning bolts as dark winged creatures sliced out with gleaming swords against screaming mortals racing to flee their wrath.

Seneca went along the wall, searching for the doorway. Along the rim of the mural, he finally pointed. "It's a magic mirror made from black volcanic stone. The stolen stone holds the universal language of the angels and is the doorway. We found it, Oliver."

"I'm curious. How will you enter without the demons knowing?"

"They'll know the instant we penetrate their fortress. We must return and inform our team. Hold my hand."

He held Seneca's hand, and they returned to the barn.

The angel placed his hands on the top of Oliver's head. "You won't remember anything from today. Issuing you a memory wipe is the only way to keep you safe. Go home. You'll meet Lee and Harry Saturday at the designated time to open the gates to Sacred Heights Sanatorium."

Oliver nodded, left the barn, and drove home.

Inside the kitchen, he made a fresh pot of coffee and wondered what happened to the time.

HARRY WENT with the boy-like angel outside.

With a wave of his hand, Simon replicated the Sacred Heights grounds. He pointed to a tree next to a white wicker chair. "That's the tree where Oliver found Nadine. Once the door is open to Hades, we'll make our way to that spot. The tree is an exit point we're using to forward the souls to the In-Between, then Michael will take the souls for debriefing before they ascend to Heaven. Do you understand?"

"Um, not exactly, but I'll catch on. Where's the In-between? What do you want me to do?"

"The In-Between is the AAF headquarters between Heaven and Earth." The angel pulled a royal blue bag from his armor pouch. He handed Harry several blue spheres of energy. "The spheres are designed to kill demons but could level a city block."

Simon waved his hand again, and lifelike angel statues appeared on the simulated grounds. "The practice spheres you hold in your hand aren't full strength. So, I hear you made all-state pitching?"

"Seven years ago." He did several stretches then threw the first sphere at the statue furthest from them, making immediate contact. The figure exploded into dust particles.

"Hot dog. I knew I picked a winner." Simon somersaulted. "Throw another one."

Harry threw the spheres until his arm hurt. "I better stop, or I won't be able to throw Saturday night."

The angel ran his hands across Harry's shoulders and down both arms, removing all the soreness created during practice.

He moaned in delight. "Simon, you keep rubbing my arms like that, and I'll marry you instead of Lee."

Simon roared with laughter. "I like you, mortal man. Let's see how fast you can run."

The angel had him sprinting for the next hour, weaving in and around the statues until his legs grew tired. Simon leaned down to place hands on Harry's legs.

He stepped back and threw his palms up. "Nope, don't rub my legs. I won't be responsible for my actions."

Simon chuckled again. The replication of Sacred Heights disappeared. Next to the barn, the angel boy placed one finger into a trough, creating a whirlpool of hot water. "Jump in. It'll restore your muscles."

"What? Naked? What if someone sees me?"

"Silly man, no one will see you. I'll even turn my back."

Harry quickly took off his clothes and stepped into the hot swirling jets of water. He placed his arms on the sides and leaned his head back. "Simon, this is a start to a beautiful relationship."

"You're all right, mortal. Come into the barn when you're up to it." Simon vanished.

LEE AND ERINELLE sparred for most of the practice. First, they fought with swords, then daggers and lastly a combination of both.

Sweating, she bent over and gripped her knees. "I need to practice time-walking."

"You remember time-walking?"

She leaned against the wall of the barn. "The Spirit of Man joggled my memory. I traveled to the Garden of Eden."

"Did you see my good friend, Metatron? He guards the Tree of Life, but don't confused it with the Tree of Knowledge. If any human reached the Tree of Life they would be immortal."

"I didn't see any angels. The Spirit of Man stated my DNA came from The Creator, the angels, and my mortal parents. If I'm part angel, where do I fit in the hierarchy? And why don't I have wings?" She slid to the ground and placed the palms of her hands on the dirt floor of the barn.

Erinelle's wings disappeared as she sat next to Lee.

They waited on the others to arrive.

"We don't have much time, so here's a crash course of the angel system. The highest order of angels is called the Seraphim replacing Luc's worship angels. They praise The Creator continuously."

Erinelle cupped her hands and blew an image of the Cherubs in a vehicle, not from this world. "Cherubs aren't babies with wings. They're fierce angels with four faces representing wild animals, domestic beasts, mortal humans, and the birds of the air. The Thrones, with all-seeing eyes, are the chariots of fire driven by the Cherubs. They help to protect the Garden of Eden with Metatron."

"Really? I always picture the famous painting of two cherubs by Raphael. Has anyone ever told you the chariots look like a flying saucer?"

"Well, they do fly between worlds." Erinelle said, "And most humans think of the chubby babies with wings. The artist was named for our Raphael."

"But I'm not just a human, am I?"

"No, you're not. You're different but in a good way. Hm, where was I, oh yeah, the second order of angels is led by The Dominions. They resemble humans but rarely engage with them. They're in charge of the lower order angels. The Virtues perform miracles. My team and most of the AAF are a part of The Powers, warriors protecting not only Earth but the Universe."

"Am I a lower order angel?"

"The Chosen do not fall within the traditional hierarchy. And you're a new creation, so the short answer is no. The Principalities govern nations or groups within the Universe. The archangels like Michael and Raphael are first in power. The chief angels are Michael, Raphael, and Gabriel, plus Jegudiel, Selaphiel, Uriel, and Barachiel. They oversee humanity events like the military, politics, and the economies of the world."

The other teams started materializing inside the barn.

"So, Michael and Raphael are helping our team because it helps maintain the order of our lives?" Lee asked.

"We try to maintain order on Earth and throughout the Universe. As the end of an age gets closer, more chaos will ensue. Our main goal is to save souls. The Creator considers humanity as one of His greatest achievements, although Luc's trying to destroy it."

They joined the group as Michael entered the center of the arena.

The commander extended his arms to reveal the updated blueprints of Sacred Heights Sanatorium. "Please open your eyes so you may see, open your ears so you may hear, and open your mind to all possibilities as we chart our course for Saturday night."

Harry sidled up to Lee. She looked at him, then circled her arm around his waist. She didn't deserve him, but she was glad he was at her side. She prayed silently for the success and safety of their mission.

She'd never forgive herself if something happened to him during the battle. Thankfully, Harry would fight outside of the facility, and from what she learned of Simon, he was in competent hands.

After the training session ended, Lee and Harry went back to the house.

Inside the kitchen, Carol Ann made breakfast while Blaine read the newspaper and Eva sipped coffee.

"Something smells mighty good," Lee said.

Carol Ann frowned. "Where did y'all go this morning?"

Harry grabbed a piece of bacon. "We strolled up to Campbell Ridge to watch the sunrise. It was quite spectacular."

"Sublime." Lee kissed his cheek.

"Aw, I'm so glad you two finally got together." Eva sighed. "Carol Ann and I had a bet. She won."

Harry chuckled. "What did you bet, Mother, dear?"

"I bet you'd never get the courage, and Carol Ann bet Lee would make you see the light."

"You are so right. Lee made me see the light. I've loved her most of my life and come to find out she loves me too. We're getting married."

Lee's mouth gaped. She'd asked him to wait until after the battle. He winked at her.

Carol Ann squealed with delight while jumping up and down. "I'm thrilled. Oh my gosh. We're going to be real sisters, after all." She dropped the spatula and ran to Lee, hugging her.

The front door opened, and her parents walked inside, laughing and smiling like two teenagers. "We're missing the party, Jenny," Joseph said. "And who's getting married?"

The blood rushed to Lee's face. "I suppose Harry and I are getting married. I asked him to wait until..."

"Until never. I want us to spend our whole life together. And I want ten kids."

She spat out her coffee. "Only if you're giving birth." She grabbed a napkin and soaked up the mess. The room erupted in laughter. She glanced around at their families. She'd do anything to protect them.

Harry scooped her up and twirled her around. "How about one boy and one girl. Work for you?"

She kissed him soundly on the mouth which released a round of clapping and whistles from their families.

With her arms around his neck, she leaned in and whispered, so no one else heard, "I'll give you children if we survive."

He rubbed his face next to hers and whispered, "We're going to kick some demon ass."

CHAPTER 13

"THERE'S NO TOMORROW"

*L*ee made it on time to work even after the theatrics of her family's reaction to her engagement. She parked in Oliver's garage and went into the kitchen to make a pot of coffee.

He was nowhere in sight. She walked down the hall and heard moaning from upstairs.

"Oliver, are you all right?" she yelled up the stairs.

He gave no reply.

She hadn't been upstairs and hesitated. She called out again, "I'm coming up."

She crept up the stairs with her hand gliding along the wrought-iron railing leading to an open second-floor plan. She glanced around the room and found him passed out on the couch. An empty bottle of vodka lay on the floor. "How in the world did you drink so much since this morning?"

He waved. "Skal."

"You have patients this morning."

He slurred his words. "Cancel them."

"What happened?" She knelt on the wood plank floor next to the couch.

"I'm a terrible person. I deserve to go to Hell."

"Only true evil deserves Hell. No more alcohol. Good grief, Oliver, we have a major battle tomorrow. You need a clear head. I'll bring you a cup of coffee then I'll reschedule your patients for next week."

"Won't be here next week. I'll be dead, in Hell." He scrambled for the empty bottle, but she retrieved it.

"I'll be back in a few minutes."

She raced downstairs into the kitchen and poured him a cup of black coffee. She glanced at the grandfather clock on the wall. She had forty-five minutes to reach the first patient. She placed one of the boxed scones, and the coffee cup on a food tray then made her way upstairs.

"Wake up, Oliver, and eat some breakfast. Drink some coffee." She placed the refreshments on the side table. "I'll be back as soon as I cancel your appointments."

Over the next hour, she contacted the patients by telephone. Most graciously rescheduled for next week. But what if next week didn't come for her or Oliver?

She shook off the negative thoughts. She placed the closed sign on the front door, then flipped the deadbolt.

By the time she made it back upstairs, he had slumped on the arm of the couch looking much worse for wear than when she first saw him this morning. "Tell me what happened?"

"I made a deal with the devil. I promised to deliver you to Luc in exchange for Nadine."

She took a deep breath, pushed him over, and joined him on the couch. "We knew you made the deal."

His brows popped upward. "You did?"

"Yes, Oliver. You're helping the AAF. We're going to save Nadine's soul or die trying, but you must run interference with the staff while we attack. The AAF has everything under control."

"Do you know what Luc told me?"

"No."

"Luc said Nadine never loved me, or her family. He stated she belonged to him because she gave up her soul's right when she killed herself." He nailed her with a look of hopelessness. "I read her chart. I spent time with her. I fell in love with her."

"Luc is a master of lies."

"What if he's telling me the truth?" He rubbed the back of his neck. "What happens to her soul if she did kill herself?"

"I'm not the Almighty, but I think a person in their right mind would never choose to take their own life. I believe tortured souls with altered states of mind have recourse with The Creator. I don't believe they go to Hell because they hurt so badly and can no longer endure their torment." She said, "To me, those souls have experienced Hell on Earth. I don't believe The Creator's warriors would breach Luc's portal if they didn't believe the same way."

"So, you think Nadine has a chance at freedom?"

"One hundred percent. Take a shower because you smell, and I'll make us some lunch?"

"I have a splitting headache." He swayed, getting to his feet. She steadied his balance. "Would you mind terribly grabbing one of those powders I made for your mom. You'll find them in the top right-hand drawer closest to the kitchen sink."

"Sure thing. Oh, Mr. Desmille brought you eggs, lettuce, tomatoes with a slab of bacon yesterday. I'll whip up some sandwiches. You must stay strong for Nadine and yourself. Tomorrow night is going to be extremely difficult. We need you on your toes."

"I'm sorry, Lee. I don't deserve your friendship, but I am thankful for it."

"Do you have a photo of Nadine?"

"Over on the bookshelf, beside her silver hand-mirror, you'll find a picture I took of her reading. After dressing, I'll meet you downstairs."

Lee watched him walk down the hall with his shoulders slumped, and his head bowed. She worried he might be a liability to the operation if he didn't get it together soon. She'd alert Erinelle.

She stepped over to the white painted bookshelves with rows of medical journals, books on herbs, and several books of fiction. She picked up the framed photo of Nadine and froze. It was like looking at a reflection of herself.

She picked up the silver hand mirror and instantly traveled on the cords of light. Millions of multicolored strands of light swiftly carried her through the entrance of Hades. Mental images flashed through her mind so fast it made her extremely nauseous.

Looking left and right, she was astonished.

In college, she'd read Dante's epic poem, *Divine Comedy,* about a dream sending him into the nine circles of Hell. He'd appeared in the middle of a dense forest. He tried to climb a mountain, but ferocious animals chased him, driven into what she assumed was the Eternal Darkness.

She ran the poem through her mind and realized Dante must've seen Hades firsthand. She stood on the banks of a vast forest, frantically looking for demons, but instead found individuals milling around the first circle.

Hugging herself, she glanced around for Nadine, then proceeded with extreme caution.

In the center of the first circle, she found an enormous pavilion. She heard collective sighs and periodic screams throughout the sinister place. The lost souls lived separately from The Creator, forever singing a gruesome song of woe.

One single light burned brightly on the far side of the pavilion through the dark and eerie woods.

The light must come from the innocent souls.

Lee made her way toward the light, and several individuals turned to her. She lightly touched the arm of a priest. "I'm looking for the innocent soul sent here before her death."

The priest bowed his head, reverently. He wailed, "Woe to those condemned to this place. Those you seek wait together in the right-hand corner of the first circle."

"Will you take me to them?"

Following the priest, she went along a narrow path dimly lit by molten lava of a nearby volcano. The black iron sign at the entrance of the forest read The Lost Souls of Hell.

Swarms of insects raced toward them, and the clergyman darted into the hollow of a large tree next to the pavilion, pulling her with him. "We must wait until the insects pass. They eat the skin and there is no good treatment for it."

A cold shiver went down her spine.

The longer she stayed within the first circle, the more despair crept into her heart. A great sadness filled her spirit, and she inwardly cried for the lost souls.

"I'm Nicodemus," the clergyman said. "I served the church my whole life, and never truly accepted The Creator's truth. I was sorely wrong. The Bible tells us many *strive to enter the narrow gate to Heaven and will not.* I should have believed in His word. Who're you that you're able to enter this realm alive and the demons don't devour you?"

"I'm not completely sure why the demons don't see me. I'm part of The Creator's Chosen sent to save souls of the innocent used as pawns in the angelic war. The person I seek is Nadine Vaughn."

The insects changed direction to a group of naked people running on the beach.

Nicodemus motioned for Lee to follow him. "Many of the individuals here do not understand they're dead." He pointed to those on the beach. "They think they're on a vacation which took an ugly turn of events. It may take decades before they understand Luc sealed their fate."

In the right-hand corner of the pavilion, Lee spotted Nadine curled into a ball, her thumb in her mouth. "I see her, Nicodemus."

He didn't listen but wandered off, crying and shaking his head. Wailing, "Woe is me. Woe is me."

"Excuse me, are you Nadine Vaughn?"

They locked eyes, and Lee knew beyond a shadow of a doubt, the female was her angel twin.

Nadine jumped to her feet and hugged her. "Leeel, it is so good to see you. Why have you come?" She whispered, "Luc will win the war if he finds you here. He'll have the both of us."

"We're twins from Heaven?"

"We are angel twins. Luc drained most of my powers but hasn't taken my angel light. We're doomed if he gets you too."

"I'm here in spirit, but with some physical properties," Lee explained. "I traveled on the cords of light once I picked up your mirror."

"My mirror? I don't understand. Why can't the demons see you?"

"I have no clue why they don't see me. Um. Oliver Pedersen has a photo of you next to your silver hand mirror on his bookshelves."

"Oh, Oliver. What a dear, sweet man. How is he? Please tell him I'll love him, always." Her chin quivered. "He tried to help me. Tell him, I'm sorry I dragged him into the conflict."

"He's a train wreck, but he is helping us with a plan to extract your soul."

"But how?"

"Sacred Heights is a portal." She lifted her chin. "I'm coming with warrior angels from Heaven to set your soul free. Do you remember the AAF?"

"We fought with the AAF before The Creator changed us. I fought on Earth too. The demons took my warrior angel and locked me in Sacred Heights. I didn't kill myself. They murdered my husband and child. The demons torture me day and night."

Lee's heart sunk to her toes. "I'm so sorry, but tomorrow night, we come with an AAF legion to set free the souls of the innocents. Where are the others with you? Two teenage boys went missing from my hometown. Asher and Dick?"

"They're here." Nadine glanced around nervously. She pointed. "All the innocent souls are locked within The Seven Doors of the Devil's Castle. They sent me here as a spy. They sensed an angel of light. They sensed you. The Giants are watching me. The beasts guard me."

"What beasts?"

Her eyes widened with fear. "They're everywhere. Don't you see them? They're coming for you. You must leave, now," she cried.

"Don't give up, sister. We are coming back."

Everything seemed to fall into place.

Lee was meant to find out her true nature to save her sister. Angel twins spoke the same language. Their thoughts linked by the cords of light. It would help her to navigate the legion into Hell and save the innocent souls.

"You will return to our heavenly home."

"Be careful, sister. Luc is much stronger in Hell than above ground."

Lee made her way cautiously through the forest, sensing the beast's presence. She didn't run but floated on the cords of light through the pavilion toward the crossover ferry. The closer she came to the boat, the more beasts she heard growling, snarling, and roaring her name.

She looked up and saw an angel on a boat. The Sea of Dead tried climbing on board.

"The dead cannot harm you," the angel said.

Lee flew to her. "Who are you?"

"My name is Sharon."

The choppy and turbulent waters nearly capsized the boat, but Sharon didn't waver. She pointed to the multicolored strands of light near the shoreline. "Jump to the strands of light."

She went to the cords of light and focused her mind on the silver hand mirror. In a split-second, she stood next to the bookshelves.

Her knees buckled as Oliver entered the room.

He ran to her. "Lee, what's wrong?" He picked her up and helped her to the sofa.

"I time-walked into the first circle of Hell. I found where they're holding Nadine and the other innocents. The demons are aware we're coming, and they're waiting." She called out, "Erinelle, I need you."

The female warrior appeared. "You entered Hades? Are you insane to go alone?"

"I didn't plan the trip. I picked up Nadine's mirror, and I was just there. Did you know she's my angel twin? I believe The Creator knew this would happen and sent me to save her. I will lead our forces to save her tomorrow night."

"I knew you had an angel twin, but I had no idea it was Nadine. You are ready for the battle in Hades. Because once we breach the portal, the fallen will come."

Fury filled her heart from the mental image of her sister's suffering. "I am ready. Have you ever been to Hades?"

"Only once a thousand years ago."

"Great sorrow fills my soul with such heaviness." Lee said, "Hades is real. No one should ever have to enter that horrid place when all they must do is believe. The people in the first circle are good too. I met a priest."

"It's so sad those in the first circle never took the time to believe and accept His truth. They don't suffer like the ones who willfully turned their backs to Him or those mortals that join Luc's forces, exchanging their souls to gain earthly desires. All will seek justice after the final battle."

"So, there's hope?"

"I cannot say. But we're retrieving the living souls who believe. I must meet with Michael. The offensive tactics must change. One legion may not be enough to fight Luc's army."

"Luc is using the innocents' light. Nadine stated his powers are stronger near the gates of Devil's Castle. Who are the Giants?"

"They are the hybrids Luc created with the daughters of man, pre-flood. They guard the entrance to the castle. Don't worry, Lee. The AAF has an unlimited amount of resources at our disposal. We will succeed."

"I'm not worried about myself. I am concerned about my sister. I can't believe it. I have a sister." She turned to Oliver. "Nadine didn't kill herself. She loves you, she told me so."

"She's in Hades because I didn't listen to her. I didn't have faith in myself to believe the supernatural is possible. I am a man of science, but I see science and the supernatural work together." He hugged Lee. "Thank you for finding Nadine, but what if Luc wins? What happens to her?"

"I won't concede the battle before it starts, Oliver. I am going in with the mindset of a winner. I am entering Hell to save my sister. I will die if necessary."

Lee read Erinelle's thoughts. *"Luc wins some of the battles, but he will not win the war. He has the advantage in Hell. The only way he will succeed*

Saturday night is if he captures you. Michael may pull you from the operation. With you and your angel twin, Luc would have the DNA to create others like you."

"I am the only one who can find Nadine. We are connected. I will fight for her."

A memory of long ago flashed in her mind. She had betrayed Nadine before the fall.

She had attended the rebellion meetings with Erinelle, and Nadine found out. They fought bitterly over the ideals of the angelic system. The rift between them grew threatening to tear their relationship apart.

In the end, Lee removed herself from the rebellion meetings at Nadine's request. She betrayed The Dragon. She chose to fight with the AAF.

Did Luc know they were sisters?

Had he learned the connection?

The Creator gave her another chance to redeem herself.

She wouldn't fail her sister again.

This time, she meant to rectify her wrongs at any cost.

CHAPTER 14

"DEARLY BELOVED"

*L*ee left Oliver's a little jittery from the time-walking experience into Hades and from the revelations of her past. But her powers grew stronger each day. She had sensed the beasts in the forest, and she heard the roar of monstrous creatures in the abyss.

Hades was a fearful place, but she wondered how many of the wails and screams were real and how many of them were fake, used merely to intimidate the lost souls.

Maybe Luc used similar tactics with his army. He thrived on the pain, suffering, and despair of others. He lived and breathed to conquer all in his quest to be the Supreme Being of all.

After arriving home, she jumped into the tub and soaked for thirty minutes until her fingers were all shriveled and wrinkly.

Harry had been working on Glenn Hall's renovations. He phoned and wanted her to ride with him to Murfreesboro. She needed a diversion from the trauma of the day.

Whenever he placed his arms around her, his strength rubbed off. She needed him in so many ways, and the fact he was willing to lay his life down for her made her both happy and sad. She didn't want him hurt or worse, dead. However, just knowing he would be there with her tomorrow night gave her strength.

He kept her together, glued with love.

He met her at the steps, and they walked to his car. He opened the door for her.

"Where are we going?" she asked before she slid inside.

"I know you wanted to wait until we completed our Sacred Heights mission to marry, but honestly, we have no idea the outcome or if either one of us will survive." He leaned in and caressed her cheek. "With your permission, let's get a marriage license and then visit my friend, J. D. Johnson. He's also the local Justice of the Peace." He shut the passenger door then went to the driver's side and got in.

"I *do* love you." She sighed. "After my day, I agree with you. I don't want to wait either." She hesitated to tell him about her angel twin.

"Thank goodness because I already called J. D. at home earlier, and he's waiting on us."

"I guess it's a good thing I agreed."

"We'll wait if you have any reservations, but I thought I'd ask anyway."

"Nope. Not one. There are no guarantees in this lifetime, and I don't want to waste another second not being yours." Her stomach did a quick flip. She'd dreamed of marrying him for so long she didn't care when or where if it meant being together. "Life goes by in a flash in the grand scheme of things."

She pushed thoughts of Nadine away.

Harry deserved her undivided attention.

The late afternoon sun shot beams of light through the scenic landscape. They passed by large homes with immaculate lawns. Everything seemed to take on a surreal quality as the car whizzed along the road toward Murfreesboro.

She squirmed in the seat with anticipation of their nuptials. "Harry, may we stop by the flower shop?"

His brilliant grin went wide, and his eyes lit with excitement. "Done it. My sister created a beautiful bouquet, and I placed it in the trunk of the car. It's full of blue hydrangeas, white and pink roses mixed with eucalyptus from Mother's garden."

Her hand flew to her mouth. "Carol Ann and I promised to be each other's maid of honor. She's going to be furious with me."

"Carol Ann and Pugs are going to be our witnesses. They're meeting us at J.D.'s."

"You are good. How did you know I'd agree?"

"I didn't know you'd go for it, but since we face insurmountable odds tomorrow night, I thought I'd give it a whirl. Married, you and I become one in all things. My heart and soul are tethered to you."

"Darling, Harry, I am tethered to you too. You are strong and courageous. You by my side gives me courage. You give me strength." She rubbed his right shoulder. "I wish I wore something a little nicer, though." She looked at her twill pencil skirt and a collared shirt. Not precisely the wedding dress she envisioned while growing up.

He gave her a sheepish grin. "Carol Ann helped me retrieve your graduation dress. The dress is blue, not white, but it's beautiful and brings out your eyes. She even packed your dainty blue shoes and a few other things. I made a reservation at the B&B on Main Street to spend the night. Carol Ann also told your parents so they wouldn't worry when you don't come home tonight."

"I was going to call them later. So, what's next?"

"We'll get our license, head over to J.D.'s, and afterward we'll grab dinner, then go to the B&B."

"How romantic. When did you plan it?"

"After you left this morning, I made the calls, and as luck would have it, everything worked out." He pulled into the County Clerk's office and turned to her. "So, you'll have to change in the ladies' room."

"Not a problem."

He reached for her hand. "No regrets?"

She shook her head. "Nope. Let's get hitched."

After exiting the car, he opened the trunk and took out the bag with her dress and shoes.

She peeked inside the box of flowers and inhaled. "They are

gorgeous, and the scent's divine. Eva is going to shoot me for not including her."

"And what about your parents? Joseph isn't going to be happy either, me stealing his little girl away without a word."

"We're engaged. Our parents will get over our elopement, eventually."

Lee went into one of the restroom stalls to change clothes. When she opened the door, her angel twin's face stared back at her from the mirror. Her fingers began to tremble as she reached up and placed her fingertips on the smooth glass surface.

I'm a fraud. I've lived a lie my entire life.

She gripped the sink counter, petrified with fear.

Harry knocked on the restroom door. "Honey, are you okay?"

Not able to respond or move. She just stared at the reflection.

He entered quietly walking up behind her. "What is it?" His hands trailed down her arms. "What's the matter, honey? Cold feet?"

She swiveled in his arms. "I-I'm not worthy of your love, Harry. I found something out about myself today. I'm not worthy of fighting with the angels either."

"Darlin', you are more than worthy. What happened? Why are you second-guessing yourself and us?"

"Nadine Vaughn and the innocents are held in Hades. She's my angel twin from Heaven. I betrayed her. I betrayed The Creator. I was following the Morning Star before the rebellion. I listened to his words. She and I fought. We had a horrible argument, and it's the only reason why I didn't join the rebellion with the others. It's why I didn't fall."

His eyes went wide. "I don't understand." She glanced at the rapid pulse in his throat.

"I'm a crossbreed. Before The Creator sent me to Earth, I was an angel. He changed me. He made me into a lethal weapon to fight in the war. I'm created to yield destruction. I'm afraid, truly petrified."

"I don't care if you're a crossbreed." He tilted her chin up. "I don't care if you bark like a dog. I know you, Lee Campbell. You are kind, sweet, and gentle. You aren't meant to cause destruction. If The

Creator designed you with a specific purpose to fight in this supernatural war, then I will be by your side. Who and what you were before you came to Earth doesn't matter because you're not that person anymore. You may have an angel twin, but you also have two wonderful mortal parents who raised you right."

"What if I fail Nadine again?" She swallowed hard and fought the urge to cry. "What if I fail you?"

"The Creator wouldn't place such trust in you if He didn't think you could do the job. He also gave you a chance of being a mortal. You are mortal too, aren't you?"

She nodded. "Well, part of me is mortal."

"The best part. The part I love, the part I want to spend the rest of my life with. I'm not privy to all the divine knowledge you have inside that spectacular brain, but I do know what's in your heart. I've watched you most of my life. Do you trust me?"

"Uh-huh."

He held her hands. "Is it mandatory for you to fight tomorrow night?"

"No. When I told Erinelle, she threatened to pull me from the mission, but I can't let Nadine down again. We're connected in this crazy cosmic drama, and I know here"—she placed her hand over her heart—"I have to save her."

"Well, it seems to me, you've made one choice. Now, it's time for you to make another, and I won't hold it against you if you want to wait."

Her eyes searched his eyes. "You won't be disappointed in me."

"What? If we don't marry? Probably."

"Oh, Harry, I meant disappointed in me as your wife. I don't want to disappoint you."

"Never." He cupped her face in his hands. "We're made for each other, and I don't need to be an angel to know it."

She took a deep inhale and exhaled. "I love you, Harry Glenn."

"And I love you more." He tilted his head. "So, is that a yes or no on the marriage thing?"

She grinned. "It's a yes. Yes, yes, yes, yes."

Harry waited for her to change clothes in the bathroom stall then he took her hand, and they exited the restroom.

"Thank you for listening to me without judgment."

"It's what husbands do." He whistled then moved his hand back and forth. "And wowzah, you look good enough to eat."

"All in good time, my dear Harry, all in good time."

They strolled into the clerk's office just before closing time, giddy as two kids.

The clerk asked, "I need the date of your birth."

Harry replied, "August second."

"What year?"

"Every year." He chuckled, and Lee goosed him in the ribs.

The court clerk looked over the rim of her glasses. "Like I haven't heard that one before."

"We're eloping." Lee placed her palms on the counter. "And we're a little excited."

"I certainly hope so," The court clerk said with a hint of mirth.

He waggled his brows. "Now, who's the funny one."

With their paperwork in Harry's hand, they raced down the hallway to the car. The clock on the courthouse square chimed five thirty in the afternoon.

"What time are Carol Ann and Pugs meeting us?"

"They should've arrived at J.D.'s at five. Are you ready, darlin'? To become my wife to have and to hold?"

"In health and sickness, until—"

"Don't say it," He said.

"Until time meets eternity." She couldn't contain her excitement. Warmth radiated throughout her body.

He opened the door, then circled his arm around her waist, pulling her up for a kiss. "Your love weaves a magic spell, a rhythmic spell pounding my heart so hard and loud."

"Oh my wonderful sweet Harry, you hold my heart, forever."

"Are you afraid of what tomorrow's battle may bring us?"

"Not anymore." She slid into the car, and a few seconds later, he followed. "We are soul mates, Harry."

"Not star-crossed?"

"Soul mates. Many wouldn't stand by me the way you have and face immortal enemies in the realm of demons, no less. You are a courageous man, full of honor, and it doesn't hurt you're cute too."

"Cute? I think dashing, and maybe add a little daring." He drove down Main Street then pulled into the home of J.D. Johnson.

Carol Ann and Pugs waved from the front porch veranda.

Lee and Harry got out of the car. He retrieved her flowers from the trunk and handed them to her.

Her best friend ran down the steps. "Oh my gosh, I can't believe it." She hugged Lee. "You're marrying my brother. We're sisters in our hearts, and now it's going to be legal."

J.D. stood next to his wife, or at least that's what she assumed. "Well, my boy, are you ready to take the plunge into matrimony?" he asked.

Harry rushed to greet his friends. "The water looks fine to me. Hey, I can't thank you and Ethel enough for marrying us on such short notice. And you too, Pugs."

"This isn't a shotgun wedding, is it?" Pugs chortled.

She narrowed her eyes at Harry's best friend. Pugs had a knack for saying what was on his mind regardless if he hurt anyone's feelings. "Sounds like something you'd say, but to answer your stupid question, no. We didn't want the hassle of a big wedding." She wasn't going to tell their friends they may not make it through the weekend, and she didn't want to think about it, either. She would try to make the most of every second with Harry even if they had only one night.

Carol Ann linked her arm with Lee's. "Pugs is just jealous because no one will marry him."

"Speak for yourself, little sister." Pugs snorted.

The ceremony was brief yet tenderly sweet.

To Lee's surprise, Ethel cooked dinner, and J.D. opened a bottle of Imperial Moet & Chandon. "I saved this baby since 1941 and tonight is a great way to celebrate. Here's to Mr. and Mrs. Harry Glenn." He popped the cork to cheers.

Pugs pounded the dining room table. "Hear. Hear."

Ethel poured the champagne.

Carol Ann raised a glass. "I'm a bit selfish, but you two are most important to me." With a hitch in her voice, she said, "Lee, you and I have been best friends all our lives. Oh, the times we had playing dress-up, and the countless sleepovers when we dreamed about our weddings."

She turned to Harry. "Lee's always dreamed of you." She winked at Lee, and continued, "It's true, and the fact you're my much-loved brother, who's kind, compassionate, and funny, I'm doubly blessed. All joking aside, I'm thrilled for you both."

"Thank you." Lee mouthed.

"Here's to my brother and his lovely bride, wishing you many years of happiness."

The wedding party raised their glasses in a toast then sipped champagne.

Pugs went on a tangent about Harry learning all his womanizing skills from him, causing a hilarious outburst from the ladies.

At the end of the evening, Harry and Lee left their friends with full hearts.

Driving to the B&B, neither spoke.

The electricity in the air between them surged through her body. There was an irrepressible tug drawing her to him with intense ferocity and a little trepidation. The seductive glances exchanged between them defied any self-control she had left.

The blooming desire building inside of her made her nerve endings tingle. She was his wife. She still couldn't believe it. It created a ripple of positive emotions unparalleled to any other experience in her mortal life so far.

Being slightly intoxicated from the champagne, and the delicious scent rolling off her husband, made her giddy and a tad bit light-headed. She wanted to drown in his scent, to taste his body in ways she'd only read about, but now was going to experience firsthand. She anticipated his lips on hers.

Their dawning love opened a new world to Lee. A world where she and Harry would face life's ups and downs together.

He pulled into the parking space and turned to Lee. "We're here."

"It's wonderful."

Morton's Manor's Queen Anne exterior and the interior's eclectic sense of style reflected a slower bygone era. A heady scent of fresh flowers mixed with a hint of lemon filled the house.

After checking in, they practically raced each other upstairs to the honeymoon suite.

He unlocked the door, then scooped her into his arms before crossing the threshold. "Um, I dreamed our first time would be our honeymoon with an ocean view somewhere, but this ain't bad."

He released her and went back for their baggage before closing the door behind him. "Carol Ann packed for you, but if you need anything, I can run to the store. It stays open until eleven."

The suite had a large bedroom and private bath with excellent views of the historic downtown. "Everything is perfect." She plopped on the bed and rolled over onto her back, then kicked off her shoes. She looked at Harry, then outstretched her arms. "Kiss me."

He joined her, then leaned in and kissed her softly. His tongue traced across her lips before he gently tugged her lower lip. He trailed kisses across her cheek, down her neck, before licking her throat at the pulse point. He came back to her mouth, brushing his lips against hers.

With a throaty whisper, he said, "You're so damn beautiful."

She arched against him, and he trailed kisses down to her cleavage.

"You're giving me goosebumps." She snickered.

"I'm going to give you more than that." His playful nature was one of the things she loved most about him.

She pulled him on top of her. "Promises, promises."

His hand skimmed her calf muscles and up the back of her thigh. "My girl is soft and strong in all the right places. Do you like my hand under your dress?"

She nodded. "Uh-huh."

"May I kiss you behind your knees?"

She squirmed under his touch. She ached for it and throbbed for more. "Please."

He started at her ankle, kissing her, and moved along her inner thigh, continuing to the back of her knees. He licked, nipped, and kissed along her smooth skin. "Do you like it?"

"Very much. I love your kisses."

"I love your dress, but I'd love it more off." He lay beside her.

She rose, propped by her elbows. "Have you been with many women?" she asked.

He shook his head. "Darlin', you can't speak of other women when I'm making love to you or my equipment won't work."

She burst out laughing. "You are too funny."

"And laughing at me doesn't help either."

She stood then reached around to the back of her dress to unzip it. She pushed the fabric off, revealing her white lace bra and panties.

His eyes widened, and his breath quickened. "You're going to be the death of me yet."

"Not funny."

He took her back into his arms, kissing her hard and fast while she fumbled with the buttons on his shirt. He broke from the kiss, took a step back, and practically ripped his shirt off, toeing off his shoes, then undid his pants.

She wet her lips. "You're beautiful too, Harry. May I?" She traced her fingertips down his muscular chest, then started on his low back, working her way up to his shoulders. "Make love to me, husband of mine."

He unfastened her bra, and she slipped off her panties.

"Lie back for me, darlin', I don't want to hurt you."

Lee frowned. "Why would you hurt me?"

"Um, normally, the first time hurts a woman."

She crossed her arms over her breasts. "And I suppose you learned that firsthand too. Who, Harry? Who have you slept with?" Her heart skipped a beat.

He sat on the bed and threw her a blanket. "Good grief, Lee, we're on our honeymoon, and why does it matter?"

"How would you feel if I made love with someone else?"

He turned abruptly. "Have you?"

She clenched a fist and hit him in the chest. "No."

"Ouch." He rubbed the spot. "You need to dial your temper down. I'm not discussing my previous sex life, nor would I want any details about your escapades, young lady."

"No escapades until now, Harry, and as long as you didn't diddle Catherine."

"Diddle?? Oh, good lord." He rolled his eyes.

She gave him a thunderous scowl. "You made love to Catherine? Didn't you?"

He paced about the room, shaking his head, talking to himself under his breath. "I'm not discussing my sex life with you, but I vow from this moment on, I'm yours for the rest of our lives and beyond. Look, sweetheart, I have a past, I won't pussyfoot around it, but I swear to all things holy you are my true love, my only love, my wife, forever."

Her breathing leveled out. She removed the blanket and stood before Harry naked. She lifted her chin slightly taunting him. "Then prove it."

"Miss Bossy. Part of our problem is we've been friends since infancy. I get you're curious about me, but for you and me to work, our relationship starts now with a clean slate. Deal?"

They shook hands.

"Deal. Oh, I read the Hindu text on eroticism."

It was Harry's turn to belt out laughter. "You mean the *Kamasutra?*"

"The art of making love is a beautiful and wondrous thing. Carol Ann and I found a copy at college."

He stuck his fingers in his ears. "La, la, la, la, la. I can't hear anything about my sister and sex, understood?"

"Well, I'm ready for the challenge."

"Geesh, Lee, this isn't a test."

She wrapped the blanket around her again and joined him on the bed, placing her head against his shoulder. "I'm sorry. One more question."

He waved his hand in agitation. "Why not?"

"Are you saying sex will hurt because I'm a virgin?"

"Yes."

She circled her arm around his waist. "Well, not a problem."

He dipped his chin to his throat. "What?"

"Not that, silly. Dad bought Princess when I was thirteen. She was wild the first year or so and one day we took off flying across the back forty, and she threw me across a fence. Remember my arm in a cast?"

He rubbed her back with tenderness. "Yeah."

"Well, the fall also broke my hymen."

"Seriously?"

"Yeah, I'm serious. I started bleeding badly, so my parents took me to the hospital. You don't have to worry about hurting me. Can we start over?" She tented her fingers in prayer mode. "Pretty please with ice cream on top."

He pressed kisses along her shoulder. "Whatever makes you happy."

"But it'll make you happy too?"

"Very." He released a moan as he palmed her breast. "Perfect, you are perfect." He stared at her for the longest time. He moved his hand up to her jawline, tracing his thumb over her bottom lip.

She twisted her fingers into his thick dark hair, jerking his head back, and covered his mouth with her lips in a searing kiss.

He's mine.

He scooped her up and threw her back on the bed.

Their love blazed through the night like a shooting star.

His voice was husky and deep. "I love you so damn much."

"I love you too." She clutched the sheets in her hands as he took extra time to make sure she was satisfied. The incredible sensation made her insides clench and throb until she finally broke free and shuddered with the most significant release of pleasure she'd ever known. She felt his smile against her skin.

He made love to her slow and easy at first, rocking her gently with sublime rhythm.

"Are you okay?" he panted.

Gripping onto his biceps, she labored for breath. "I'm fabulous." A complete sense of euphoria swept over her. She poured every ounce of love and tenderness she had for him into the love they shared.

They knew and understood each other so well. He pleasured her with every touch, every stroke, every thrust. The intimacy between the two of them sent her to a higher plane of consciousness. The stars, planets, and the Milky Way had nothing on Harry.

It was as if they could read each other's thoughts, anticipating each other's needs before their own. Their connection went beyond her expectations, cutting her to the core of her soul with emotion that no mere words could describe.

Making love with Harry was everything she dreamed it would be. She understood the meaning, and *they shall become one*. They were one. They fit each other perfectly. The love they shared was powerful yet vulnerable, tender, but passionate.

Blood pounded through her veins to the point of sweet agony. "I love you so much."

He adjusted her angle slightly. "You are mine." He gripped her thighs as she tilted her hips upward to meet his thrusts.

Moments later, he collapsed onto her chest.

Both spent. Both sated.

She couldn't stop grinning.

He rolled off to the side, propped by an elbow. He stroked her cheek. "I'm sorry. I couldn't control myself."

She placed her hand on top of his. "Don't apologize. Harry, you're an incredible lover."

He shook his head with playful confidence. "Why thank you, darlin'. I aim to please." He kissed her again.

She pushed away from him and crawled out of bed. She flushed with heat just thinking about making love to him with such boldness.

Her soul filled with a sense of exhilaration. "I'll be back."

She went into the bathroom and turned on the water. She grabbed a cloth from the linen closet to quickly bathe. Lastly, she brushed the tangles out of her hair.

He dozed when she slid between the sheets, nudging her face into the crook of his neck. "I'll be a happy woman if I die today. Harry?"

He blinked a few times. "Yes, love?"

"Can we do it again?" she asked with shyness.

He had the best smile. "Give me a minute, and I think I can manage."

She had fallen in love with his smile, his humor, his sense of right and wrong as a young girl. She knew the night on the back stairs of Glenn Hall that she'd marry him someday.

They spent the night in bed, talking and sharing their innermost secrets along with hopes and dreams for their future. They sipped soda pop and nibbled on fruit, cheese, and desserts that had been left in the room by the staff.

They made love again before drifting off to sleep.

LEE WALKED *into a room trimmed with gold and crystal walls. Crimson curtains hung from the ceiling and pooled on the floor. Thousands of flickering candles levitated in the air, lighting the gossamer screen room with dark gold cushioned seating arranged in a semicircle. One wall opened to reveal a theater-like screen.*

She clutched her throat the moment the battle scene began with flocks of angels tearing each other apart and then she saw a much older version of herself charging the grounds with her sword and daggers cutting through demons quickly until a searing cry released from one of her team. She catapulted through the air and ran the demon beast through.

Fire exploded into her back.

Lee woke with a start, sweating profusely, and stared at Harry. The recurring dream had plagued her throughout her life, except this time, it rang with a feather of truth.

"Oh, my darling husband, I'm going to die," she whispered.

THE NEXT MORNING, Lee traced her fingertips along his jawline, and

Harry stirred, slipping his arm around her waist and pulling her next to him.

"Did you sleep well?"

She played with the tufts of his chest hair. "Not exactly. Another bad dream. I've had it before."

"Dreams have a way of bringing to the surface our fears and concerns with life. They don't necessarily mean they're true."

"Pretty sure this was an omen of the future. I'm not sure I can change it."

The look of love in his eyes grounded her. "Remember the scripture we memorized in Sunday school, *'Do not worry about tomorrow because tomorrow will take care of itself.'* Or something to the effect."

"Erinelle tells me the same thing. It's part of my human nature to worry, my mortal weakness, I suppose. Changing subjects, let's speak with Dad about moving into Granddaddy's cabin to have a place of our own."

"I finished my training with the electric department so we can always buy a house."

"I love Everglade Farms. I can't imagine not living there."

"Everglade Farms it is. Come here, dumplin' and give me some more sugar."

"Gladly."

She made love to him again, savoring the taste of his lips, the saltiness of his neck, the scent of his masculinity, and pushed away all the thoughts of her demise.

Thunder rolled across the heavens, followed by a slow and steady rain.

Afterward, Harry ran a steaming hot bath into the Victorian-era cast-iron tub supported by feet shaped like lion's claws clutching a ball. They eased down into the water and took turns lathering each other with pink Camay soap scented with French perfume.

She grabbed several extravagantly thick towels from the table next to the tub as they stepped out on the carpeted rug to dry off.

After dressing, they ate a delicious meal prepared and discreetly delivered to the honeymoon suite by one of the staff members while they had been indisposed.

The underlying tone changed between them as the clock ticked away the minutes of the afternoon.

In silence, Lee packed her bag, then went to the tall window and looked toward downtown.

His arms slid around her waist, and she leaned against his chest.

"The rain's stopped."

"Look, a rainbow." She turned to look up into his gorgeous face.

"A positive omen."

She released a breath. "It's time."

"Yeah, I know."

Before they closed the door of the room, she circled her arms around his neck. "Don't do anything heroic tonight. Leave it to the warrior angels."

"I won't say ditto. We have to trust those whom The Creator sent us."

She nodded. "Yes, yes, we do."

They left Morton's Manor and drove to Everglade Farms. She wanted to see her parents in case the battle went awry.

CHAPTER 15

"I'LL BE SEEING YOU"

The road home seemed to take forever. The storm had passed, and the clouds rolled away, giving way to a dramatic sunset of fiery oranges and reds. Topping Campbell Ridge, Lee looked at the farm silhouetted against the sky. Many times, she'd looked at the view, but this evening, she pressed the image into her memory bank.

Her parents joined by the Glenns met them on the porch with hugs, kisses, and well-wishes.

"I'm so happy for you both," Jenny said.

Joseph clapped his hand on Harry's back. "You better take care of my baby girl."

"I will, I promise."

Joseph pressed his lips together, then smiled. "I'm holding you to your promise."

"We're going to throw you kids one heck of a wedding reception once the renovations on the house are complete," Eva excitedly proclaimed.

Blaine said, "Now, Mother, don't press the kids."

Harry coughed and added, "We're not kids anymore, Dad."

Joseph reached for Lee's baggage. "You're no longer children, but you'll always be kids in our eyes."

Her mom entered the living area. "True. Are you hungry? May I make you something to eat?"

"No, thank you. Morton's Manor food filled me to the brim." She sat on the sofa and Harry scooted in by her side.

He interjected, "Um, we're going to get some clothes and stay in the pool house for some privacy."

She looked at her father, pressing her hands into her lap. "We'd also like to fix up the old cabin and move in, with your permission, of course."

Joseph clasped Jenny's hand. "Yes, yes, what a wonderful idea."

Over the next hour, the families reminisced about the days gone by and discussed their marriage, future offspring, and the beach trip to Florida. They allowed their parents to make plans, knowing full well the events of the night might change them.

Lee excused herself and went to her bedroom to pack some clothes and toiletries. She pulled on the warrior bodysuit and boots, then slipped on an ankle-length dress to conceal them.

Carol Ann stuck her head inside the door. "May I come in?"

"Sure." She kept focused. Time was running out.

"I've known you all my life, and something is wrong." Carol Ann's brows wrinkled into a frown. "Did something happen last night you want to talk about?".

She snapped the luggage shut. "Harry and I are perfect. Some things are happening in our lives which I'm not at liberty to discuss, but I have one request, pray for us tonight."

"Always. Whatever is upsetting you, I'm here for you."

"We must leave, but we'll talk tomorrow. I love you, sister."

Harry entered the room and pointed to his watch. "We gotta go, baby." He grabbed the handle of her luggage. "Thanks for everything, sis." He kissed the top of Carol Ann's head.

"I love you two so much, and you're scaring me. I sense something bad. Tell me what's going on."

Energy shot to Lee's fingertips. Without thinking, she placed her hands over Carol Ann's eyes and planted happy thoughts, taking away her sister-in-law's fear.

She wondered what other powers would materialize to her by dawn.

Lee went to the barn with Harry to see Princess. "Hey, girl, I won't be gone long, and Dad promises to give you treats."

Erinelle materialized before them. "There's been a slight change of plans. Lee, you're coming with me. We have a double spy in Luc's camp who's given us new intel. We intend to attack by time-walking into the fourth-four towers of Sacred Heights Sanatorium."

Simon appeared next to Harry. "I'm riding with you."

Harry's face paled. Lee could see his fingers trembling. She placed his hands in hers. "Darling, we can do this. You must follow Simon's lead. Remember, I need to concentrate on the battle."

Swallowing hard, he replied, "This is real. Oh my god, before now, it was abstract thinking. Please, please, come back to me."

"We'll meet again when the battle is over. I love you." She kissed him.

"I love you more. Take your advice. Don't be a hero. Come on, Simon, let's go."

Erinelle placed her hand on Harry's forearm. "Hold on a minute. You and Lee will meet us where Campbell Ridge Road meets Highway 99. We don't want to raise concerns from your families if you leave alone. Simon brought you warrior gear to help prevent injuries."

"My body armor is under my dress, and I'm wearing my boots." Lee raised her dress and stuck out her right foot.

Harry pulled Lee into his arms one more time and kissed her. "Please take care of yourself. Don't take unnecessary chances. Lean on your angels."

"I'll do my best." Knowing the whole time, she would lead the angel forces into Hades to rescue her angel twin and any other innocents. She and Nadine shared a common link transcending space and time. She turned to Erinelle, straightening her spine.

She raised her chin. "I'm ready."

CHAPTER 16

"PRAISE THE LORD AND PASS THE AMMUNITION"

*T*he Battle of Sacred Heights Sanatorium

Lee motioned for Harry to pull into the driveway of an abandoned house at the corner of Campbell Ridge Road and Highway 99. She squeezed his knee, then took his face in her hands and kissed him. "I'll see you before dawn." She reached for the doorknob and exited the vehicle.

He got out of the car, placing his hands on the top of the roof. "I'm going to hold you to that darlin'."

Simon handed him his gear, and Harry turned and, without looking back, went to the side of the house to change clothes.

She watched him disappear in the shadows, then turned to Erinelle.

She held Lee's hands. "I'll guide you to the In-Between. Michael is waiting for us in the situation room."

Lee nodded. "I'm following you."

Instantaneously, they time-walked into a large room with tiered seating packed with seasoned warrior angels. As one, the angels turned to look at them. The beautiful and lethal beings made her pulse race, but her breathing remained steady.

Time was irrelevant in the heavens, but their military campaign ticked in synchronization with Earth's time and more specifically the Central Time Zone reflected by a large clock levitating in the air.

"Incredible. This place reminds me of a college lecture hall. Um, except for the warrior angels and the delicious scent of sugar mixed with vanilla. It smells like Mom's baking cookies."

The tiered glass-enclosed room held the fiercest looking angels— not the depictions of church murals or the Sistine Chapel. Humanity tended to paint peaceful-looking angels in pastel colors.

The seasoned warrior angels in front of her reminded her more of the paintings by the 16th Century artist, Michael Damaskenos. These angels prepared for another battle in their quest for victory against The Dragon—Luc.

Erinelle placed a finger over her lips and pointed toward the solid gold door silently sliding open.

The warriors stood at attention when Michael strode into the room. "At ease, please sit down."

Michael was known for his exceptional strength and bravery. The hilt of his saber glowed brightly against his blue-gray mesh armor with a dark crimson sash across his breastplate. His divine shield was secured to his back.

He stepped over to Lee and Erinelle, then bowed. "Welcome, Lee Campbell-Glenn. It's been some time since we talked. Do you remember me?" He touched the side of her face giving Lee total recall of their last conversation.

Lee met Michael in Heaven's Rose Garden, a social gathering place for angels to catch up. In those days, she'd been known as Leeel, a warrior angel recently assigned to The Chosen division of the AAF.

Sitting under the rainbow tree, he said, "Most angels shift from holographic forms to physical ones easily. Our spirit form allows us to be everywhere and anywhere at the same time, but The Chosen live as humans. You will regain some of your angel characteristics once you receive your trigger stone and it releases your memories along with your powers from Heaven. I need you to remember your direct link to The Creator is through the Trinities double helix. It is how He hears human cries."

"I am happy to serve the realm in any capacity," she replied.

"You are wise and full of power. Your generous spirit is full of love, and humanity needs all the love it can get."

~

LEE BOWED BEFORE THE ARCHANGEL. "Thank you, Michael, for allowing me the chance to serve under your command."

"Please grab a seat as I outline our war plan to retrieve the innocent souls." He went to the crystal podium and addressed the legion. "Luc holds the captives for their eternal light. We'll use aerial smoke screens to provide concealment from his soldiers as well as the civilian population. Shields will prevent the mortal staff and patients from witnessing the battle. Precisely at midnight, each mortal will be placed into a deep sleep with one of our sentries posted at every door."

She wanted desperately to take notes but would rely on her recall ability. She listened intently as Michael described their plan of attack using charts, maps, and coordinates.

"Ground troops under the command of Simon will surround the perimeter of the Sacred Heights property. Three battalions of soldiers will descend on the fourth-floor towers in forced concentration as I open the sky. Our reserve legion will carry out the aerial attack. I'll send soldiers into Hades to replenish any injured warriors entering the first circle, but be aware the moment we enter Hell, Luc, and his army will attack."

He added, "Keep moving forward. Lee will guide you to the location of the innocent souls. Follow her and Erinelle across the Sea of Dead that will lead to the Pavilion of Intelligent Minds. From there, we'll storm the Devil's Castle." He placed life-size images on the wallboard from her recent trip into Hades in perfect order for the extraction.

"Luc rarely engages, but I assure you, he will be in attendance.

Keep on your guard. We will move with one purpose and think as one mind to secure our victory."

The angels in the room roared their approval, pounding the tables and stomping their feet. The sensation reverberated throughout Lee's body.

She shivered.

Last time, she escaped Hades without being caught.

This time, Luc would be looking for her.

Trapped twin angels would give him added leverage in the war. He knew of the planned AAF attack, and like a mad dog, he'd tear out throats of his enemies to protect what he thought belonged to him.

Protection shields cloaked Lee as she time-walked with the first battalion to Sacred Heights Sanatorium at midnight, the AAF's covert mission initiated at Michael's command.

Her fingers tingled with sparks of electricity.

Her heart pounded so loud she could barely hear herself think.

She remembered fighting demons, the moment Michael tore open the portal to Hades through the magic mirror.

The legion descended along with Heaven's griffons brought to battle Luc's beasts guarding The Devil's Castle.

A supernatural fire erupted on the fourth-four towers as demons clashed sabers with the AAF.

Lee fought demons literally coming out of the woodwork. Her mind released more powers as she entered Hades.

You are a lethal weapon.

You have the power to blow up the state of Tennessee.

Electrical currents rolled off her body.

She allowed her connection to Nadine to pull her in the right direction with a beam of light radiating from the castle on the mountain.

The Sea of Dead rolled violently. The molten lava heated the water to boiling. Scalding screams from the dead made it nearly impossible to think, as the AAF engaged telepathy as their primary form of communicating with each other.

Erinelle extended her fingers across the convoluted sea, allowing the first battalion to enter a replica of a Viking longship that material-ized out of thin air. Lee, along with other warrior angels, climbed into the vessel.

The Creator built the ship for speed along with the symmetrical bow and stern, allowing her captain, the Archangel Jegudiel, to maneuver the craft with expert ability toward the pavilion.

Jegudiel ran the ship aground.

Each AAF warrior reached for their battle shields, spears, swords, daggers, bows, and arrows made by The Creator and readied them-selves for battle.

Demons charged the AAF team as soon as their feet touched the sand.

Lee raced to the dark forest following the path leading to The Pavilion of Intelligent minds where righteous non-believers of The Creator's Trinity resided. The residents cowered from the AAF while pointing, whispering and shaking their heads.

The fallen angels engaged in a counterattack with a myriad of weaponry, but she remained focused as fire rained down from the dark skies. She had a vision revealing Nadine's position and the other innocent souls inside the castle through one of The Seven Doors of Hell.

But which door?

Bitter fighting broke out close to the castle.

Erinelle fought ruthlessly and protected Lee's back while Jegudiel flanked her on the other side; both angels shielded her from injury. They climbed the rocky and treacherous terrain of the mountain leading to the castle guarded by Luc's fearsome and merciless beasts. They possessed three heads, a lion, a ram, and a black wolf with red eyes as large as a saucer, the torso of a stallion and feet and legs of a dragon.

The Griffons flew in squawking to fight the beasts while Lee and her team remained on course to the castle entrance.

The battle raged on.

Michael arranged for new legions to swarm into the area. The AAF intercepted the injured angels before the demons could send them to the Eternal Blackness. The healers took the wounded to the In-Between's Treatment Centers.

Lee didn't focus on the casualties falling around her but kept moving forward as Michael instructed. Luc's giants engaged her team at the top of the mountain. Some of the monsters appeared to be over fifty feet tall.

The AAF sent in winged horses. Divine fire blazed from their eyes paving a route to the castle.

Black volcanic stone structure protected the gate. A dozen AAF members crossed their spears, creating bolts of lightning to obliterate the stone as they stormed Luc's palace. The closer the AAF came to the captive souls, the more fierce and tenacious the demons fought.

Lee sensed the presence of Luc with sickening dread. He tried breaching her mind with the shrillest, raucous sound. The screeching from within the walls of the castle caused her searing pain and threatened to burst her eardrums.

She called on Michael using telepathy, and the archangel blocked Luc's entry to her brain. The pain subsided.

On the second landing of the castle, she found the seven doors in a rotunda. The supporting walls consisted of gemstones in varying shape and size. Upon a closer glance, the stones held elongated heads of creatures not from her realm of Earth. Their screams seemed frozen in time, but she sensed the souls lived in hellish torment.

Which door held the innocent souls?

One wrong decision could be catastrophic.

THE NERVE-WRACKING DRIVE to Sacred Heights Sanatorium had Harry on edge. His new bride left with the AAF to fight a supernatural battle with no clue of the outcome. He prayed fervently as Simon rattled on about the procedures of war.

He wore gold body armor with a breastplate covered in carnelian, emerald, sapphire, lapis lazuli, and jasper. Simon had told him the gemstones held magical properties. The armored suit fit him like a second skin with matching gloves and laced-up military boots.

"Harry, you must pay attention to me. Our ground troops will appear the instant my feet hit the Sacred Heights Sanatorium alerting the demon forces. You must always stay close to me. The power belt you're wearing contains the blue spheres of energy with an endless self-replenishing supply needed during the battle. You have a great arm. Use it wisely."

"I will. I'm worried about my wife." The vehicle fishtailed in the gravel road leading to the gates of Sacred Heights Sanatorium.

Simon placed his hand on Harry's shoulder. "Allow my energy to give you courage, man. Lee's fearless, and so are you." The energy flowing into Harry's body calmed his insecurities.

Oliver waited with two orderlies at the gate. He motioned for them to enter. The orderlies had odd-shaped black eyes with no sclera.

Simon yelled, "Floor it. They're demons."

Fear spiked his heart.

His adrenaline coursed through his veins igniting his fight or flight instincts while he spun out, spraying gravel into the air. He glanced into the vehicle's rearview mirror as the orderlies' clothes shifted into red and black scales, with some type of armor, and black wings jutted from their backs.

"Park next to the male staff building."

Harry did as Simon commanded and skidded to a stop. He threw the car into park and they quickly exited his car to engage the enemy. He reached into his power belt, retrieving a half-dozen spheres.

Simon placed his fingertips over Harry's eyes. "I'm lifting humanity's protective film so you may witness the fight as a warrior angel. Stay alive, my friend."

A thin barrier lifted from his eyes with a cooling sensation.

Harry blinked a couple of times. The surrounding landscape changed drastically.

The night's veil opened, and AAF warrior angels descended into the earthly realm spawning violent winds and spontaneous tornadoes.

Lightning bolts lit the sky.

The AAF wings created such a roar of winds swaying and bending the trees to a near breaking point.

The clouds hid the moon and stars as an eerie silence fell on the land from all of nature's living creatures big and small, seemingly aware of the presence of the angels.

It took all his strength to lean into the wind, forcing himself to move forward to Nadine's tree as rain fell in sheets pelting him.

He swiped the wetness and looked up at the towers. The fourth floor blazed with unearthly fire. Coils of terror snaked through his stomach. Lee was up there, and he couldn't reach her.

"Keep moving, Harry," Simon shouted, "We're almost there. Remember, the demons have black wings."

During Harry's AAF combat training, Simon instructed him to go to the tree where Nadine died which served as a portal for the innocent souls using its living branches to transport them to Heaven.

Luc's fallen angels resembled the AAF, but with terrifying features.

Rounding the main building, he saw a tree lit up with what resembled inextinguishable Christmas candles. Its branches thickened in real time before his eyes.

Nadine's tree.

A groundswell of troops from both sides entered the battlefield as Harry fired the blue energy spheres at the demons' heads causing them to explode into ash particles that singed his armor while blisters formed on his face.

Harry had fought in Korea.

Tonight's players were supernatural, but the campaign used similar strategies.

War in any arena was horrific.

He'd carry the images to his grave.

CHAPTER 17

"SMOKE GETS IN YOUR EYES"

*T*he Seven Doors of Hell

Lee held out her hand and turned the iron ring to open the first door. She entered in a flash. Neither Erinelle nor the AAF team followed her inside. Divine sword in one hand, she reached behind her back with the other hand, pulling the protective shield around her.

Inching forward, she listened for any word from Nadine.

Smoke rose from a lake of fire streaming by the charred trees and limbs giving off the only light in the gloomy place. White ash fell from the darkened skies like snow.

The rotten flesh from dead carcasses of half-eaten animals lay in decay on the ground creating a horrible stench.

She edged along the gruesome path. "Nadine, are you here?"

The further she went into the Pits of Hell, the more her mind played tricks. Her senses attuned to every sound.

"Help me, Lee. I'm hurt," Harry called out to her several times that she ignored. It couldn't be him. He was with Simon. The Dragon used mental manipulation.

A massive, terrifying shark beast jumped from the acid-spewing fire intent on eating her.

She double-stepped to get away from its jagged teeth, using her shield to keep the lava from splashing her skin. She glanced over her shoulder, searching for a way to escape.

Out of nowhere, a fire-breathing dragon swooped from the top of the smoldering mountain. "Did you come to play with me, Leeel?"

Through gritted teeth, she yelled, "Where's Nadine?"

In the form of an enormous red dragon the length of a football field from nose to tail, Luc circled her as prey. "Ah, Nadine is not the delicacy for my palate, but you are her angel twin as I had suspected all along. My spies confirmed it by searching Heaven's historical archives this morning. Now, I have you both."

He cornered her between a massive boulder and the lake of fire. "Demon fighter, you don't have what it takes to battle an archangel. I will give you a choice. Drop your weapons and vow allegiance to me, and I will allow you to return home to dear, sweet, and straight from the South, Harry. Or deny me, and I'll throw you into the lake of fire that never dies, and your thirst will never quench. Your skin and bones will melt into the river flowing with millions of other lost souls including Angels of the Light."

She assumed the AAF used her as bait while they retrieved the innocent souls. She wouldn't hesitate to kill the beast. She'd rather die than allow Luc to capture her.

Instinctively, Lee sheathed her sword and slung the battle shield to her back. She extended her palms out, releasing white energy bolts of lightning from her hands. She made a direct hit to The Dragon's chest, making him turn head over tail, twice.

Someone yanked Lee's arm hard, and she was back inside the dome of the seven doors. The AAF slaughtered all manner of creatures large and small, but more demons and creatures of the dark kept coming.

Erinelle released her arm and shouted, "Where did you go?"

"The Dragon's pit. Give me a second."

"We don't have a second." Erinelle slashed through several of the fallen, beating them back away from Lee.

Lee heard Nadine sobbing.

She blotted out all the other stimuli around her and zoned in on her sister's tears as each one hit the ground with hissing steam.

Nadine was close.

"Where are you, Nadine? What door are you behind?"

Her sister whimpered, "I'm not supposed to tell you."

Lee placed her hand on each door until her connection with Nadine locked. "Back away from the door. We're coming for you." She blew the door open using telekinesis and flew through the next door of Hell.

Again, she was alone.

Why wasn't the AAF following her?

She approached a labyrinth of mirrors. Her angel twin cried, but the further she went inside the maze, the farther away Nadine's voice faded out of reach.

She outstretched her hands and bumped into the glass walls. Each mirror looked identical with closed archways above her head. Multiple colored beams bounced so fast through the glass it made her dizzy.

The light of the innocent souls trapped within the fiendish mirrors radiated.

Think, Lee.

A sinking sense of dread came over her as Daglan entered the maze.

"Cupcake, I was wondering if you and I would ever dance. The innocent souls are in the center of the labyrinth. All you have to do is get by me. So let's play awhile before the real fight begins."

She stared at Daglan's once beautiful face now scarred by her sparks of energy. Red welts marred him. His hatred for her filled his expression with violence. His ice, cold stare gave her the shivers.

She went into her fighting stance. She intended on finishing the job she'd started in the doctor's office. She lifted her sword with one hand and her shield with the other. "I have no time for playing games with you, Daglan. Whoa, wait a minute." She remembered him before the fall. "Why did you follow the Morning Star? You used to sing with such a rich sound. You could switch vocal timbres flawlessly."

"How do you know me?"

"I am Leeel." She rotated the blade before she lunged, catching him off guard. Her sword sliced across his chest. He countered her advance, knocking the blade from her hand. She did a roundhouse kick to his back, knocking him to his knees.

"Bitch." He spat. "I remember you. But how in Lucifer's name do you have the scent of a mortal?" He hopped to his feet into battle mode with his blade in hand.

She summoned her blade. "I'm unlike anything you've ever seen, and I am taking the innocent souls with me."

"No, you're not. The only place you're going is to The Eternal Darkness but not before I capture you and deliver you to my master. He'll want to examine you in our weapons lab thoroughly."

They clashed blades and fought furiously, crashing into the mirrors and bringing them down one by one.

Lee kept her eyes on Daglan's sword but sensed Nadine and the innocent souls nearby.

He started laughing when sweat ran into her eyes. "Too hot? Then get out of Hell's kitchen." He nicked her face, her neck, and arms. He toyed with her. Blood flowed freely from her wounds. For some odd reason, she didn't feel pain.

She countered his moves while fending his blows and somer-saulting into the air. She raised her blade over her head, and using all her strength, lopped off Daglan's head. Black blood spurted like a water fountain.

She stared in disbelief. He didn't burst into ash but grappled for his head, putting it back in place.

Lee didn't wait for him to stand but charged him, beating him back against the broken and jagged mirrors.

He regrouped by time-walking behind her. "You can't kill me, Leeel. Hades is my turf, not yours."

He swung his blade at her head.

She dodged and blocked the blow.

Erinelle's words rang out in her mind. *The demon must die.*

She didn't relent but continued to press him as the fight surged on, blood ran down into her eyes, making it hard to see.

Daglan must have a weakness.

She couldn't time-walk to the innocents without first defeating him. She remembered somehow that females from the otherworldly realms plus Earth's women were his weakness.

She wet her lips. "Daglan, do you want me?"

He struck her again but raised a brow. "More than any other female. You are strong. You are my match, Leeel." He pressed her against the mirrored wall with desire in his eyes.

His breathing labored.

She allowed him to take the sword from her hand.

If this didn't work, she was screwed.

She inched closer while he threw their blades to the ground.

Daglan eyed her mouth and licked his lustful lips.

She kept eye contact with him just a few seconds longer. He grabbed her right breast and twisted her nipple. She bit down on her lip, not to cry out. She reached within her power belt for a blue death star, and then she shoved it into his demon heart.

Daglan fell.

His eyes widened with fear. "What have you done?"

"Yes, Daglan, you can die. My weapons are divine." Lee covered herself with her protective shield as Luc's general exploded into ash sending him to the Eternal Darkness, forever.

She picked up her sword, swiping it clean, then leaped over the shards of glass, catching Nadine's image in the mirror's reflection.

Lee closed her eyes and time-walked.

In the center of the labyrinth, Nadine and dozens of other innocent souls, including the local boys from Everglade, huddled together in abject terror.

She approached them with caution. She must look deranged covered with her blood and Daglan's. "Nadine, it's Lee. Do not be afraid. I'm here to save you."

Nadine searched Lee's eyes. "You killed Daglan?"

"Yes. We must hurry. More demons will come for us. Follow me."

Lee snaked her way back through the maze of broken mirrors. She didn't take the time to understand all the powers unleashing from her soul.

It wasn't just one or two powers, but her entire being thrummed as a weapon. And with Nadine by her side, combining their forces, any demons making contact would immediately disintegrate into ash.

At the last mirror, Lee barely recognized herself. Her chestnut hair stood on its end as lethal currents of electricity arced from her body. Her brown eyes glowed like sparkling diamonds.

She spoke softly. "Are all the innocent souls still with you, Nadine?"

Her twin nodded to the countless souls behind her.

Lee flicked her fingertips, and the last mirror vanished.

Back in the rotunda, Erinelle along with the other AAF team continued battling the demons.

Lee led the innocents to the portal opening.

She didn't understand how she knew what to do; she just did.

The Dragon circled above the castle, spewing fire and roaring so loud it caused Hades to quake. He opened another gate. Demons and giants rushed toward the dome.

Without wings, Lee levitated, stretching her arms open, and she pointed her palms in the direction of the aggressors, releasing streams of white energy.

Quickly, Erinelle along with several members of their AAF unit began placing white linen tunics over each captive soul, and one by one they spontaneously disappeared.

Nadine waited on Lee to return to the surface before putting on the tunic. She hugged Lee. "Thank you for saving us. Please tell Oliver I will always love him. Tell him I'll wait for him at Heaven's Gate."

"Nadine, the portal waits," Erinelle said.

She put on the white linen tunic and disappeared.

Lee asked, "Where did they go?"

"They went to Nadine's tree. The Creator's using the tree as an exit point to the In-Between and from there onward to Heaven. Hurry, let's get out of here before Luc opens all the gates of Hell."

She followed Erinelle racing out of the castle. She took in the magnitude of the battle. Thousands of angels fought tearing each other apart. The AAF angels glowed with the light of The Creator, and black wings with red tips marked the fallen angels.

The Angel Armed Forces dug into the trenches along the mountainside. The Creator's weaponry was decimating the fallen angels and unearthly creatures from the dark.

Without waiting for a signal, Lee launched into the fight. Swirling white energy fields released from her hands and surrounded her physical form creating a protection shield pinging off any demon's attempt to injure or kill her.

Violent screams startled her.

Erinelle yelled, "Run for the ship. Don't look back. The roar you're hearing is Luc opening the nine gates of Hell. We're outnumbered. Run, Lee!"

She didn't have to be told twice. Her superhuman speed kicked in, and she whizzed by the fallen in a blur of light.

The Dragon opened his mouth, shooting a stream of fire at her.

She dodged behind a burned-out tree.

Luc filled her with an onslaught of doubts, making her second-guess the direction of the longship.

Sweat poured down her back from the scorching heat. Her mind drifted. The darkness allowed madness to seep into her mind. She stopped and looked around, not knowing where she was or what she was doing. The scene she witnessed was straight out of the biblical narrative of the apocalypse.

Am I dreaming?

Is this real?

Erinelle smacked her hard across the face. "Snap out of it. You with me?" She tugged her arm in the right direction.

Lee shook off the brain fog as she ran next to her warrior angel. They entered the ship last.

From the longship, the AAF fired dozens of blue-energy arrows, exploding demons, and any other encroaching critters as they sailed across the Sea of Dead. Jegudiel maneuvered the vessel with expertise over the unforgiving and turbulent water. The longship threatened to capsize with the Souls of the Dead slapping and beating against the planks.

They sailed into a strong gale, but Jegudiel's sure hands kept them afloat.

Shouts came from the dark forest, and more of the enemy waited for them to dock the boat.

An undecipherable song broke out between the angels on the ship. A most beautiful melody she would later learn summoned another AAF legion.

The angels on board communicated again using telepathy.

Erinelle looked at her. "As soon the ship hits the shore, and our feet hit the ground, think of Harry. Time-walk to him. It is the safest and fastest way out of Hades, but not while we're on the sea; otherwise, you could land in an alternate timeline, and you may not survive."

Dread crept into her heart. Battling the demons was a job for supernatural beings, not a mortal.

What if Harry's hurt?

What if he dies?

"Sing, Lee. Sing." Erinelle shouted.

She opened her mouth and sang her favorite gospel song, "In The Garden," in perfect alto with lots of warmth and resonance. The longship ran aground, and the moment her feet touched the sand, she thought of Harry.

CHAPTER 18

"DON'T WORRY 'BOUT ME"

*H*arry fought hard against the demons, utilizing his pent-up frustration and anger to nail any of them coming within shot distance with the blue spheres of energy. The more he threw, the more spheres magically appeared in his power belt. He focused on one demon at a time without looking at the carnage going on around him.

The AAF sent in more recruits until every demon beast had been eradicated from the grounds of the Sacred Heights Sanatorium property. The thunderstorm kept the supernatural fires at bay.

The torrential rainfall stopped after the innocent souls reached Nadine's tree. One by one their souls released into the divine gateway created in the sky carrying them to the In-Between and onward to Heaven on multi-colored beams of light.

Then the AAF sent in clean-up crews to secure the area and ensured the safety of the staff and patients.

The battle ended.

Harry looked up at the towers. His chest constricted, and his gut twisted with worry.

Where's Lee?

He no more thought her name when she materialized in front of him, covered in blood. Her hair stood on its end like she'd been electrocuted. His heart hammered as she jumped into his arms and squeezed his neck.

"Thank God, you're alive. We're alive." She kissed him all over his face.

Blood and black goo covered her from her head to her boots. He searched her eyes. "Are you hurt? Do you need a doctor?" He shouted, "Simon, Simon. Hurry, Lee's hurt."

"I know I'm a mess, but I'm fine. A few injuries, but they've healed. The blood isn't mine. You know, Southern women don't cotton to threats against family," she said with a hint of sarcasm. "Luc's army suffered major losses. To my knowledge, the AAF had minimal casualties."

A surge of relief washed over him.

"Your hair is singed, and you have blisters on your face."

"Oh, Lee, I'm good now you're here. So, Nadine and the boys? Are they safe?" Warm light pulsated from Lee's hands as she placed them on his face and ran her fingers through his hair, restoring him from any damage of the battle.

She gave him a quick kiss, then released her legs from his waist and stood.

"All the innocent souls are en route to Heaven. Erinelle and her team deserve much praise and gratitude. Your bravery and courage will be etched in my heart forever. I'll never be able to repay you."

His shoulders relaxed. The campaign had been a success. "Let's go home. I'm sure I'll think of some ways you can repay me." He swiped the blood from her face.

Oliver inched out of the shadows. "Is it over?"

Lee turned to him. "Nadine is free. She sent her love and told me to tell you she'll wait for you at Heaven's Gate."

"Thank you, sweet Jesus," Oliver cried. "Thanks to all of you."

"You're safe too, Doc," Lee said. "I learned The Creator signed your name in the book."

"Really? What book?"

"The Book of Life. Harry and I are leaving soon, but before we go,

I'm going to give you a memory wipe. How far back do you need it to go?"

"Don't give me a memory wipe. I won't tell anyone. I want to remember Nadine. I need to remember she didn't kill herself, and she's safe in Heaven."

Simon and Erinelle appeared covered in blood and Harry wouldn't even attempt to guess what the bits and pieces were clinging to their armor.

Sunday School had taught him about the spiritual battle waged over souls. He'd assumed the struggle for the soul was silent and hidden, but tonight proved him wrong. These fantastic warriors of light put their lives on the line, and they did it continuously.

Erinelle took Lee's hand into hers. "Stupendous effort, my friend. I'm so proud of you. Epic battles like tonight don't happen as often as the day-to-day physical, mental, and emotional battles humans face. Try and enjoy your time with Harry. True love like yours is a gift most people search for a lifetime and never find. And no memory wipes for Oliver."

Simon clapped Harry's back. "You'll do for a mortal."

"Thanks, Simon. I had a great teacher." He draped his arm around Lee's waist.

"Hey, y'all, I'm fighting to stand on my feet. My body is shaking. Hey, Oliver, may I take a quick shower and change in the staff quarters?" She leaned her head on Harry's shoulder.

"Sure thing. The left wing houses the female staff. The showers are down the first corridor on the left. You'll find clean nurses' uniforms in the Ladies locker room closet. Harry, you can follow me. I think I'll spend the night here and do my rounds in the morning, but Lee, I'll see you bright and early Monday."

"Um, Oliver, we're still on our honeymoon. How about Tuesday morning? And, we brought clothes in the trunk of the car."

"Honeymoon? Boy, I'd like to be around when you tell the grand-kids." Simon cackled, and the others joined in unison.

Harry wouldn't think too far into the future. He wanted to live for each day with his new bride, count his blessings, and never complain about going to church again.

AFTER SHOWERING IN THE DORMITORIES, Lee rode with Harry to Glenn Hall. She dozed on and off on the journey. In between the wakeful moments, she relived the incredible force of power she released during the battle. Her skills activated when she engaged the demons in combat, and they intensified when Luc appeared.

Her face tightened with disgust from some of the mental snap-shots of Hades. She made a deadly enemy with Luc and his army. They'd come for her again.

When? Where? How?

She didn't sweat it. She had the power within her to protect those she loved, and she wouldn't hesitate to use it.

Arriving at the pool house, Harry unlocked the side door, and they went inside. To her surprise, a basket of fruit with a variety of cheeses sat on the table along with a bottle of champagne in a stainless bucket of watered-down ice.

She opened the card and read:

I prayed for you and Harry as you asked me too. I came over with fruit, drinks, and left a sandwich tray in the fridge. Remember, I'm here for you anytime. Love, Carol Ann

"Carol Ann is sweet. I'm starving, but I have to wash my hair, and any remaining grime away. The staff showers didn't have any shampoo or soap. Care to join me, husband?"

"Oh, yeah, I'll join you in the shower. But aren't you tired?"

"Exhausted, but also very relieved my fighting skills worked. Harry, I released some spectacular powers tonight. Erinelle trained me well, but I knew exactly what to do in situations I hadn't prepared for. I was a different person in Hell. Like I was outside looking in."

"Wanna tell me about it? And does this mean you're glad we're married?"

"Absolutely, I'm glad we married, and no, I don't want to talk about my powers except that I'll never look at a lightning bolt the same way again."

"Lightning bolts?" he asked.

"Yeah, I shot bolts of electricity from the palms of my hands. Oh, well, I need to bathe before I collapse. My energy is gone."

"Like the light, you used to heal my face and restore my hair?"

"Uh-huh, but a hundred times stronger."

"Remind me not to make you mad." His eyes twinkled with apparent mischief, and she playfully smacked his arm. "Grab some clothes, darlin'. We'll shower inside the main house. The construction crew started the renovations. It's amazing what a fresh coat of paint can do to eliminate the smell of smoke. The upstairs bathroom is working just fine. Mom has the windows open. The water out here takes forever to heat."

"Hot water sounds lovely." She opened her suitcase and pulled out her pink silk nightgown, undergarments, and slippers. She followed him to the main house, up to the back stairs, and into the bathroom.

"Shower or tub?"

"Shower, please." She peeled off her clothes and placed them in a heap while he turned on the shower faucet allowing the water to heat.

"Jump in."

She stepped under the steaming stream of water. "Gosh, the water feels great on my aching muscles."

He stepped in behind her and began to lather her hair with shampoo. She didn't look at the gunk flowing down the drain. Thinking about the demon innards made her empty stomach queasy.

He helped her to remove the black goo that had penetrated the armor and gently massaged her muscles using circular motions with a sudsy washcloth.

"You have magic fingers, but turnabout is fair play." She swapped places with him and washed his hair and delicious body.

He swiveled around, taking her into his arms and kissing her soundly on the mouth. "I'm tired, but not too tired to make love to my wife."

Water trickled between them intensifying her desires and

cranking up her need for him. The fog lifted from her brain, erasing the images of the night, replacing them with Harry's tender kisses. The man she loved and adored.

Without saying a word, each knew tonight could've been worse. They made it out alive, and Lee wanted him. She wanted to feel love, taste love, and embrace love.

They pressed their bodies tightly together. He lifted her, and she wrapped her legs around him. What started as tender lovemaking turned into a wild and frenzied passion. He took possession of her body and soul. He held her with one hand, his fingers digging into her flesh, and his other hand fisted her hair.

She released a throaty moan. The closer she came to an orgasm, she thought her heart would burst. With every stroke, every caress, every kiss, he made her feel alive.

The hot water turned lukewarm, and he carried her out of the shower and placed her on the bathroom counter. Her body begged for more. He'd been holding back when he snapped. The rhythm of their love increased with such ferocity, desperate for each other, each crying out the other's name.

He held her tightly until his release. His head fell forward, resting on her shoulder with an audible sigh. "My legs are so weak. I'm not sure I can walk."

"I know just what you mean. Think we could sleep in your old room tonight?"

"Great minds do think alike. But I thought you wanted something to eat." He released his hold and took a step back.

"I am hungry, but I need to sleep more."

He grabbed towels from the linen closet and dried her hair and body before wiping off the droplets from his glistening skin.

After brushing her hair and teeth, she slipped on her gown, while he pulled on a pair of boxers. He scooped her up and carried her into his room, placing her gently on the bed.

"Do you have any idea the countless times I wanted to sleep in here with you?"

"Yeah, about as many times as I wanted you here. You go on and rest, and I'll grab some of the eats my sister brought. Champagne or soda pop?"

"Soda pop, but I may fall asleep before you return."

"I'll put the bottles on ice, so you'll have something to drink anytime during the night." He retrieved a pair of pajama bottoms from the oak dresser and left the room.

Lee grabbed his pillow and inhaled Harry's scent, Old Spice, her favorite. After all the years of wanting him, he was finally hers.

She drifted to sleep with a smile on her face.

LEE STOOD on the top of Campbell Ridge. She placed her hand over her abdomen. She was with child and couldn't wait to see the look on Harry's face.

Suddenly, Luc appeared in a dark gray cloud. "Have you read the news lately? Listened to the radio? The world you grew up in— is over. It's only going to get worse; I assure you. Do you ever think The Creator could stop it all in a blink of an eye? Earth, humanity, all living creatures are subjects in one monstrous experiment, and as a punishment, He sent my followers and me as witnesses. His nature is to create, and He's perfecting the same experiment on other worlds that someday may collide with Earth."

He flew out of the cloud and strutted around her like a peacock. "You graduated from college. I'm sure you studied about prehistoric man. The Creator played around with many species like The Homo habilis, The Homo erectus, The Homo neanderthalensis, or what you refer to as the Neanderthals. There are many more. Shall I continue?"

He peered deep into her eyes. "Use your hybrid DNA to search the truth before your child is born. You have a chance to see my side of things. I may not be as kind to your offspring. Remember, I am always near you and yours."

Rage surged within her as she flung herself at him. "I belong to Him, who created me through His grace alone. Begone from my sight, Deceiver!"

He sidestepped her. "I see the future. And so can you. Wake up, Leeel."

~

SHE BOLTED from the bed in sheer terror, screaming at the top of her lungs.

Harry jumped from the bed. "What—What is it? What happened?"

"I'm pregnant, and Luc is watching me, watching us, and he knows I'm pregnant, Harry."

"There, there, darlin'. Don't get yourself so worked up. You had a bad dream. Maybe you see possible futures and things can still change. We have a right to nightmares after what we witnessed last night." He helped her to bed then slid in next to her. "How can you be pregnant so soon?"

She rolled her eyes. "It only takes one time. I see the future sometimes in my dreams. I'm going to have our first child in nine months."

She closed her eyes for a second. "I'm telling you I have prophetic dreams I'm just beginning to understand. I've had them most of my life. I dreamed of my death too."

With a raised voice, he insisted, "No. No. No talk of death. We all die. I want to live. I want us to live life to the fullest. Simon told me free will changes future outcomes."

She nudged her forehead against his neck. "I agree. I want to live too, but death is a part of living. I think Luc is going to kill me using my—our daughter. Her name is Ruby."

"Remember, The Prince watches over humanity, and the Spirit of Man dwells within us. *Fear not, for He is with us until the end of time.*"

"You're right. I'm probably getting worked up over nothing. Michael told me once our DNA links to the Trinity. It's how He hears our prayers. I'm so glad you're by my side in this life."

"Always. You need to rest, and I'll go to Miss Pearl's and grab some pastries for breakfast."

She fluffed the pillow and tucked it under her head. "Find out if she has any fried peach pies."

He chuckled. "Cravings already?"

"Nah, just my favorite from Miss Pearl's."

"I'll be back in a few shakes of a cow's tail." He pulled on his pants and shirt, grabbed his shoes, and quietly closed the door behind him.

"Erinelle? Are you here?"

"I'm here. Worrying has never stopped anything." She sat on the bed — her hand on Lee's thigh.

Peace washed over her in warm waves. "I'm pregnant. Aren't I?"

"Yes," Erinelle replied. "You and Harry are blessed with a son."

"And we'll call him, George."

CHAPTER 19

"LOST HIGHWAY"

*T*uesday morning, Lee arrived at work early to make coffee and straighten the waiting room. She walked by Oliver's office, and he looked haggard. "Would you like a fresh cup of coffee?"

He motioned for her to enter. "Please sit down."

She sat across from his desk in a red leather chair.

"I received news last night my father is gravely ill. I must return home to care for him and his practice. I placed a call to a colleague who interned at Sacred Heights as a family practitioner. He's willing to move to Everglade and care for its people. His name is Brandon Smith."

"I am sorry, Oliver, is there anything I can do to help?"

"Please take my appointment book and call each of my patients. Inform them of my situation. Dr. Smith stated it'll be late summer before he's able to move here. The hospital will cover my patients until he's settled."

"I'll take care of it. So, I take it I need to look for employment elsewhere?" Lee stood.

"I placed a call for you to the general manager of the telephone company, Brian Buchanan. He's waiting for your call about a position opening soon." He pushed away from his desk and went to Lee placing his arms around her. "I'm forever in your debt for helping Nadine and me. I'll miss you, my friend."

The chimes rang from the office front door, announcing the arrival of the first patient of the day. Lee squeezed his hands. "I'll never forget you. You led me to my angel twin and my first mission. I'm grateful for the care you gave my mother too. I better check in Mrs. Leatherman. She's experiencing gout issues."

"Send her on back. The doctor is in." He slipped on his white coat and grabbed his stethoscope.

She went to the front office and checked in the patient.

So much had happened since the day she met Erinelle, the same day she graduated from college, and the day Harry revealed his feelings for her for the first time.

She'd heard things happen for a reason. Meeting Oliver opened the doors to the supernatural in a way she hadn't expected. Her divine calling wouldn't end with his leaving. She would continue her lessons from Erinelle while expanding her knowledge of the angelic war.

Over the next couple of weeks, Lee and Harry helped Oliver pack and ship most of his belonging to New York by freight. Dr. Smith purchased the remaining medical equipment, supplies, office furniture, and house. The day he left for New York, the Campbells and the Glenns met him in the driveway to send him off.

Her mom hugged him and handed him a brown sack. "I packed sandwiches for the road trip. Be careful and stay in touch."

Dad shook his hand. "Everglade is losing one of its best doctors. We wish you well."

The Glenns presented him with a check. "We want you to use the funds any way you deem fit."

Carol Ann kissed him on the cheek. "You are going to make some girl very lucky."

"Be sure to call on me if you're ever in Harnsey, New York," he said.

Lee had told Oliver of Carol Ann's infatuation. She knew in her heart that day would never come.

Lee and Harry said their goodbyes to Oliver in private. They stood arm-in-arm, watching him slide into the Chevy Bel Air. They would share letters and Christmas cards for the rest of their lives.

He nodded to Harry. "Take good care of her."

"I got you, Doc. I will."

Oliver drove out of Everglade for the last time.

CHAPTER 20

"THE VERY THOUGHT OF YOU"

*G*ammie's at Grayton Beach

Lee spoke to Dr. Smith on several occasions. The new doctor arranged with her to keep a check on the office and house until he could move later in the summer.

She also interviewed and landed a manager's position in charge of the switchboard operators with the telephone company. She would start her new job when she returned from vacation.

The Glenns and the Campbells drove to Gammie's beach house on the Gulf Coast of Florida in the small village of Grayton. They rode down the oyster-shell roads passing pine and oaks until they reached the two-story wooden structure protected by natural barriers and the dunes. One of the oldest homes, Gammie's house was a treasure with a large wraparound porch directly on the white sand beach.

It had been two years since Lee's last trip.

Gammie stood on the steps to welcome them with her prize-winning Jack Russell terrier, Rusty, yapping as they parked and unpacked luggage. "'Bout time y'all got here, dinner is getting cold." She gingerly went down the steps, holding the wooden rail.

Harry's grandmother had inherited the place from Blaine's father when he passed away nearly a decade ago. She wore her white hair cropped short, and she had a winsome smile. "After y'all get settled, there's a shrimp boil with potatoes and corn in the pot on the back porch." She propped her hand on her hip. "Harry Glenn, I hear you got hitched without telling me. But I approve of Lee. She's always been a favorite of mine."

Harry picked Gammie up and hugged her before carefully releasing her back on the ground. "I missed you so much."

She smacked his arm. "You are a charmer. Come here, Lee."

She went to Gammie, and she reached for her hand.

Gammie eyed her suspiciously, leaned in and whispered, "Do the rest of them know you're with child?"

Lee whispered back, "No, ma'am. We want to tell everyone together."

"Well, I'll swan. Go on, girl. Get to it. You and Harry are on the top floor. Thought you might need some privacy, but remember, sounds carry on the waves." She snorted with laughter. "We have some celebrating to do. I'll crack open my best muscadine wine."

The families met on the back porch for the boil just in time for sunset on the ocean. It was a family tradition. Vibrant reds, oranges, pinks, and lavender stretched across the skies over the calm waters. The sight made Lee catch her breath. Beautiful didn't quite describe the image, more like divine as the sun slowly dropped out of sight. At the same time, left of the house, the full summer moon rose over Western Lake.

Light-hearted conversation filtered over the warm Gulf's briny breezes.

Harry raised his bottle of beer and winked at Lee. "We have an announcement to make."

The conversations went silent. Everyone turned to Harry. "We're having a baby."

Whistles, claps, and squeals of delight released into the night air.

Jenny and Eva hugged.

Carol Ann sat next to Lee and placed her hand on her belly. "I'm going to spoil this baby rotten. When's he due?"

"How do you know we're having a boy?" Harry asked.

Carol Ann waved him off. "I don't, but I'd rather say him than it."

"Um, I think in about thirty-five weeks." She took a sip of water.

Harry's chest puffed out. "It doesn't matter whether the baby is a boy or girl as long as Lee and the child are healthy."

Her mother ran out of the room, and Lee followed her into the guest bedroom on the main floor.

"What's the matter, Mom?"

"I don't want to be a party pooper." She sat down on the bed and sniffled.

Lee joined her and squeezed her hand. "Is it your head? I can make it better."

Erinelle appeared in spirit form. "You can't use your healing powers while pregnant. You must be strong for your mother and your child."

Dad walked into the room and shut the door. He placed his hand on Lee's shoulder. "Honey, we wanted to wait and tell you after the beach trip, but you might as well know your mom has a brain tumor."

Lee couldn't breathe. She was suffocating. She wanted to scream. How could she be happy and sad at the same time? Life could be beautiful and so unfair.

"No one ever truly dies. Souls move on."

She wanted to scream at Erinelle too. While she knew humans had X amount of days in a lifetime, rarely did anyone discuss dying.

"It is one of the reasons for her headaches." He sat next to her mom. His face seemed older. "Our girl is strong, and she needs to know the truth."

Lee swallowed hard. "I am here for you, Mom. Always."

"I want to hold my grandchild before God takes me home. I'm not afraid of dying." Mom sniffled again. "I am afraid of leaving all of you behind. I won't be there to comfort you, to babysit, or see the child's first Christmas."

Panic struck in the pit of Lee's stomach. "How advanced is the cancer? Did Oliver know?"

She held Lee's hand in her lap. "I asked Oliver not to tell you. You and Harry are very young, and I didn't want to burden you with my problems."

Lee got angry. Angry for Oliver not telling her about her mother. Angry at The Creator too for taking her mom when she needed her most.

"I understand you are angry. The Creator didn't cause the cancer. The body sometimes mutates cells."

"Erinelle, please, no rationalizations. I understand sickness happens, but doggone it— I don't want to lose my mother."

Lee gripped the bedspread and twisted the material in her hands. She didn't want her parents to hurt. "Surely, something can help."

"Oliver sent me to a specialist in Nashville. They could try and remove the tumor, but the prognosis for a bleeding tumor isn't good. He described the treatments and my chances too. I chose to use the pain meds he made for me instead of treatment. I want to be present in each moment I have left. Don't be mad at me."

"I love you, Mom. I'm not mad at you." She prayed for strength. "I think I'll go for a walk on the beach alone. I need to think."

"Cricket, your mother doesn't want anyone but Harry to know of her condition while we're here. We have time to tell our friends before her condition worsens. She didn't want you to know either, but you deserve to know the truth." Her father hugged Lee.

She pulled away, shaking her head. "I won't let her die. I won't." She stormed out of the bedroom and out the front door, down the steps, and raced to the beach. She fast-walked while trying to think.

Warm waves lapped at her feet.

Erinelle came to her. "You can't heal your mother. Sometimes, illness and disease happen. If you try to use your powers, you risk your health and the life of your unborn child."

She balled her hands into fists. "I have great powers, and I'm forbidden to use them. Why can't you heal her? Call on Raphael. Do something."

The ocean breeze blew Erinelle's long red hair off her shoulders. "I can't. Sometimes things happen, so the glory of The Creator might be revealed. Life is hard, but it is also a wonderful gift. You have this incredible place, and loved ones surround you. Enjoy the moment you're living in and not what may happen tomorrow, the next day or the next year. Live each day like it's your last with joy and happiness in your heart, and you will have few regrets."

She grabbed Lee by her shoulders. "You still have time with your mom. Use it wisely. You know Jenny will live on in Heaven, and someday you'll reunite. Don't harbor resentment, for if you do, Luc wins."

Lee knew Erinelle was right, but it still didn't make her feel any better.

Harry ran along the shoreline to catch up with her. "Do you want to talk about it?"

"My mother has cancer. She's going to die maybe even before George is born." Saying the words aloud released a rain barrel of emotions.

The sky opened, and the words echoed on the water, *"I am with you always, but I'm closer to you in your time of despair. One day, there will be no more tears, and I will fill the world with My glory forever, and ever."*

She looked up into Harry's eyes when the sky closed. "Did you hear that?"

"Hear what, baby?"

"Hold me, Harry. Just hold me."

He placed his arms around her, swaying back and forth while singing, "The Very Thought of You" under the starlit skies. She began to breathe a little easier as she snuggled against his chest. Her wedding vows—*Someone to have and to hold*—made so much sense to her.

"I have a thought if you'll hear me out."

"I'm listening."

"Instead of fixing up the old cabin, we should move in with your parents. I'm sure they'll need extra help as Jenny's disease progresses. It will give you extra time with her too. What do you think?"

She stopped walking, turned, and searched his eyes. "I'm the luckiest girl on the planet. I love you. I love the idea, and I'm sure they will too."

He intertwined his fingers with hers and lifted them to press a kiss. "It won't be easy watching your mother as she transitions from this life to the next, but it should give you peace knowing she is in His hands, and at the end of the day, love will light the way."

"Hm. Love will light the way. I heard Erinelle say the same thing. She said love is the greatest gift, and grace saves us all."

"Wise angel. Are you ready to walk back? I'm afraid Gammie Glenn will send out a search party."

"As ready as I'll ever be. Harry?"

"Yeah?"

"You're going to be a wonderful father."

"I love this child so much without seeing him yet."

Back at the beach house, Lee went to her parents and apologized. "I'm sorry for running away. Harry and I would like to live with you. I want to help you, Mom. I want to be with you as long as you're still with us."

She hugged Lee. "Honey, I would love for you and Harry to move in with us."

"And that goes for me too," her dad added.

CHAPTER 21

"LIFE'S BEEN GOOD"

*E*verglade Farms

Lee and Harry moved into Everglade Farms, carving out a life for themselves with her parents. Her mother held George the day of his birth and lived another two years before she crossed into the next realm.

During her mother's last days of life, Lee stayed at her bedside. She took care of her every need. George grew into a precocious toddler and filled their home with much love and laughter. He made it possible for Lee to let go of her mother.

In 1957, Lee gave birth to a little girl named Ruby. The angel Seneca along with Erinelle materialized, relaying the information that the infant would become one of The Chosen of Campbell Ridge.

"In the coming years, you will witness Ruby's innate abilities, but in the year of our Lord, nineteen hundred and seventy-seven, she and her friends, Anna and Sandy, will join the order of The Chosen," Seneca said. "As the war escalates, more of her friends and family will be called on to fight."

"I am willing to guide and teach her."

"No. Your and Harry's sole responsibility is to be her parents," said Erinelle. "The world is changing fast. The lines blur between right and wrong. You will continue to train with me in preparation for another battle."

"When?"

"Remember, Lee, time in the heavenly realm is not the same as Earth. Possible battles, skirmishes, world-changing events, all are subject to variations based on human free will."

"The battle of which you speak, is it the same one of my recurring dream?"

The warrior angels exchanged glances. Erinelle asked, "What recurring dream?"

"The battle where I die."

"The battle where you die? I believe the dream is a devious trick of Luc's."

Lee remembered the dream with Luc from years ago. "He said I could see the future. He gave me a choice to join his forces. I declined."

"He is the master of lies, betrayal, and trickery. I don't believe it. And the future is subject to free will too. I'll do some research in the Hall of Moses."

Lee tilted her head. "What's the Hall of Moses?"

Seneca picked up the infant, Ruby, and rocked her in his arms. "We store all the records of the Universe in the Hall of Moses. The Book of Life allows the faithful to cross realms."

She swung her legs over to the side of the bed. "So, let me get this straight. My daughter is going to fight demons, and I'm not allowed to discuss it with her? Ruby needs to know she's not alone. She'll need me."

Erinelle sat on the bed next to her. "You will help her. But allow Ruby to be a child, to grow into a teenager then as one of The Chosen. The world is different now, and when she discovers her divine calling, there's going to be a great upheaval on the planet. Ruby will need to mature longer than you did. She will need her friends to help in the fight. Her generation and the generations to come will witness miracles and attribute it to chance or science. They will look at us as alien forces, not angelic ones."

"Aliens like in Roswell?" She threw her hands out, palms up.

"Technically, anything not of this world is alien. You are alien in that respect." Seneca placed Ruby back in the bassinet as George ran into the room.

"Mommy, I caught a fish out of the pond, but Granddaddy made me throw it back." He turned to Seneca. "Who are you?"

Lee slowly stood and reached for George. "What are you talking about, son?"

He looked at her as though she lost her mind. "The bright people. Him and her." He pointed.

Erinelle ruffled his hair. "If only all humanity could view the world through a child's eyes. George, we are angels." She turned to Lee. "Innocent children before the age of accountability, see and converse with angels. That how George sees us."

"I'm going to watch Saturday cartoons until Granddaddy cooks breakfast. I miss your cooking, Mama. He burns everything." George ran out of Lee's bedroom.

She shook her head and laughed. "TV is going to be the downfall of our civilization."

"Not exactly, but close," Seneca said. "Time to go, Erinelle. Michael is waiting for us." Seneca and Erinelle vanished.

Lee picked up Ruby and placed her next to her breast to nurse. Holding the infant in her arms, she felt a sense of pride. Her daughter would be one of The Chosen. She would protect her children with her life.

Dad stuck his head into the room. "Want to come downstairs for a spell? I'll carry Ruby."

"Daddy?"

"Yeah, Cricket?"

"You're a great father and a wonderful grandfather too. I love you." He smiled. "I love you more."

～

DAYS TURNED INTO WEEKS, then into months, and the months turned into years. Lee and Harry watched their children grow, attend school and sporting events. They watched them fall in and out of love, and eventually marry. George married his high school sweetheart, Lizzie, and Ruby married a young man, named Reed.

Over time, Lee and Harry laid their parents to rest in the family cemetery. Carol Ann married and moved across the country. Glenn Hall sold to another family, but they kept Everglade Farms.

December 8, 1985, Ruby gave birth to a baby boy she named, Joseph Lee Jackson.

Lee held the baby in her arms and sang him a lullaby.

Ruby and her friends, Anna and Sandy looked on. The girls beamed with brightness and released positive vibes of extraordinary love.

"Wonder what powers Little Joe will inherit?" Lee grinned.

The girls looked amazed and somewhat confused.

"Mom? What are you saying?"

"I waited many years to tell you that I am one of The Chosen of Campbell Ridge too. I watched over you girls just like your angels. I received permission today after the birth of this little miracle to speak of my connection. Do you want to ask me some questions?"

Ruby pushed herself up to a sitting position. "Well, yeah. What are your powers? And for how long?"

"I have all the powers of the angels. I am part angel, part Creator, part mortal. I have been fighting in the angelic war since the day I graduated from college."

All three girls' mouths gaped.

"Does Dad know?"

"Of course, Dad knows. We'll talk more about it later. You need to rest, and I need a soda. Anyone else?" Lee asked.

She received no takers. She slipped out of the room and nearly slammed into a nurse.

The nurse quickly walked away.

"Stop, nurse, I need to speak to you."

In a brilliant flash of light, Luc materialized, wearing a long, dark trench coat and black turtleneck, leather pants, and black boots. His inky jet-black hair flowed over his shoulders in waves. "Hello, my old foe. It seems you are still too perceptive for your own good."

Her eyes blazed with fire. The palms of her hands tingled with white bursts of energy. "You leave my daughter, her family, and her friends alone. I will call on every angel in the AAF at my disposal if necessary." She stretched out her fingers and released the bolt of energy at Luc's head, which he deflected easily.

"Chill out, chick. Go with the flow. Peace, baby, and all that jazz." He flashed his pearly whites. He seemed to keep a perpetual smirk on his face. "We will meet again, Lee. This time, I will win, for I too see the future."

Erinelle appeared with weapons. Her sword pointed at his chest. "Leave, now, Dragon."

"Still calling me, Dragon, eh? Hm. I still love it." He batted the sword away, bowed and disappeared in a burst of mist.

She looked at Erinelle and sighed. "Luc's not going to leave us alone, is he?"

"No. I'm afraid this is the beginning of the end. Are you ready to fight again, warrior?"

"Always, and forever, until the end of an age."

"Meeting at the barn, one week from tonight. We must plan our military strategies and include the new team members."

Lee paled. "But Ruby can't fight for two years while Joe is a baby."

"The rules of engagement have changed. We need everyone, including Ruby. She is her mother's daughter." Erinelle winked and dematerialized.

Lee went back into Ruby's hospital room, and as she clutched the doorknob, a vision came to her:

Sandy investigated the death of Nick London, a local businessman in downtown Nashville and found a leather-bound book she placed in her arms. On the cover, Lee saw a serpent-entwined rod with metal embellishments at each corner. The worn vellum pages contained the names of the damned. Sandy found Luc's Testament, which placed a target on her head.

Lee pushed the door open. She watched Ruby, Anna, and Sandy cooing over her grandson. "I didn't have exact change. Hey, girls, I think we should schedule a meeting with the AAF angels in charge of The Chosen of Campbell Ridge. A battle is brewing."

Sandy's brows furrowed. "What battle?"

She squeezed Sandy's hand, revealing the vision she witnessed.

Sandy withdrew her hand and leaned against the hospital wall. Her hand flew to her mouth. "Hold on a damn minute. You have visions too? Cole Steel is one of the men I'm investigating in a story about downtown businesses closing. Nick London owns one of the few local businesses left. Is he going to die? I believe it connects with a string of murders on Music Row. I have a hunch, Cole Steel and his henchmen committed the crimes."

"I dreamed about him." Ruby said, "Be careful, Sandy."

Sandy straightened her spine. "I am not afraid of Cole Steel, and I have a pretty tough guardian angel watching out for me."

Lee nodded. "Baldric is a great warrior, but I'm afraid his judgment isn't great concerning you."

Sandy's face flushed. "How so?"

"I'm clairvoyant too." She winked.

Anna stepped in between them. "Ruby needs to rest."

"No arguments from me," Lee replied.

Anna and Sandy said their goodbyes while Lee sat with Ruby until Reed came into the room.

"Hey, Mama Lee. Our baby boy has your eyes, I think." Reed picked up the infant and placed him on his shoulder, gently patting the baby's bottom.

"I'll stop by your house and get it ready for your arrival home tomorrow, and I'll cook your favorite meals." Lee pulled on her coat, gloves, and grabbed her purse.

Ruby yawned. "Mom, please don't overdo it, but I appreciate your help."

"I'm as near as your phone." She hugged and kissed Ruby, then placed her hand on her abdomen, healing her instantly from the after-effects of childbirth. Ruby would need all her strength to fight in a supernatural battle.

Lee kissed Reed's cheek, then gently patted the sleeping baby. "May love light the way, my children." She walked out the door.

She stepped into the elevators and waited for the doors to close. *"Erinelle, I know you listened. Sandy is going to get herself in a lot of trouble. Is there any way we can prevent her retrieving Luc's Testament?"*

"I'm not sure where he keeps the book, but if Nick London has it, he's a dead man walking. I'll check with headquarters to see if we have any intel on its location. Baldric is staying pretty close to Sandy."

The forbidden and budding relationship between Sandy and Baldric may result in problems for the whole team. However, Lee kept her mouth closed.

On the drive home, light snow mixed with freezing rain. Lee pulled into the newly built garage connecting to the kitchen by a breezeway. The scent of buttered biscuits hit her nostrils when she opened the back door. She placed her purse on the baker's rack next to the mudroom, hung up her coat, and slipped off her boots.

Harry cooked on the stovetop. "Supper is ready. Are you hungry?"

She circled her arm around his waist, placing her face against his back.

He turned off the stove then whipped around, taking her into his arms. "Darlin' spill the beans."

She searched his eyes. "You read me too well. Luc masqueraded as a female nurse outside of Ruby's room. I chased him into a corridor where Erinelle materialized, and he disappeared."

She released from his embrace. She sat in one of the kitchen chairs next to the walnut dining table. "When I went back into the room, I had a vision of Sandy. Another battle is coming, Harry. One like Sacred Heights. Erinelle and I want a team meeting, but I also want Ruby to enjoy her time with Little Joe before facing a supernatural battle."

He leaned against the cabinet gripping the counter. "Stop worrying if you can't change anything. It will only make you sick."

"How can you say that? You know what it's like to fight. We've been fortunate to keep the clashes between realms small, but the one coming is much larger. I'm worried about the girls and Jerry. They're all in the mix now."

He brought over two plates of food and poured sweet tea into the glasses. "One day at a time, darlin'. Otherwise, you'll not sleep a wink tonight."

"You're right, but I have a nagging dread I can't shake loose."

He joined her at the table and took her hands while he said grace. He held a spoonful of food to Lee's mouth. "I cooked this delicious chicken casserole, and I want your opinion."

"I'm famished." She took a bite, which melted like a stick of butter. "You should consider cooking all our meals. Superb. So, are you still going out of town with this weather?"

"Yeah. One night and two days. Teaching safety classes is a cushy job, and I'm so close to retiring. I'll swing by the hospital in the morning to visit my babies before driving to East Tennessee."

"I can't wait until you retire. I don't like sleeping one night without you."

His grin went wide. "You're buttering me up for a slice of chocolate chess pie, aren't you?"

"Honey, you keep cooking like this, and I'll have to buy new clothes."

"I like my wife with meat on her bones. I'll prove it later."

"You can still make me blush like a girl."

"My girl." He squeezed her hand.

After putting up the leftovers and placing the plates into the dishwasher, they made their way to the bedroom.

She gazed into his eyes. "You never age. It isn't fair."

"Oh, I'm old. I hide it well." He pressed his face into her neck, nipping and biting. Rustling under the covers, he made her giggle again and again until they laughed uncontrollably like teenagers.

Fifteen minutes later, Harry snored like a freight train.

Lee slipped out of bed, put on her robe, and quietly exited the room. She went downstairs. The embers in the hearth had died down, so she added a log and stoked the fire to blazing. She made a cup of tea and eased down on the couch. Holding the cup in her hand, she stared into the flickering flames.

Harry was right. They had a beautiful life. She'd try her best to enjoy the little moments in life like tonight and think about the war tomorrow.

CHAPTER 22

"KNOCKIN' ON HEAVEN'S DOOR"

*L*ee increased her training regime to every day after the vision in the hospital, and after six weeks, her body responded like a much younger woman's. She met with Erinelle daily and had staved off the team meeting until tonight. Ruby and her friends would find out their real potential and meet the angel forces sent to The Chosen's aid.

After cleaning the house, she made a large pot of vegetable soup and two skillets of cornbread for the crew, Ruby, Reed, Anna, Jerry, and Sandy. Harry agreed to babysit during the meeting.

She heard a car door slam. She went to the front door, wiping her hands with a dishtowel. Snow steadily fell on the ground. "Sandy, honey, you must be freezing to death. I made soup and cornbread plus I bought buttermilk just for you. Are you spending the night?"

Sandy held Luc's Testament in her arms. "I need to get back to Nashville to work on my story." She shrugged out of her winter coat and toed off her snow boots.

They went into the kitchen.

"The book is dangerous. Luc will come for it. Not to mention, the longer you keep it, the darker your soul becomes. I don't want to touch it. Place it on the baker's rack and wash your hands. I'll get you a bowl of soup and some cornbread." Lee stirred the pot.

"Mama Bear, you worry too much, and Baldric's already read me the riot act. The book is going to nail Cole Steele's ass to the wall. My story about Nick London may save lives. I promise to give the book to Baldric and the AAF as soon as the story airs."

Ruby came in the back door with Little Joe bundled up. "Something smells great, and I'm starving." Little Joe wailed. "He's a little colicky." Sandy took the baby for about two seconds before handing him to Lee.

Lee took off his winter bunting and then placed him on her shoulder, patting his back until he belched. "Good baby. Feeling better now?"

Harry came into the kitchen and took the baby from Lee. "How's Papa's big boy, huh?" Something about his demeanor made babies calm.

Jerry and Anna entered from the kitchen door, hanging their coats up in the mudroom.

The room filled with chatter.

Lee whistled loudly to get their attention. "We have fifteen minutes to get to the barn. Eat up and don't be late. Erinelle is a fierce leader and expects one hundred and ten percent from each of us."

Ruby slurped soup. "Mom, we get it."

"No, my darling, you won't get it until we meet in the barn. Be on time, and that includes you too, Jerry."

"Geez, Miss Lee, I didn't say anything."

"Yeah, but you were going too. Sandy, I left clothes in Ruby's room if you need them."

Lee left the group to finish eating while she quickly changed into her workout gear.

INSIDE THE BARN, the rafters filled with warrior angels bringing their light and warmth into the arena. The Chosen of Campbell Ridge met them for the first time. She listened to Erinelle explain their objectives when Reed strode into the area. Harry must've said something to Simon because he took Reed under his wing.

After the intense practice session, the group dispersed except for Sandy. Lee convinced her to spend the night. She stayed in Ruby's room.

After Sandy retired for the evening, Harry filled the bathtub with hot water for Lee, and she gingerly submerged into the steamy bubble bath.

He sat on the toilet seat. "Luc's Testament is the catalyst to the battle. The one you dreamed about, right?"

"I think so. I discussed the dream with Michael, including the minute details. Luc will send his demons if he doesn't come himself. Sandy is in grave danger. She's placed us in danger when she brought that book into our home. Surely, Baldric is watching her closely. Erinelle has a legion of angels protecting the farm."

"I don't like it. I should fight too."

She placed her arms on the side of the tub. "You'll need to guard Little Joe. He is one of The Chosen too. I'm sure he's on Luc's radar. His guardian angel is Thane, and Humiel will have the back-up duty."

After washing her hair, he helped her out of the tub, drying her off with a towel. He worked the lotion into her shoulder muscles. "We're not as young as we used to be. But, dang, woman you look good. I'm worried about you, though. I think it's time to allow the kids to take over. They're young and strong. Why do you have to fight?"

She raised a brow. "Are you saying I don't have the strength to fight? I beat Reed tonight."

"Reed isn't a demon with supernatural powers."

"Well, not exactly true. Simon is training him."

"Geesh. Sometimes, I wish we were normal."

"What's normal?" She cupped his face. "Let's cross that bridge when we come to it. Deal?"

Harry lifted her in his arms and carried her to bed.

No words were necessary.

~

TWO DAYS LATER, Lee turned on the morning news. Sandy reported her story in front of Steele Enterprises. "Harry, Sandy busted Cole. The District Attorney is opening an investigation. I am proud of her courage, but going against Cole is standing against Luc."

The telephone rang, and Harry answered, "Hey, baby girl, how are you doing? Mom? She's here. I'll put you on speaker."

"Mom, I had a dream. Sandy is in trouble. I think Cole has her. I called her, but now she's not answering."

Her pulse raced. "Where's Baldric?"

"I can't reach any of the angels."

"I'll try and reach Erinelle. Don't go anywhere by yourself. Call Reed and you two come here with the baby. It's safe here."

"I'll pack and be over soon. Mom, I'm scared."

"Me too."

Erinelle appeared. "We have a breach. Michael and Baldric are in a closed meeting with The Creator. He and Sandy paired last night. It's taboo. From the intel I gathered at headquarters, one of Luc's lead demons, Caiojezeal, staked out Sandy and descended on her parents' home as soon as Michael summoned Baldric. A surprise attack took the warrior angel subbing for Baldric. The demons took Sandy. Luc is after the book, but he also knows of her connection with The Chosen. He's holding her captive at his foothold in Arrington."

Lee paced in front of the fireplace, wringing her hands with worry. Her thoughts went to Nadine and the suffering she endured in the Devil's Castle. "We need the team here. We must retrieve Sandy fast."

Erinelle shook her head. "The battle may be worse than Sacred Heights."

"Worse than Hell? How?" she asked.

Harry slammed his fist on the oak side table. "How did the AAF allow this to happen?"

The angel placed her hand on his shoulder, and he relaxed. "It's war. I'll get the AAF operations and team members of Campbell Ridge here by dusk. You and Lee call in The Chosen." She dematerialized.

By nightfall, AAF warrior angels, The Chosen along with Michael filled Everglade Farms. He took over the operations, setting up charts, and surveillance. "We are a well-oiled machine, and I do not, repeat, do not want any mistakes."

Baldric ran out of the house and returned thirty minutes later with information from Caiojezeal, Luc's right hand angel. "He is going to work with us to retrieve Sandy. Luc has the book, but he's holding Sandy in a room next to his bedroom. Caiojezeal said Luc intends on taking her as his bride." Baldric roared and stomped his foot, shaking the whole house.

"Can we trust a demon?" Lee asked.

Baldric looked at Michael. His face was full of fury. "We don't have a choice. He's willing to turn against Luc in exchange for clemency. He wants to go home."

"He is lying." Erinelle shouted, "You can't trust a demon."

Baldric's shoulders slumped. "Yes, we can. He's in love with Sandy, too." He stormed out of the house, and Erinelle followed him to the barn.

Noisy chatter filled the house.

Michael shouted, "Enough. The plan is ready to implement. Lee's son, George, is a savvy electrician but a full-bloodied mortal. He's agreed to help. Once he places bugs in Luc's house, we'll meet again to set the rules of engagement. I suggest The Chosen retrieve their belongings and remain at Everglade Farms until the battle is over. We have legions protecting our base of operations here for this battle."

LEE RODE WITH ANNA, Jerry, Ruby, and Reed to Nelson Doune Farms situated next to Luc's estate. She could almost hear the thrumming heartbeats of the passengers. Reed stared out the window while Jerry drove the Chevrolet Suburban.

Lee and Harry said their goodbyes last night, both understanding the possible outcomes of the day.

Ruby blamed herself for not reacting sooner with The Dragon

Dream. Against Lee's and Reed's wishes, she decided to fight for her best friend.

Lee's adrenaline pumped as she went over Michael's plan in her mind for the AAF special ops mission. They would take out the outbuildings along with the mortal guards first. At Michael's command, the units would attack Luc's home in Arrington guarded by seasoned demon warriors, and ruthless, cutthroat mortals. Caiojezeal gave them a detailed drawing of the underground cave systems which gave Luc direct access to Hades.

The AAF would have to fight in the nine circles of Hell again if he escaped with Sandy.

So, Erinelle was right. It had the potential of being more dangerous than Sacred Heights.

During the reconnaissance mission, George discovered Luc held several captive wards and AAF angels. Their purpose was to enter Luc's fortress and retrieve the captives while Baldric freed Sandy.

Lee and Reed paired up with Erinelle and Simon.

Luwenia would lead Jerry's team with the arrows of destruction. Ruby went with Seneca in the third line of defense. Anna worked with Raphael and the other angel healers.

In theory, they had a sound plan.

Minutes seemed to last hours as they drove through Nelson Doune Farms. Tennessee Walking Horses filled the front barn lot. Lee didn't care about the mansion or thoroughbreds. She cared about the people in the vehicle. She didn't care about the farm, but she'd called and thanked Mr. Doune earlier for helping George.

George had gone into Luc's home with no supernatural gifts besides Simon and Celina, George's guardian. Nelson's hired hands helped to distract the mortals while he cased the house and planted listening devices. His bravery helped to forge the AAF plan of attack.

As they rounded the barn, the rough terrain jostled the group in the vehicle. Minutes later, they stopped.

Jerry placed his arm on the console. "No one's here."

"Wait until we get out of the truck. Be on your guard, and remember, don't hesitate. You must destroy the enemy, or the enemy will destroy you."

Legions of angels appeared in the misty meadows as they exited the suburban.

Jerry chuckled nervously. "Well, that's something you don't see every day."

The Chosen went into the hunting cabin to gear up for the battle. After changing into the angel body armor, The Chosen met up with the assigned AAF teams. Lee nervously shifted one foot to the other, waiting for the sound of the trumpets.

Michael gave the signal and led the charge.

The AAF overtook the outbuildings and barns. The surprise attack wiped out the human guards. Baldric's group cut through the front line of the demon angels' defense, charging Luc's gardens into the main house. The inky night sky faded into the rising sun spreading pale pinks, and yellows along the horizon.

Michael shouted orders for more legions as the demon floodgates opened.

AAF soldiers fell on the battlefield, but the healer angels quickly repaired the damage.

Lee went into battle mode, blocking out all the noise. With total focus, she lunged at the first demon, slicing him in half, exploding the beast to ash. Heart pumping, she pressed onward, charging, slashing, retreating and blocking, making her way forward to the front line.

In her peripheral vision, across the meadow, Ruby fell to the ground, then everything went into slow motion.

Lee's recurring dream was coming true.

Erinelle flanked her beating back demons. "Go to Ruby. I'll be right behind you."

She ducked, fought off a demon and weaved before kicking her superspeed into overdrive.

Ruby's eyes widened with fear as she approached. She opened her mouth, but Lee heard no words.

She released the power of an electrical force field projecting it around her daughter, leaving herself vulnerable. Her protective shield saved Ruby's life.

Lee and Reed locked eyes as demons attacked them from every direction, but unlike her dream, Erinelle and Simon fought with them side by side. She didn't have the time to relax.

She reached for Ruby at the precise moment the demon's blade pierced her back, spreading fire and unbelievable pain throughout her body. She glanced as another beast plunged a dagger into Reed.

They both dropped to their knees and fell to the ground. She lay on her side and searched Ruby's eyes.

"Mama, Reed, don't leave me. Help, someone help!"

Anna appeared. With the face of a stone, she looked at Ruby and said, "Reed or your mom. You have seconds, or they're both dead."

Lee mouthed, "I love you" and closed her eyes.

HER EYELIDS FLUTTERED. One. Two. Three. Lee woke in a vast white room. White walls, white furniture, white bed, and linens. She remembered Erinelle and the flight to Everglade Farms, but then things got a little fuzzy.

She died.

Her dream realized.

She didn't cry. She was at home.

Nadine sat in a chair next to the bed, holding Lee's hand. "You're back, sister."

"How are you?"

"The question is, how are you?" Nadine grinned.

Lee shrugged. She hadn't the time to process the implications of her death.

The Prince entered the white room, His light more brilliant than she remembered.

She tried sitting up, but He waved his hand. "Rest, daughter."

She pushed against the headboard then straightened.

The Prince in all His glory sat in a white chair opposite of Nadine.

He wore a brilliant white tunic cinched with a golden belt. His smile warmed her inside and out. He nearly blinded her with His magnificence. His beauty was beyond mortal words.

The Prince took her hand into his. "Thank you, my good and faithful servant. You didn't save yourself, but you saved many others."

She swallowed hard. "My family, our friends, are they safe?"

His grin warmed her heart and soul. "Yes. Don't fret. Everyone is safe. You miss Harry?"

She blinked several times too choked up to speak.

"Why are you crying? Don't you understand life on Earth is only a blip in the big picture of the Universe? However, as your Prince, I am giving you a choice. You may stay here in Heaven or return to Earth for a time before coming home for good."

"Is there a wrong answer?"

"No wrong answers here." He chuckled.

She leaped from the bed and hugged his neck. "I want to return to my family—to Harry."

Lee's life went into hyper-rewind. No grieving. No graveside services. No funeral. No fiery pain. She was back inside her bedroom.

Erinelle prayed in the undecipherable language of the angels.

Harry burst into the room.

They locked eyes, and Lee bolted from the bed. She jumped into his arms, kissing him hard while holding onto him for dear life.

Erinelle exclaimed, "Praise to the Trinity for this miracle."

"I died, Harry, just like my dream." She wept happy tears. "But—but The Prince gave me a choice, to stay in Heaven or return to you and my family."

His voice quivered. "You came back to me." He placed his palm on the curve of her cheek.

"Always, Harry. It's you and me, forever. How's Ruby? George? The baby?"

"Honey, everyone is fine. But"—he reached for the bedside phone and dialed—"talk to Ruby. She thinks you died too."

Ruby was right. She had died.

With a trembling hand, Lee placed the receiver next to her ear.

Ruby picked up after three rings. "Hello."

"Honey, it's Mom." She heard Ruby sob. "I'm okay, sweetheart. Better than okay. I'm great. How's Reed?"

Harry watched her every move.

Ruby's voice broke. "Oh, Mom. Thank God, you're okay. I thought they killed you. I thought you died protecting me. I love you. Reed's out of surgery. Anna is with us. She's healing him. And Sandy and Baldric just walked in." She paused, the phone muffled, and she heard, "Mom's alive, y'all. She's okay."

The room erupted in cheers, and Lee grinned.

She released an exhale. "Great news. Give everyone my love, and we'll take care of Little Joe until Reed's better. Take care of yourself, baby girl. I'll see you soon."

"See you soon, Mom." Ruby hung up.

"Erinelle, did I move into an alternate lifeline?" Lee asked.

The angel tilted her head. "Well, I don't know." She seemed perplexed. "I'll search the archives. Oh, you mean the night you were supposed to dance with Harry under the stars at Glenn Hall. It is quite possible."

Lee learned many lessons over her lifetime, but the biggest lesson was never to take life for granted. She would return to her home in Heaven again. But for now, she basked in the knowledge The Creator blessed her with a loving husband, family, and great friends, and through His grace, love saved her. He gave her Erinelle as a teacher, guardian, and friend.

Erinelle read her thoughts. She jutted her wings toward Heaven. "Your lessons aren't over, yet."

EPILOGUE

"GOLDEN YEARS"

*2*007
Everglade, Tennessee

JOE ENTERED Everglade General Store and waved to the checkout clerk, Rose. "Where is she?"

"Miss Ruby is in her office. I'm sorry I missed your graduation, but it's tourist time, and someone had to mind the store."

"No worries, Rose. I know you love me." He chuckled and threw her a peace sign before he walked down the candy aisle toward the back of the store. He stuck his head inside his mother's office. He grew up in the store and hoped someday to talk his mom into retiring and letting him take over the family business. He didn't want to work for his father. They were too much alike and butted heads regularly.

Joe rapped his knuckles on the door. "Hey, Mama Bear. Checking to see if you need anything."

"Oh, Little Joe, go check on mother for me. I haven't stopped all day, and I'm worried about her." Ruby sat behind her desk, clicking away on her keyboard.

"Please call me Joe, Mom. I'm six foot four and weigh two hundred pounds. There's nothing little about me. And what's going on with Mama Lee?"

She pushed away from her desk and opened her arms. "Give us a kiss."

Joe picked up his mom and squeezed before releasing his embrace, then kissed her cheek. "You know, I have a business degree. You should make me the store manager. You've worked hard, and you should enjoy your golden years."

"Geez, Louise, I'm fifty. I have years before I retire, but I'm thinking about expanding since Everglade is busting loose at the seams. Have you seen all the new subdivisions around here since you got home?" She went back to her chair, placing her forearms on the desk. "What do you think about opening a new store on the other side of town? We own some land where the new highway is under construction."

"That's a great idea. What does Dad say?" He sat in the chair opposite the desk.

"He wants me to quit and sell the store. But I love it. I love the people. I mean, I know we don't make the money he does, but my store is paid for, and I've saved quite the nest egg. I've crunched the numbers. I could do it with your help."

"Count on me, Mom. We'll team up on Dad. So, what's the matter with Mama Lee?"

"Dad asked me to take her car keys. He's afraid of doing it." Ruby sighed. "She's gotten lost several times, and once the sheriff had to follow her home."

"Do you think she's getting Alzheimer's?"

"I have talked with her doctors. She has early signs. It makes me so sad. My mother's the strongest person I've ever known. I've been doing some research. The best thing is keeping her routines the same. I've stuck a few subtle sticky notes on her fridge, and in the bathroom as reminders of things, like to brush her teeth. Or make sure the stove is off."

She leaned back in her chair. "Would you mind checking on her?

Or better yet, drive her up the ridge on the Gator. She loves it, up there, and it'll get her outside in the fresh air and sunshine."

"Sure. I love spending time with Mama Lee. Papa Harry is afraid of her?" Joe hadn't noticed any changes in his grandmother. He and his little sister had spent most of their summers with them.

"Dad isn't exactly afraid of Mom, but she's had him wrapped around her little finger for decades. And you're the best. Oh, Rose made lasagna with a salad and strawberry shortcake for dessert for Mom and Dad. It's in the kitchen. I'll stop by on my way home. Alisa and your dad are doing a marketing event for Jerry, so they'll be late. By the way, Jerry did ask me if you had a job. You could probably make more money working for him than me."

Ruby's cell phone buzzed. She glanced, then clicked off the sound. "Vendor. I'll call them later."

Uncle Jerry ran a multimillion-dollar software company. He really wasn't a blood uncle, but Anna and Sandy were his mom's besties. He'd referred to them as aunts and uncles all his life. "If you choose not to open the new store or don't need me to work this one, I might think about it. I love the store too, Mom."

Her face softened. "I know you do. Hey, text me when you get to Everglade Farms and let me know Mom's okay."

"You got it. I'll see you at home later." He left her office and went into the store's kitchen to grab the boxed food. On the way out of the store, he nearly slammed into Elena. He hadn't seen her much since they broke up after high school. She'd been furious when he went away to college instead of staying local.

Elena's cheeks flushed, but she held the door open. "Hi, Joe. I heard you were back."

"Yeah, I didn't see you at my party, only your parents and Eric. Where were you?"

She narrowed her eyes. "I know it's a shocker the world doesn't revolve around Little Joe Jackson, but I'm interning at the TV station over the summer. Good to see you, though." She went to push by him, but he blocked her.

"What is wrong with you?"

With exasperation, she said, "Me? You want to get into this now in the store?"

"Yes, I don't understand why you're avoiding me." He shifted the box in his arms.

"Well, for starters, you dumped me the night before you moved to Knoxville. You never emailed, sent texts, or friended me on Facebook. I figured you moved on. So, I did too. Look, I'm picking up some things for my mom. Would you please let me pass?"

"Wait a minute. I did try to email you. I'm not on Facebook, and my cell service sucks in the mountains. And when I moved to Knoxville, I didn't want you to wait for me. I wanted you to live your own life. I didn't do it to hurt you. I—I..."

"What, Joe? What can you possibly say that will change what you did to me?" She placed her hand on her hip and tapped her foot impatiently.

He glanced at her left hand and noticed a large white gold diamond ring. "Are you engaged?"

"Yes, I'm engaged." Elena shoved her hands into her jean pockets.

Through gritted teeth, he asked, "Who? And when is the wedding?"

"Sterling, and we haven't set a date yet."

"Sterling Forrester? Are you kidding?" He couldn't believe she'd fall for a pompous ass like him.

"Don't you dare say anything negative about Sterling. He picked up the pieces of my heart and helped me to live again. You broke me, Joe. You never called me. You never came home to see me. What did you expect? That I'd wait forever?"

"Eric told me you didn't love me anymore. He told me you had a serious boyfriend. Um, excuse me—fiancé." The first college break Joe came home from Knoxville, Eric, Elena's twin brother, told him she had another boyfriend. So, he left her alone even though it killed him inside. She hadn't made any of his family's holiday functions.

"Well, your first mistake was asking my brother and not me."

Ruby stepped over to the door. "I could hear y'all yelling at each other from my office. If you're going to shout, take it out back." She reached over and kissed Elena's cheek. "I have your mom's order ready. Rose has it behind the counter."

"I'm sorry, Ruby." Elena frowned. "I have nothing left to say to your son." She whipped around, and Joe watched her go inside the store without looking back.

God, he forgot about Elena's hot temper. He forgot about how hot she was period.

Ruby lifted his chin with her fingers. "She's not married yet, but you have some major ice to chip away from her heart. Elena still loves you, or she wouldn't have shouted."

"I don't know about that, but I'll call you when I get to Mama Lee's."

He jogged down the steps and slid into his black Jeep, placing the box of food in the passenger seat, then drove to Everglade Farms.

He must decide his best course of action to win Elena back. She couldn't marry Sterling. She had promised to marry him but that was long ago.

Joe planned on speaking with his grandparents about moving into the log cabin since his Uncle George and Aunt Lizzie moved to Gammie's house in Florida.

Topping the ridge, he exhaled. He loved the farm. He waved at Papa Harry on the tractor, cutting hay. He pulled into the driveway, grabbed the food, and made his way up the low sloped hill to the kitchen door.

Joe opened the door with one hand, balancing the box of the food with his other hand. Stepping inside, he smelled something burning. He quickly placed the dinner on the table and looked for the source of the smell.

On the stove, an empty pot rattled on a red coiled eye. He grabbed a hot pad and moved the pan to the back of the oven, then turned the knob to off. "Mama Lee, are you here?"

～

227

LEE STARED out her bedroom window and hummed. She startled when Joe tapped her shoulder.

"Mama Lee, are you all right?"

She turned and smiled. "I'm fine. Do you hear them singing?"

"Hear who?" He looked around. "I don't hear any music."

She touched his forearm then grinned. "The angels are singing for me, Joe. It's almost time for me to go home."

"You are home, Mama Lee." He tucked her arm in his while helping her down the stairs one step at a time. "Maybe you and Papa Harry should move your bedroom downstairs. Hey, I brought supper. But I thought you'd like to ride with me on the Gator to the cave. I haven't seen it since I came back."

"I'd love to see the cave. Get one of the fold-up chairs out of the mudroom. Now, what did I do with my walking stick?" She looked around the den and moved into the living area before finding her cane in the kitchen. "My goodness, something's burning."

"Yeah, the water in the pot boiled out. I threw the pan away. It's ruined."

"Dad-blame-it. I put on the water to make tea. I swear half the time I can't remember what I forgot." She wrung her hands nervously.

"It's okay. How would you feel about me moving in with you and Papa for a spell?"

"Oh, what a splendid idea. You could move into your mom's old room, or George's room has an upstairs balcony looking out over the farm. You'd have a private entrance with the outside stairs."

"Sounds perfect. I'll talk to Papa. I don't want to intrude."

She leaned on her cane for support. "Oh, Joe, you could never intrude on us. So, you might want to get the ATV out of the barn and pick me up at the back steps. I'm not so steady on my feet anymore."

"You got it."

Lee stepped onto the back deck and watched Joe run toward the barn.

"Erinelle, are you here?"

"Always, Lee."

"Does Joe receive his memory stone today?"

"Yes, I thought you'd like to see the torch pass to your grandson."

"You mean before I go home. What about Harry? I don't want to leave him behind."

"You won't. I promise."

She watched her grandson drive the two-seater Gator up to the sloped hill. He parked it next to the new deck that Reed and Jerry added onto their house last year. Harry bought the ATV so they could tour around the farm since her arthritis made it difficult to walk.

Joe hopped out and helped her to enter the vehicle's passenger side. He placed her walking stick, chair, and blanket into the cargo bed.

Heading up the ridge, he opened the throttle wide. Tooling over the well-worn path, Lee felt a familiar exhilaration and freedom as she used to when she rode her beloved Princess, who'd died decades ago.

Everglade Farms had changed little over the last seventy-eight years of her life. Even the fresh summer breeze seemed to possess the tranquility of spirit.

"You're worried about Elena?" she asked.

"Reading my mind, again?"

"Uh-huh. I wouldn't worry too much. Elena may be engaged to the Forrester boy, but she is still in love with you. There is a difference. You tell her how you feel, son, and don't wait. Time is of the essence in matters of the heart." She gripped the door handle as he made the last turn toward the cave.

"I saw Elena today. She's pretty mad at me, but I swear all I wanted to do was kiss her."

"Hm. Might I suggest you try it? What's the worst that could happen?" She thought about Sandy's twins, Elena and Eric. They were hybrids like her. She'd overheard Sandy telling Ruby about a sparring match between the twins and they sprouted wings.

Elena hadn't told Joe, and neither had his best friend, Eric.

Lee heard a choir of angels singing as Joe came to a stop next to the lazy stream near the cave. "Do you hear them, son?"

He got out of the ATV and stopped in his tracks. His tilted his head to the side and his eyes widened. "I hear singing. Someone must be up here with a boom box. Look, there's a light inside the cave. Mama Lee, stay put, I'm going to check it out. Use my cell if I don't come out soon." He reached into the storage bin and withdrew an oversized flashlight.

She grabbed his hand. "Do not be afraid, Joe. You're not alone."

"I'm not afraid. But I am curious to see who's in the cave." He kissed the top of her head. "I'll be back."

Erinelle appeared next to Lee in the driver seat of the Gator. "He's a good boy. He's powerful and courageous. He'll be fine. I won't let anything happen to him. You don't have to worry."

"What about the twins? Have they received their memory stones?"

"Not until Joe gets his first. He will bring his little sister Alisa, Sandy's twins, Elena, Eric, and Anna and Jerry's daughter, Amy, to the cave. They're the new recruits."

Lee sighed. "Campbell Ridge's Chosen continues."

"Yes, with the help of their parents."

Nearly an hour passed before Joe exited the cave. He stumbled over the rocks in the stream but didn't fall. He looked at Lee as he approached the vehicle. His face paled. His fingers trembled. "Um, you knew what I was walking into, didn't you?"

She nodded. "Do you have questions for me?"

He placed one hand in his jean pocket, and the other hand gripped the roof of the Gator. "Do you still fight? Do you have powers? Does my mom? And how long have you known about me?"

"Sit next to me, my darling boy."

He slid behind the steering wheel of the Gator. "Tell me, Mama Lee."

She told him the story of The Chosen over the next hour and a half or so.

"My powers aren't strong anymore. I read your thoughts today. Even though my memory is bad, I still have visions. I hear the angels sing. Your grandfather and I are at the end of our journey, and you are at the beginning. I offer this bit of advice: listen to your heart, listen to your angel, you will know when the time comes what to do. Be wary of strangers. Angels walk among us but so do demons. The end of my age is over. You and the other Chosen will fight, and you will win."

Joe rubbed his face with his hands. "Elena is a hybrid like you? But so am I, right?"

"Your mom has my DNA, which she passed on to you along with your father's. I can't see your future, Joe. Hm. Sandy, Anna, and your mom kept a journal they called, Ditch Lane Diaries. May I suggest you ask for it. Read it. Lean on your angel, Thane."

Thane and Erinelle appeared.

The female warrior bowed to Joe. "I am Erinelle, Lee's warrior angel. I will continue to work with you and The Chosen after your grandparents pass on."

Joe turned to Lee and grabbed her hand. "Are you dying?"

"Dying is a part of living. My spirit will live on. Remember, the laughter. Laughter is the key to true happiness." Her internal struggle was real. She hated to leave her children and grandchildren, but she'd lived an extraordinary life. She would see them again.

"I will. I will remember everything. I will carry on your legacy. I'll fight for the light."

Lee leaned against Joe's shoulder and patted his hand. "You're going to be a great light in this world. I will always be near you. My spirit may soar in a cardinal, or the wind that tinkles a wind chime, or maybe in the laughter of a baby. The most important lesson I learned is everything on our planet is related. It is worth the good fight."

LATER IN THE EVENING, Lee lay in Harry's arms. They talked for hours about their lives together, about their children and grandchildren. She told him about Joe's awakening with his stone.

"We've raised our children well, Lee. Joe's brave and strong. He has determination and a tender heart. He may look like Reed, but he reminds me so much of Ruby."

She rubbed his chest, then searched his eyes. "Erinelle told me I'm going home soon. Do you want to go with me?"

Harry rolled onto his side and caressed her cheek with his hand. He leaned in and kissed her gently, then whispered, "Wherever you go, I will follow."

EXCERPT FROM THE WITCHES OF HANT HOLLOW

Prologue

Present Day

Jasmine peered into her dressing table mirror and froze. Her mind's eye watched Jonathan step out of the cabin. He flew through the midnight air over treetops and neighborhood homes. She connected with his rush of emotions heightened by fear of crashing to the ground.

Not a car or truck in sight on the lonely country roads.

The woods of Hant Hollow rapidly became apparent as she watched him lower altitude. A small clearing came into view revealing the Doanhart mansion's asymmetrical design and gambrel roof with arched windows illuminating a golden glow on the achromatic facade.

He tried to run as soon as his feet hit the ground, but someone grabbed him, digging fingernails into his upper arm, drawing blood. He fought to no avail.

The massive front porch with elaborate classical elements loomed and distorted in Jasmine's view as she watched Jonathan stumble up the steps. His eyes widened as the red double door open of its own accord.

Bile rose from her stomach, but the knot in her throat pushed it back down.

An unclear voice, neither male nor female, laughed. "Sick? Angry? Hurt? Go ahead, and tell me what you really think."

An invisible force pushed Jonathan inside, making him fall on the foyer's marble floor.

Pushing up on his hands and knees, Jonathan released a deep breath and screamed, "I hate you for stealing my life, for killing my wife, and for manipulating me into doing something you wanted so desperately. But your plans backfired, didn't they? Do you really want to know what I think? I want to wrap my fingers around your scrawny neck and choke you to death."

The sinister laughter echoed in the empty house. "Who said my plans backfired?"

A hooded figure came into Jasmine's view and gripped Jonathan under the arm and dragging him up the mahogany spiral staircase with an ornate balustrade. On the stairwell landing, portraits of women, centuries old, came to life nodding and whispering to each other as if they knew a secret Jasmine didn't, yet.

Hundreds of candles flickered and floated in the air on the third floor ballroom. The walls and bookshelves contain antiquities, oddities, and sculptures. The sculptures seemed almost lifelike with terror filled eyes.

The hooded figure put Jonathan in an ancient Egyptian throne made of ebony and inlaid with gold and precious stones. Glowing ropes mysteriously bound his wrists and ankles securely to the chair.

Jasmine glanced away for only a second and Jonathan shouted, "You, it was you this whole time?"

Out of the corner of his eye, Jonathan turned, and she screamed.

She shouted but no vocal sounds enunciated from her lips. The hooded figure spelled her.

Jasmine summoned the Mouijah Stones.

∽

1915

Rockvale, Tennessee

Jonathan tethered his two-horse team to the hitching post and went up the stairs into the General store to pick up supplies and staples for the farm.

He glanced to his right, and a stunning woman stood next to the fabric bin. Her copper curls hung loosely over her shoulders. She turned slightly lifting her gaze to meet him.

He tipped his Stetson. "Ma'am, I don't believe I've had the pleasure. My name's Jonathan Rogers."

She smiled and lifted her chin. "Everyone in town has surely been hospitable since our arrival. I'm Mae." She extended a gloved hand, and he looked down and for a second thought about kissing it but instead placed his hands over hers and held it a might too long.

She politely withdrew and raised a brow. "My father is the new bank president. Perhaps, you've heard of him? Anthony Morgan? You should stop by and open an account."

Jonathan chuckled while rubbing the rim of his hat. "I mean no disrespect, but I don't trust bankers with my money."

Mae's mouth gaped open then she frowned. With a distinct Southern accent, she huffed, "I'll be sure to pass along the information to my father." She turned her back to Jonathan and picked up a bolt of fabric.

He liked Mae straight away but left her to her business while he attended to his shopping list. Once he completed his task, he purposely ignored Mae as he walked toward the door carrying several boxes of goods.

Out of his peripheral vision, he noticed Mae stared at him with both hands on her hips in apparent vexation as he left the store. He chuckled again and made a mental note to attend the Saturday night dance.

After loading the buckboard, he took off his hat and wiped the sweat from his face with a red and white bandanna. He heard boys shouting and cursing up a storm behind the store.

He ran around back and found three teenage boys throwing rocks and dirt at a young woman.

Jonathan shouted, "Stop it right now, or I'll haul every blasted one of you to Sheriff Watson." He stepped in front of the frightened woman, and she cowered behind him.

One of the boys yelled, "She's a witch. Her Grannie put a curse on my daddy's backside, and he broke out with blisters full of pus."

Jonathan placed his hand on his hip. "Get while the getting's good, boys. Last chance." He pulled out his Colt and fired a round in the air. The boys took off like white lightning and disappeared down the back alley.

He knelt before the crying woman and dried her tears with his fingertips. "It's okay. The boys are gone. By the way, my name's Jonathan, and you must be one of the Doanharts." He noticed the clumps of dirt on her dress and the swelling of her right. "If you'd like, I'd be happy to give you a ride home."

"Those boys are mean. Oh, I'm Jasmine—Jasmine Doanhart." Her green catlike eyes widened as she pressed her lips tight with a slight quiver in her chin.

Jonathan tried dusting off the light blue Gunne Sack Dress. "Yup, they're mean alright. I'm afraid you're going to have quite a shiner on your right eye. So, how about that ride?"

With a look of fear, she shook her head no. "My grandmother wouldn't like that at all."

"I'll tell you what. I'll give you a ride on my way home, and drop you off just before Hant Hollow. Is this your basket of apples?" He swiftly picked up the shiny red apples scattered on the ground and placed them back into the brown wicker basket.

Jonathan had never been to the Doanhart's house, and for that matter, the people venturing there at night never recalled the location.

"Yes, I was taking the apples and cider to sell at the store when the boys cornered me. They broke the cider bottles and threw rocks at me shouting, Witch."

Jonathan pushed his hat slightly off his forehead. "I don't believe in witches. People make up things they can't quite put their finger on."

"Why are you so kind to me?"

"That's how my daddy raised me."

"Oh, okay. If you're sure it won't be too much trouble, I'd love that ride." Jasmine reached for the basket as he helped her into the buckboard.

"I've been craving Dutch apple pie so how about I buy the apples from you."

Jasmine smiled and nodded. "Oh, thank you. But I can't take your money. How about we trade the apples for the ride?"

Jonathan threw his head back and laughed. "You got yourself a deal."

On the road to Hant Hollow, the horse's hooves clipped-clopped in a steady rhythm with the jingle-jangle of the harness over the occasional whinny and neigh. The buckboard jostled over the occasional pothole.

He chatted with Jasmine about the new horror film, *Dr. Jekyll and Mr. Hyde with James Cruze* opening at the town's nickelodeon. "Have you seen the spooky posters and decorations added to the outside of the building?"

"Oh, no, my grandmother doesn't allow us to attend any of the pictures. I'd love to see one, though."

"You've never been to any films? They're wonderful."

She gripped the side of the buckboard as it rolled over the grooves on the dirt road. "The people in town shun us. They call us names and cross to the other side of the street when one of my family members approaches. And what happened today isn't the first time one of us has been attacked in town. But they'll sneak to our house in the dead of night for a healing herb when one of theirs is sick or fetch us to help with the delivery of one of their brats."

"That's horrible. Most of the people in town were kind to my father, and still are to me, but after my dad died, I sold our house and bought a small farm in the country not far from Hant Hollow." He didn't mention his weasel of a cousin stealing the family business from him.

"How did he die? Oh, I'm sorry, maybe I shouldn't have asked that question."

He didn't want to broach that topic until he found out what happened to his father. He kept investigating even though the town doctor ruled his death as a heart attack.

His cousin, Dale had been trying to gain control of the family mill and the property that went with it. Dale had something to do with his dad's death. Jonathan felt it in his gut, and one day he'd prove it. One day he'd get the mill back. He didn't want the house—too many memories, and too many ghosts.

On the edge of Hant Hollow, Jonathan pulled on the reins. "Whoa, Ida. Whoa, Dick." He turned and placed his right arm on the back of the buckboard's seat. "That's a story for another day."

Jasmine burst into laughter. "Your horse's names are Ida and Dick?"

"Yep. I didn't name them. The quarter horses belonged to my father." He pulled on the brake and the horses whinnied and shook their heads. He hopped down and walked around the wagon to help Jasmine.

She held onto his hand and jumped to the ground. "Enjoy the apples, and thanks for sticking up for me."

"No thanks needed. You head along now, and be sure to watch out for those knuckle-headed boys." He paused for a second then asked, "Hey, you want to go to the movie with me?"

Jasmine blushed and briefly glanced to the ground before locking those incredible green eyes with his. His stomach flipped.

She reached up on tiptoe and kissed Jonathan's cheek. "I appreciate the offer, but I have to decline. Although, you're like a knight in one of the Grimm stories."

He took off his hat and placed it on his chest. "Milady." He climbed back into the buckboard and snapped the reins. "Get along. Let's go home." He watched Jasmine disappear into the thicket of Hant Hollow.

Shaking his head, the day had taken much longer than he intended. The Doanharts had never given him any problems. Besides, gossip thrives in a small town, and he never gave the witches rumors any credence.

On the ride home, Jonathan thoughts returned to his dad's death. The foreman of the mill worked for their family for twenty odd years, and he arranged to get a copy of the office key for Jonathan.

He muttered to himself, "I'll leave early on Saturday night and make a stop by the mill before going to the dance. Just maybe, Dale left something behind that will implicate him."

The day his dad died was like any other day in their small town. Except over breakfast, Thomas mentioned he'd met with an attorney to draw up documents naming Jonathan as a full partner. He'd worked for his father since he graduated high school. His father had been the epitome of good health and in the prime of his life. A heart attacked seemed unlikely.

And Dale lost his shares to the family business in poker game years ago, and he never forgave Thomas for claiming the debt. Dale produced legal papers at the hearing of the will naming him the sole heir to Rogers Mill. It seemed too coincidental to Jonathan.

Turning the team down the farm road, Jonathan shook his thoughts about his family and whistled *Hello, Frisco.*

The clouds disappeared, and the sun beat down on his face.

Things seemed to be looking up for a change.

He met two beautiful women today.

Buy The Witches of Hant Hollow online at your favorite bookstore or go to DFJonesAuthor.com.

ABOUT THE AUTHOR

2017 IRC Book Awards for Best Paranormal Romance

D. F. Jones began her career as a broadcast consultant at the ABC Affiliate in Nashville, which led her to open an advertising agency over twenty years ago.

Writing not only is a source of creative expression, but it also releases stress. Writing takes her to a place where anything is possible, and fiction is a place made of dreams.

D. F. Jones is happily married to the love of her life with two gorgeous sons. Besides writing and reading, she loves attending music concerts and the theater. She's an avid fan of the Tennessee Titans, MT Blue Raiders, and enjoys working in her flower gardens.

Whether it's angels or demons, time travel adventures, witches and wizards, or ghosts, her books are action-packed with supernatural, suspense, and romantic elements.

Get book updates, buy links and social media:
http://dfjonesauthor.com/